"You were watching me, checking into my personal life."

Kim's stomach churned, her entire life turned inside out. She'd trusted him, loved him, and he'd repaid her by using her!

Jake's jaw grew rock hard. "I was trying to help."

She shook her head. "That wasn't it. It was your need for vengeance, wasn't it? That's why you seduced me," she concluded, tears burning her eyes. "To get back at Robert by getting close to me and digging up anything you could get on him. Well, I hope you had a good time, Jake, because it's over!"

Dear Reader,

Welcome to the Silhouette **Special Edition** experience! With your search for consistently satisfying reading in mind, every month the authors and editors of Silhouette **Special Edition** aim to offer you a stimulating blend of deep emotions and high romance.

The name Silhouette **Special Edition** and the distinctive arch on the cover represent a commitment—a commitment to bring you six sensitive, substantial novels each month. In the pages of a Silhouette **Special Edition**, compelling true-to-life characters face riveting emotional issues—and come out winners. All the authors in the series strive for depth, vividness and warmth in writing these stories of living and loving in today's world.

The result, we hope, is romance you can believe in. Deeply emotional, richly romantic, infinitely rewarding—that's the Silhouette **Special Edition** experience. Come share it with us—six times a month!

From all the authors and editors of Silhouette **Special Edition**,

Best wishes,

Leslie Kazanjian,
Senior Editor

LISA JACKSON
With No Regrets

Silhouette Special Edition

Published by Silhouette Books New York

America's Publisher of Contemporary Romance

SILHOUETTE BOOKS
300 East 42nd St., New York, N.Y. 10017

ISBN: 0-373-09611-9

First Silhouette Books printing July 1990

Books by Lisa Jackson

LISA JACKSON

was raised in Molalla, Oregon, and now lives with her husband, Mark, and her two sons in a suburb of Portland, Oregon. Lisa and her sister, Natalie Bishop, who is also a Silhouette author, live within earshot of each other and enjoy each other's criticism and support.

Chapter One

"You can't do this to me!" Kimberly Bennett's fingers curled around the smooth oak arms of her chair. She stared, dumbfounded, at her attorney.

"And here I thought you'd be the first to offer congratulations!" Diane Welby, petite and blond, leaned her chin on her clasped hands. Her elbows were planted firmly on the top of her wide desk, and her eyes fairly sparkled. "I'm getting married, for God's sake!"

"I know, I know, but why *now*?" Kimberly asked, seeing all her plans go down the proverbial drain.

"Because Scott asked me." Diane had been widowed for seven years.

Kimberly's brows drew together in vexation. "Fine. Congratulations. I'm glad you're getting married, Diane, really, but do you have to move out of the state?"

"Scott's job is in L.A."

"But your practice is here and I need you!"

Diane sighed. "You don't need *me*—you need a good lawyer."

"You *are* a good lawyer. The best," Kimberly said, a slow panic spreading through her when she thought of her ex-husband and his most recent demands. She shivered. There was a side to Robert she hated to think about—a deadly side. "Robert's not kidding. He's threatened to take Lindsay away!"

Diane grew sober. She tapped her pen on her desk. "Look, Kim, he doesn't have much of a leg to stand on. The court already decided to grant you custody."

"But that was before he cared," Kimberly pointed out, feeling her hands begin to sweat. As soon as the divorce had become final, Robert had married his mistress, a gorgeous woman who was blind to Robert's flaws—just as Kimberly had been, years before.

"And now he cares?" Obviously Diane didn't believe it.

"Yes!"

"Why?"

Kimberly's throat felt tight. "I guess Stella can't give him a son, either."

"And now he'll settle for a daughter?" Diane asked dryly.

Hot injustice swept through Kimberly's veins. "So it seems."

Diane's mouth clamped together thoughtfully. "You know, I wouldn't just abandon you. I know Robert and how...determined he can be. The man who bought my practice is a lawyer—the best—and he's agreed to either take my pending cases or refer them to someone else."

"I don't want some man I've never met," Kimberly insisted, trying to hang on to her rapidly escaping calm. "I want you." Unnerved, she stood, folded her arms across her chest and walked past Diane's desk to the window. She watched a few dying maple leaves fall to the wet asphalt of the parking lot. In the past few years Robert had changed, and his reputation had become black as ink. No court would give him custody—or would it? She couldn't trust fate. "Maybe it's crazy, but I'd rather have a woman represent me."

"Why?"

Kimberly shrugged.

"Let me guess. You think a woman can better understand your maternal feelings?"

"Yes!" She glanced over the shoulder of her black suit. "A man might sympathize with Robert."

Diane scowled. "I doubt it. And as for Jake—"

"Who?"

"Jake McGowan, the lawyer who bought me out."

"Oh."

"He can help you. And he'll do a damn good job." Diane's voice was filled with admiration.

"He works on custody cases?" Kimberly asked without much interest.

"He used to."

"Used to?" Kimberly whirled, her blue-green gaze pinned on Diane's face. "What's that supposed to mean?"

Diane lifted a shoulder and slid her gaze away from Kimberly's. "That he concentrates on corporate law now. You know—taxes, mergers, that sort of thing."

"Yeah, I know," Kimberly said, thinking of the bevy of lawyers who were retained by the bank for which she worked. And then there were the attorneys who had worked for Robert. It seemed as if half the lawyers in Portland had been on her ex-husband's payroll at one time or another. She worried her lip. The name McGowan was familiar—but not as one of Robert's gophers. No... but there was something...

"At one time Jake McGowan was the best domestic relations attorney in Portland."

"'Was' seems to be the operative word," Kimberly challenged.

Diane twisted in her chair so that she could stare up at Kimberly and hold her with her frank blue gaze. Her forehead creased thoughtfully. "I wouldn't refer you to him unless I had absolute faith in the man. He's the best, I tell you. The man you need. There was a time when he hadn't lost a case."

"And what happened?"

Diane hesitated. "He had a few personal problems."

"Oh, great."

"But they're in the past. Listen, Kim, would I refer you to him if he weren't the best? He'll go up against anyone Robert hires and come out on top."

"You're sure?"

"As sure as I am about anything."

Kimberly felt Diane was holding something back—something important. "What is it you're not telling me?"

"Nothing. As I said, at one time he was the best in the business. He still could be."

"If..." Kimberly prodded.

Diane's mouth tightened. "If he were properly motivated."

"'If he were motivated,'" Kimberly repeated with more than a trace of cynicism. "This isn't some case in one of your textbooks, you know. This is my life. *My life* and Lindsay's."

"That's why you need Jake."

Kimberly wasn't convinced but forced a thin smile and raked her fingers through her long hair. A headache was building behind her eyes. "You know, I think it's wonderful that you're getting married again. Really."

"You have a funny way of showing it."

"Maybe I'm just envious."

"You? The woman who's sworn off men for life?"

Kimberly managed a thin smile. "Yeah, but Scott's a great guy, and I'm sure you'll be happy breathing all that smog in L.A.—"

Diane laughed.

"I'm just disappointed, that's all. I was counting on you."

"So, count on McGowan. Believe me, he can help you. Better than I can. I'll leave a note with Sarah—she's staying on—and she'll set up an appointment for you in the next couple of weeks." Diane touched Kimberly on the shoulder. "Trust me."

"I guess I have to," she said, feeling as if she had no other choice.

"You'll like him. I guarantee it."

"And if I don't?"

"You'll be the first woman who didn't."

"Oh, great. A lady-killer." Kimberly wasn't impressed. Robert had cured her of that.

Diane shook her head. "It's not intentional," she said.

"Good. Not that it matters. He wouldn't get to me."

"Oh?"

Kimberly skewered the lawyer with a suspicious look. "I'm not in the market for a man—any man. If Robert taught me one thing, it's that I can only depend on myself." She offered Diane a small smile. "I'm just interested in McGowan if he can help me keep my daughter."

"He can." Diane was firm.

Kimberly's answer was a skeptical smile. She gazed out the window, noticing that the dark sky had opened up and rain was pounding the horizon in furious, windblown waves. Raindrops drizzled in jagged rivulets across the windows.

The gutters of the old cottage-turned-office gurgled. Ever-widening puddles appeared on the uneven asphalt of the parking lot. Kimberly's thoughts were as dark as the slate-colored sky. Could anyone really help her if Robert decided to follow through on his demands? Or worse yet, would Robert ignore the law, as she suspected he had in the past, and just steal Lindsay away? Kimberly's fists clenched. Never!

If it was the last thing she ever did, she'd keep Lindsay safe with her. And if it took Jake McGowan or an act of God to do so, then so be it.

Robert, whether he knew it or not, was in for the fight of his miserable life!

She left Diane's office and headed home, stopping for groceries before driving through the dark, rain-slickened streets to her neighborhood, an older section in the southeast section of Portland known as Sellwood.

Her house, built in the early twenties, was a story and a half, painted white, trimmed in beet red and mortgage free. Though a little cramped inside, the rooms were cozy and big enough to accommodate a single mother and an energetic five-year-old. The fenced yard was surrounded by a laurel hedge and was equipped with a sandbox, picnic table and swing set. True, the house wasn't nearly as grand as the massive brick colonial she'd shared with Robert during their marriage, but the little cottage would do. And do nicely. If only Robert would leave things as they were.

As if expecting Robert or one of his shady underlings to be watching, she glanced nervously over her shoulder, then shook off her case of nerves. She couldn't afford paranoia—not now.

She locked the car, then, balancing two grocery sacks, ducked under a dripping clematis and hurried up the cracked concrete walk to the back door.

"I'm home," she called as she stepped into the kitchen and shook the rain from her hair. She heard a high-pitched squeal and the scamper of excited feet as Lindsay clambered through the hardwood halls to the kitchen.

"Mommy!" Two blond pigtails, their ribbons long gone, streamed behind an impish face and sparkling blue eyes. Lindsay flung herself at her mother.

"How're ya, pumpkin?" Kimberly asked, scooping her daughter into her arms and kissing Lindsay's flushed cheek.

"Hungry!"

"Oh, don't tell me, Arlene doesn't feed you?" Kimberly guessed, laughing as she pointed to the stains from lunch on the front of Lindsay's sweatshirt.

Lindsay's lower lip protruded. "She doesn't feed me enough!"

With a chuckle Arlene Henderson, a neighbor who took care of Lindsay while Kimberly worked, entered the room. An energetic, whip-thin woman of fifty-five, Arlene seemed taller than her five feet two inches. With frizzy, steel-gray hair and twinkling brown eyes, she winked broadly at Lindsay. "She's just mad 'cause I won't let her have a cookie until after supper. We made pumpkin cookies today, didn't we?" she asked a still-pouting Lindsay. "Even though Halloween's long over and Christmas is just around the corner."

Kimberly chuckled, but Lindsay's brow pulled into deep furrows. "I'm starving," she complained, rubbing her stomach theatrically.

"You'll survive," Kimberly predicted. "We're going to have hamburgers in less than a half an hour."

"At McDonald's!"

"No—here."

Lindsay frowned again, then squirmed out of her mother's arms. "I like McDonald's better," she pronounced, sneaking a sly look up at Kimberly.

"I know you do."

"And they've got fries and McNuggets and—and fruit pies!"

"We'll go on Saturday," Kimberly promised.

"Tonight!"

"Then not at all."

"Saturday!" Lindsay cried.

"Fair enough."

Mollified, Lindsay cast a suspicious look over her shoulder and wandered back into the living room. Once there, she began assembling Legos in front of the television.

"Robert stopped by today," Arlene said when the child was out of earshot.

Kimberly felt a cold knot settle in the pit of her stomach. "What did he want?"

"To talk to Lindsay, which he did." Arlene scowled as she slipped her arms through the sleeves of her oversize jacket. "Of course, I didn't leave the room. I don't trust the man."

Kimberly fought down the panic that crawled up her spine. "What did he want?"

"Well, actually he asked about you."

"He knows I work—"

"I know, but he stopped by the bank and you weren't there, so he assumed . . ." Arlene shrugged.

"I was with Diane."

"I didn't mention you had a lawyer."

"Good—because I don't," Kimberly said, kicking off her heels.

"No lawyer? And why in heaven's name not?"

"It's a long story—I'll fill you in later. Just tell me about Robert."

"Well, the pixie was glad to see him."

"She should be—he's her father," Kimberly said woodenly.

Arlene rolled her eyes. "If you can call him that. Anyway, he didn't stay long, just said hello, hugged her and asked about you."

"Was anyone with him?"

"Two men. But they waited in the car."

His bodyguard and chauffeur. In recent years, Robert was never without either man.

"Lindsay wasn't upset?"

"No," Arlene admitted grudgingly. "And I guess he does have the right to call his daughter, but..." She shrugged her slim shoulders.

"Of course he does," Kimberly said, ignoring the ridiculous panic that chilled her to the very bone. She'd been married to Robert for less than two years, and he'd been a stranger. She hadn't known him at all. The marriage had been a mistake from day one. They both knew it. And now, suddenly he wanted Lindsay. Ignoring the tightness in her chest, she reached for one of the cookies still cooling on racks near the window.

"Well, he isn't much of a father, and don't you stand up for him!" Arlene didn't even try to hide her dislike for the man. "You and I both know he walks on the dark side of the law."

"It's never been proven," Kimberly said, defending him instinctively, as she had for years. She couldn't believe some of the stories she'd heard about him—wouldn't. And yet...

"No, but then he didn't do right by you. Carrying on with that Stella woman while you two were married."

" 'That Stella woman' is his wife now."

"And now she wants *your* daughter."

"She won't get her," Kimberly said, though she felt the familiar fear knotted in her stomach.

"Diane tell you that?"

Kimberly frowned. "No," she admitted, explaining about her visit with her attorney.

"So Diane's remarrying—that's good," Arlene said, scratching her head. "But what do you know about this McGowan character?"

"Not much, except that Diane's sure he's the man for the job."

In the living room Lindsay giggled loudly, and Kimberly's heart turned over. She glanced down the hall and spied her daughter. Lindsay, tired of her building blocks, was trying to do headstands on the couch. She tossed her legs into the air, tried to balance against the wall and ended up flopping back on the couch, only to start the process all over again.

"Things'll work out," Arlene predicted with a steadfast smile. "The Lord will look after you."

"I hope so," Kimberly said.

"I *know* so!" Arlene snatched her umbrella from the floor. "Don't you worry, and if you take Lindsay outside, you bundle her up good. There's already a foot of snow in the mountains. Winter's coming early this year."

"I'll remember that," Kimberly replied.

"Good. I'll see you tomorrow." Waving, she hurried down the hall and called a quick goodbye to Lindsay.

As Arlene shut the door behind her, Kimberly snapped the blinds shut and thought ahead to meeting with Jake McGowan. Why did she feel there was something she should know about him? What was it?

"Come on, Mommy! Let's cut paper dolls!" Lindsay gave up her balancing act, turned off the television and, dragging one tattered, fuzzy pink bunny, dashed over to her mother. "Please, now!"

"I thought you couldn't wait to eat."

"We can do both!"

Kimberly laughed, forgetting about Jake McGowan for the moment. "I don't think so," she said. "I might get confused and cut my hamburger with the scissors and pour ketchup all over the dollies."

Lindsay giggled. "That's silly!"

"So are you, pumpkin," Kimberly said, poking a finger in Lindsay's belly. "So are you!"

"No way!" Jake growled, disgusted. His shirtsleeves rolled over his forearms, his tie strung loosely over the back of his chair, he sat amid boxes, pictures and framed awards that had been stacked against Diane Welby's desk. With a flourish he signed the contract for the house and grounds that Diane had owned. A second document took care of the legal practice. "You know how I feel about custody cases."

"She needs your help," Diane insisted.

"She doesn't need me. There are several dozen lawyers in the yellow pages." For emphasis he thumped his fingers against a scribbled-upon copy of the telephone directory.

"Humor me, Jake—meet with her." Diane skimmed her copies of the agreement, deed and contract before stuffing all the papers into a file and jamming them into her brief-case. Satisfied, she snapped the black leather case closed. "The movers will take care of all this—" she motioned to the office debris she was shipping to Los Angeles "—on Thursday."

"Good."

"Now, about Kimberly—give it a shot, okay?"

Jake's lips compressed, and he grew thoughtful. "Oh, I get it," he drawled. "This is a 'special client,' right? Maybe a friend or a friend of a friend, and she's upset that you're abandoning her.''

"Something like that.''

Shaking his head, Jake said, "Find someone else.''

"Just meet with her. If it doesn't work out, refer her to Dennis Briggs or Tyler Patton. They're both good. Not as good as you are—''

"As I *was*.''

"You could be again if you'd stop wallowing in self-pity.''

"Is that what I'm doing?'' Jake asked, feeling his lips curve downward. He really didn't give a damn.

"Yes! And it's such a waste. You could've been—could still be—the best!''

"Maybe I don't want to be,'' he said, scowling darkly.

"Suit yourself. But this time someone *needs* you.''

"Humph.''

Diane slid her case off the desk and walked to the door. Her hand rested on the knob. "Do yourself and me a favor—meet Kimberly Bennett. I'll have Sarah set up an appointment next week.''

"I'm going skiing next week.''

"Then the next.''

"It's a waste of time.''

"I don't know why I bother with you.''

"Neither do I.''

Diane sighed, opened the door, then closed it again and, holding her briefcase in both hands, said, "Fine, consider it calling in my markers—okay?''

Jake's jaw clenched, and the knot in his stomach twisted. Diane Welby had helped him pick up the pieces of his life when he needed her most. Again the horrid grief seared his soul. There was no period in his life he'd rather forget more. The days and nights had seemed to run together in pitch darkness. And the pain! God, the pain had been so intense—so all consuming. He would have given up and accepted a fate of living in his own hell, had it not been for Diane.

At the time, Jake and Diane had worked at a large firm in Portland. Diane had covered for him at the office—given him the time he needed—and comforted him when he didn't want anyone around. She'd even helped him make the move from domestic to corporate law just so that he could function again. Finally he'd managed to pull himself back together to the point where he could go on with his life. And he owed Diane Welby—he owed her big.

A grim smile tightened his lips. He shoved his hands deep into his pockets. "I guess I owe you one, *Dr.* Welby."

Shaking her head, she laughed. "More than one, but who's counting?" Opening the door again, she glanced over her shoulder. "And it won't be Dr. Welby much longer."

He laughed. The pet name he'd given her when she had cared for him would always stick. "Dr. Donaldson just doesn't have the same ring."

"Work on it. I'll see you at the wedding next week."

"I wouldn't miss it for the world," Jake said with a cynicism too ingrained for his thirty-five years. Through the window he watched Diane slide into her bronze Mustang, and he wondered if she had any idea what she was getting herself into.

Marriage, he thought with the same stygian anger that always consumed him when he thought of his own tragic, short-lived union, *who needs it?*

Chapter Two

He was late. Checking his watch and frowning, Jake drove his pickup into the parking lot of his new office building. Tall maple and fir trees separated the lot from the main road, and the building itself, a putty-colored stucco cottage with sloped roof, gables, moss-green shutters and several chimney stacks, reminded him of country homes he'd seen in Europe. Without the wooden sign swinging in the front yard, no one would guess this quaint little retreat to be a lawyer's office.

Perversely the offices appealed to him, though he'd bought Diane Welby's practice on a whim because he was tired of the run-as-fast-as-you-can pace of downtown Portland.

He parked the pickup near the door and climbed out. Rain lashed at his neck and tossed his hair away from his face. Hiking the collar of his denim jacket against the wind, he lowered the tailgate and pulled out the first box of books he could reach.

Despite a plastic tarp, the box had got wet. The cardboard sagged as he carried the awkward crate through the lot and down a mossy brick path to the door. Cursing as the box began to split, Jake shouldered his way into the building.

He dropped the box on his desk and rubbed the crick from the small of his back. As he surveyed the spacious room with its mullioned windows, fawn-colored carpet, unused fireplace and plaster walls, he wondered if he'd made a mistake.

But he'd been bored with the rat race of the city, and was sick of high rises, chrome, glass and crisp white shirts beneath neatly buttoned wool vests. He'd had it. If he never saw an athletic club again, or walked into a boardroom of self-important executives surrounding a hardwood table and puffing on cigars, or spent hours reading through the latest books on tax loopholes, it would be too soon.

"So, here you are, McGowan," he muttered as he spied a half-full bottle of Scotch shoved into his soggy box. His lips curled into a sardonic smile. Ignoring the fact that it wasn't quite noon, he dusted off the bottle, twisted off the cap and, mentally toasting this new turn of his career, muttered, "Cheers."

He took a long tug right from the bottle. As the liquor hit the back of his throat and burned a path to his stomach, he grimaced. Without bothering to recap the bottle, he strode outside.

Sooty gray clouds moved restlessly across the sky. The wind whistled through the fir boughs, and rain peppered the ground. Growling to himself, Jake climbed into the rear of the pickup, threw back the tarp and yanked on a heavy crate. He'd overslept, got a late start packing these final boxes and now he couldn't possibly drive to Mt. Bachelor by night-fall.

Hearing the purr of an engine, he glanced over his shoulder.

A sleek black Mercedes wheeled into the lot. The driver, a woman, yanked on the emergency brake, cut the engine and climbed out. Clasping a billowing black cloak around her, she headed straight for the cottage. She didn't even glance his way, but sidestepped the puddles and walked crisply along the path. Once inside the open door, she stopped dead in her tracks. "Hello?" she called in a voice so low he could barely hear it. "Sarah? Are you here?"

Jake vaulted from the bed of the pickup. His eyes narrowed on the rich woman in her raven-black cape and matching boots. He hauled the box off the back of the truck and followed her path just as she, perplexed, walked back outside. Statuesque, with high cheekbones, skin flushed from the cold and mahogany-colored hair dark with the rain, she stared at him through the most intense blue-green eyes he'd ever seen. "Excuse me, I'm looking for Jake McGowan," she said, offering a tentative smile.

"I'm McGowan."

"You?" she repeated as if she didn't believe him. Her gaze moved from his wind-tossed hair to his scuffed boots. "But I thought—the man I'm looking for is a lawyer...."

"As I said, I'm Jake McGowan," he repeated flatly.

Kimberly didn't know whether to laugh or cry. *This* was the hotshot attorney Diane had told her about? **This man** dressed in worn denim, in desperate need of a **shave** and smelling slightly of alcohol? "There—there must be some mistake."

"If you say so." He shifted a huge box full of **books and** desk paraphernalia and carried it down a short hallway—to Diane's office, or what had been Diane's office.

Wary, half-expecting him to own up to the fact that he was the groundskeeper or janitor, Kimberly followed a few steps behind, noting the man's broad shoulders stretching taut a denim jacket, his lean hips, low slung, extremely faded jeans and well-worn leather boots.

He dropped the crate in the one empty corner of the office, then turned to face her, resting his hips on a large walnut desk and crossing his arms insolently across his chest. "What can I do for you, Ms.—?"

"Bennett. Kimberly Bennett. I have an appointment with Mr. Mc—you—this morning."

Something flashed in his eyes. "So, you're Kimberly Bennett," he drawled as if her name were distasteful. His gaze moved slowly from her head to her feet, then he glanced through the window to the parking lot and her car.

"Diane told you about me?"

"A little. But your appointment is *next* Monday."

"This is the second—"

"Sarah told me the ninth."

"Oh, no." Kimberly thought ahead to her schedule at the bank. Next week was overbooked with trust clients starting to put together their year-end information. "I don't know if I can make it then . . . look, I'm here now. Can't you just see if this is going to work?" she asked. "I don't know if I can get away next week."

He smiled as if at some private joke.

Kimberly plunged on. "Diane must have mentioned how desperate I am," she said nervously. "I don't want to lose my daughter."

"Not even to her father?"

Why did he sound so bitter? "Not to anyone. Lindsay's only five. The divorce was hard enough on her, and Robert and I agreed that I should have full custody."

Jake's brows shot up.

"But he's changed his mind."

"Why?" His strong, chiseled features were taut beneath his tanned skin.

Kimberly's shoulders squared at the antagonism charging the air. He hadn't said as much, but she felt as if he didn't trust her, didn't believe her, though they'd barely met. "He claims it's because he remarried and his new wife can't conceive children." Her lips twisted at the irony of it all. Robert, the man who had once thought she should consider abortion as the solution to her surprise pregnancy, now wanted his daughter all to himself. "Robert claims Stella doesn't want to adopt."

"He *claims*?" Jake repeated. "You don't believe him?"

"It's difficult—with Robert."

"Why?"

Kimberly bristled. Damn, but these questions were personal. *What did you expect?* "He, uh, was less than honest while we were married."

Jake's mouth twitched. "And now he wants full custody?"

"That's what he says." She felt herself shaking inside, shaking with a rage that gnawed at her often during the nights when she couldn't sleep. "He told me he'd go to any lengths, even if it meant proving me unfit."

"Could he?"

"Prove me unfit? No! Of course not!" Her cheeks flushed angrily. "I mean—it's not true. He has no proof, no evidence—and I don't even think he'd go through with it, but I don't know. He's been obsessive about Lindsay lately."

"Lindsay's your daughter?"

"Yes."

"And Stella's his wife—have I got it straight?"

"Right."

His silvery eyes were cold, his gaze intense. "Wasn't Robert 'obsessive' with your daughter while you were married?"

"No—not at all." She cleared her throat. "At times he acted as if she didn't exist."

"And yet, now that he's changed his mind, he'd go as far as to claim you're unfit?"

Was this man baiting her? "I believe him."

"Because of his track record?"

That did it! "Look, I'm just telling you what he told me—okay? That's what he's threatened."

Scowling to himself, Jake plowed one hand through his wet, near-black hair. Then, noticing the condition of the room for the first time, he muttered something under his breath, cleared a dusty stack of files from a nearby chair and waved her onto the cushion.

Kimberly perched on the edge of the chair.

"I wouldn't worry about the unfit business," he said, rubbing the back of his neck.

"Why not?"

"If there's no proof, your husband's attorney won't go along with it."

"His attorney would jump off a cliff if Robert told him to."

Jake actually grinned—a crooked smile twisted by derision.

Kimberly smiled back. "Will you take my case?"

"I don't usually handle custody or domestic problems—"

"You did once. Diane said you were the best in Portland."

"She's stretching the truth."

Kimberly's eyebrows raised. "And why would she do that?"

"I don't know. Maybe to satisfy you."

"I don't think so, Mr. McGowan. She seemed to think that you could help me."

"Any attorney can help you," he replied evenly.

"I want the best."

"Then try Ben Kesler," he suggested coldly, feeling the irony of the situation. The bastard had been Jake's wife's lawyer. "He's gained quite a reputation for himself as a divorce attorney."

"Can't do it," she said softly. All the color drained from her face, and her voice threatened to give out.

"And why not?"

"Kesler is my husband's lawyer."

Jake froze. His shoulders bunched, and pain flickered across his angular features before he looked away quickly, through the window to a flock of geese flying south in an uneven V. "Then you've got problems."

"That much I already know," she snapped. "Listen, this wasn't my idea. But Diane Welby seems to think you're the best attorney around. I don't know you from Adam, but I trust Diane." Kimberly rose to her feet and took two steps closer to him. The pointed toes of her boots nearly brushed the scratched leather of his. "I'll do anything I have to for my child," she said in a low, determined voice. Her chin angled upward mutinously. "Do you have any children, Mr. McGowan?"

His breath hissed between his teeth. "No," he replied. He knew his expression was giving too much away, and he pressed his lips together.

"Then you can't possibly understand what I'm going through. Until you've experienced the vulnerability of having a child—"

"I understand," he said swiftly.

"Do you? Do you know what it's like to think you'll never see your child laugh again? Do you know how you'd feel if your daughter were scared at night? Can you imagine how much it hurts to think you've inadvertently caused your child some pain—"

"I get the picture," he cut in.

"What I'm trying to tell you, Mr. McGowan, is that I'm afraid—downright scared—that I'll lose my daughter."

"To her father," he whispered.

Kimberly drew herself up to her full five feet six inches, then pinned him with her sea-green eyes. "I have the right to be afraid. Robert doesn't like to lose."

"No one does."

"But it's deeper than that."

"Meaning?"

Kimberly hesitated, thought for a moment and then said with forced calm, "Robert accused me of being unfaithful to him. He claimed he knew who my lover was, had a private detective follow us and could name places and times when we'd met."

"I'm not interested in your love life," he said flatly.

Apparently Kimberly wasn't about to stop. Not now. "There is nothing to be interested in, Mr. McGowan. That's the point. I never cheated on my husband. But the fact is he has the gall to accuse me, intends to bring it up in court, then pay off anyone to lie. To put it frankly, Robert's put the fear of God in me."

"Nice guy, your ex."

She clamped her lips shut and glared at him. "Obviously this is a waste of my time."

"I didn't say that. But you paint him as an ogre."

Smiling bitterly, she ran shaking fingers through her hair. "I didn't know him—at least not well enough. And he changed…" She stopped, knowing it sounded trite, though it was true enough. During the course of their short marriage, Robert's business connections had taken a different direction, had turned a corner that frightened her. She swallowed against a suddenly dry throat.

"And now he's going to create a phony case against you, then perjure himself to get his kid back, is that right?"

"Yes." It did sound bizarre, even to Kimberly.

"Who *is* this guy? If he's lying, it's easy enough to prove." He crossed his arms over his chest and stared at her long and hard.

She was ashamed of the weak little wife she'd once been— the girl with her head in the clouds. She'd been blind and foolish. But no more. "My marriage was a mistake, and the only good thing that came from it is Lindsay. And I assure you, Mr. McGowan, I don't intend to lose her," she vowed, her fingers curling in conviction. "He can drag me through hell and back, but this time I intend to fight him every step of the way! Now, either you can help me, or I can find someone else!"

Jake stared straight at her, and though subconsciously he knew that he should hear her out, trust her wide-eyed innocence, he didn't listen. He wasn't about to be dragged into this mess, whatever it was. Maybe she was a liar, maybe her husband wasn't such a bad guy—and maybe she was telling the truth. Whatever the case, it didn't concern him. "I'm sorry, Ms. Bennett," he said levelly. "But I think you'd be better off with someone else. Tyler Patton—"

"Has worked for my husband."

Jake's brows pulled together. Something in the back of his brain clicked together. "What's your ex-husband's name? Robert Bennett?"

"Fisher," she said. "I took back my maiden name when the divorce was final."

Jake didn't move, but just stared at her. His eyes narrowed suspiciously, and he felt every muscle in his body stiffen. When he finally spoke, his voice was low. "Just one question."

"Shoot."

"Why did you marry him?"

"Because I was young and stupid," she answered. "He represented everything I didn't have as a child—money, power, looks, sophistication. What I didn't realize is that all those things don't add up to love." As if she were suddenly embarrassed, she looked away, glanced pointedly at her watch and frowned. "I've got to go, Mr. McGowan...." She handed him her card and met his gaze squarely. "Can you help me?"

His mouth was thin and tight. "I don't know."

She let out an exasperated breath. "I see. I guess Diane was wrong about you." With that, she headed for the door. "I'm sorry I wasted my breath and your time. Just send me a bill for—" she gestured with one hand "—this." She swept out of the room.

She shoved open the door, and a blast of damp wind blew into the room, snatching at the hem of her cloak and tangling her hair. Without looking back, she marched determinedly across the puddled parking lot.

Jake caught up with her at the car and grabbed the crook of her arm. "Wait." He tugged, whirling her around until she was face to face with him again, her eyes level with his chin. "Look, I said I didn't know if I could help you, but I told Diane I'd try and I will. If—if it doesn't work out, I'll find you someone else."

"Don't bother. I'm tired of being passed around like yesterday's trash! Diane said you were the best, and that's why I'm here. If you can't handle the job, I'm perfectly capable of finding someone who is."

His throat worked, and the grip on her arm tightened. "Diane didn't have all the facts."

"Meaning?"

Scowling, he said, "Meaning that there are other people more qualified."

"She didn't seem to think so."

"As I said, I'll look over your file, make a few inquiries when I get back into town next week—"

"Don't bother!" she muttered, jerking her arm free and sliding into the interior of her car. "I'll find someone myself!" She slammed the car door shut and turned on the ignition.

Surprised, Jake stepped back and watched as she threw the car into gear. She glanced back once. Intense blue-green eyes focused on him without blinking, and Jake, who'd sworn never to trust another beautiful woman again, especially a beautiful *rich* woman, realized with fatal dismay that he wanted to help her. Kimberly Bennett with her black Mercedes, expensive cloak, auburn, rain-dampened hair and high cheekbones now flushed from the cold, had gotten to him. Even though she'd fairly oozed money.

Robert Fisher's money.

Money made from Fisher's illegitimate business deals. Drugs, smuggling, you name it—Fisher was reported to be into it these days. Somehow, though, he managed to keep his distance from the actual crimes. And no one in his organization talked. At least no one had. But maybe that could change.

Jake's gut tightened as he watched the sleek car roll onto the main road and disappear. His fists clenched impotently, and he shoved them into the pockets of his jacket.

Kimberly's Mercedes and her expensive clothes made sense. Robert Fisher was one of the wealthiest men in Portland. He owned real estate in the west hills, several restaurants downtown, held the majority interest in three lumber mills outside the city and was allegedly one of the kingpins of organized crime in the Pacific Northwest.

Nothing had ever been proven, of course. Fisher was too slippery, his attorneys too slick. No, Robert Fisher always managed to keep one step ahead of the law—even when the law had been Jake's half brother, Daniel Stevens.

Rain drizzled down Jake's neck and slid beneath his collar. He didn't notice.

So, Diane's friend, Fisher's ex-wife, wanted to do Robert Fisher battle. For that, Kimberly Bennett had Jake's grudging approval. And she was willing to fight not only Fisher, but his attorney, Ben Kesler, a man Jake would personally nominate for bastard-of-the-century.

Well, more power to her. If nothing else, Kimberly Bennett had guts. And if she was going to take on Fisher, she'd need all of them.

Shoving wet hair from his eyes, he walked back to the pickup, unloaded another crate of files and headed back inside. Once in his new office, he dropped the crate and pawed through Diane's files until he found one marked, Bennett, Kimberly L. He noticed the bottle of Scotch and a glass tumbler. Well, why not? he thought with one glance at the rain outside. He poured himself another drink and smiled grimly.

Leaning back in his chair, wet boots propped on the top of his desk, he began to read all about Robert Fisher's intriguing ex-wife. He probably couldn't help her, but he'd make a stab at it, for Diane if nothing else. After all, he had promised Diane.

And the prospect of nailing Robert Fisher's hide to the wall was appealing—if purely selfish and vengeful.

The only problem was the child. She was an innocent in all this. She shouldn't have to suffer.

He eyed his drink. He had a few days to think about Kimberly Bennett and he could run a check on her. In the meantime he had other plans. As soon as he was unpacked, he was going to take a short skiing vacation to clear his mind. When he came back, he'd have a decision on the Bennett/Fisher custody case.

Taking a long swallow from his glass, he felt the liquor burn the back of his throat. He glanced down at the open file folder and began to read all about Ms. Kimberly Bennett.

Kimberly wheeled into the parking garage of the bank where she worked and slid the Mercedes into her spot. "Idiot," she muttered, cutting the engine. She took a minute to compose herself. There were other attorneys, she told herself, hundreds of them in Portland alone. She'd find one who would help her, someone who would care, someone who didn't seem to be prejudiced against divorced mothers and someone who wouldn't be cowed by the thought of riding roughshod over Robert Fisher.

She winced a little at that and glanced around the parking lot of the bank where Robert still did business. Hadn't she gotten her job here because of Robert? Didn't the bank president himself consider Robert his personal friend? Weren't Robert's companies the biggest depositors in First Cascade?

"So get another job," she told herself for what had to be the thousandth time. She glanced at her reflection in the rearview mirror. Worried sea-green eyes stared back at her. "There are other banks, just as there are other lawyers."

Frowning at the thought of Jake McGowan again, Kimberly quickly finger-combed her hair, hoping to tame the wayward auburn curls. Then she grabbed her briefcase and made a beeline for the elevator.

In the trust department on the third floor, Kimberly weaved her way through a maze of desks. Computers hummed, telephones rang and snatches of conversation floated in the air. The walls were polished cherry wood, the carpet plush forest green, and brass lamps and fixtures added to the image of money that the bank tried so hard to preserve.

Kimberly's secretary, Marcie, was typing frantically at her desk. Her fingers flew over the keyboard of a word processor. A black headset creased her perfect, honey-blond pageboy.

She glanced up at Kimberly's approach and ripped off the headpiece. "Thank God you're back!"

"That sounds ominous," Kimberly remarked.

"It was meant to."

"What happened?" Kimberly picked up a stack of messages on the corner of Marcie's desk. "Miss me?" she asked.

"Everything!" Marcie stage-whispered, "It's been a *zoo*—I mean an honest-to-goodness zoo—around here. Zealander's on the warpath again, claims you're stealing *his* clients."

Kimberly smothered a smile. Bill Zealander was always worried that Kimberly was climbing the corporate ladder a little more quickly than he. He blamed it on her looks, women's rights and the fact that their boss, Eric Compton, had asked Kimberly out several times since her divorce. "I can handle Bill," she said, hoping to calm Marcie down.

But Marcie was in no mood for calming. "And then there's Mrs. Pendergraft," she rattled on. "She fell and broke her hip and is in a nursing home. The trust has to pay her expenses..." Marcie went on and on, filling Kimberly in on office gossip as well as client problems. When she'd finished, she sighed loudly.

"Why don't you take a break?" Kimberly suggested, glancing around and spying Bill's secretary. "Heather and I can hold the fort."

"If you're sure . . ." But Marcie was already reaching for her purse.

"Positive. And when you get back, send Mrs. Pendergraft some flowers with a note from the bank, and whatever you do, *don't* charge her account for it!"

"Will do," Marcie promised.

Smiling, Kimberly walked into her office. She hung her cape on the brass hall tree near the window just as Marcie popped in and set a steaming cup of coffee on the desk pad.

"I thought you might need fortification."

Kimberly sighed gratefully. "I think I needed this two hours ago, before I went out."

"So, the meeting with the new lawyer didn't go well?"

"That might be the understatement of the century," she said wryly.

"Can I help?"

Kimberly took a sip from the hot coffee and thought aloud. "Can you find out all the attorneys who work directly or indirectly for the bank?" she asked. "Anyone who's on the board, or done real estate work or that sort of thing?"

"I suppose so. But it'll take time."

"That's okay," Kimberly said, frowning a little. "I just don't want anyone even loosely connected with First Cascade."

"Will do," Marcie said. "I'll get on it the minute I get back from break." With a wave she hurried out of the office, and Kimberly was left holding her steaming cup of coffee between her hands. McGowan hadn't said he wouldn't represent her, but Kimberly wasn't certain she wanted him. She needed someone dedicated, someone who had Lindsay's best interests in mind, someone committed.

And that left Jake McGowan, with his unconventional good looks and cynical disposition, out of the running.

Chapter Three

Jake wiped the dabs of shaving cream from his jaw and told himself he was the worst kind of fool.

The past three hours he'd done nothing but dwell on Kimberly Bennett and her custody case. He'd even given up unpacking his office and had driven home to shave and shower before he caught up with Kimberly again. And that was just plain nuts. If he had any brains at all, he'd leave Ms. Bennett and her problems alone. But he couldn't. Maybe it was because she'd been married to Robert Fisher, a man Jake had sworn vengeance against, or maybe it was because it had been long enough to bury his own personal demons and practice the kind of law he loved again. Or, he thought, frowning at his reflection, maybe it was because she was the most beautiful woman he'd seen in a long, long while.

Whatever the reason, he was back in his little cottage on the shores of Lake Oswego, shaving and dressing as if he cared what she thought.

Muttering to himself, he slid a cream-colored sweater over his head, then started for the door. He ignored the open suitcase on his bed and the stack of ski clothes he intended to pack.

Tonight he would call Kimberly Bennett's bluff—find out just what her game was. He'd read all the typewritten pages in her file, even deciphered Diane's illegible notes to herself, but there were still a lot of holes in Ms. Bennett's case.

Why was Fisher so interested in his daughter now? Some latent paternal feelings? Bah. Jake's lips twisted, and his stomach tightened as it always did when he thought about Robert Fisher. Fisher was capable of only one motive—greed.

If he'd wanted his kid, why had Fisher let his wife have full custody over three years ago? What had changed his mind?

Stuffing his arms through a battered leather jacket, he reached for his keys and tried not to dwell on Robert Fisher. A part of him knew it was best to let sleeping dogs lie and let the police department handle Fisher. Eventually they'd catch him, and there wouldn't be a loophole big enough for him to slip through.

Unfortunately patience wasn't Jake's long suit. And the thought of nailing Fisher's hide to the wall was more than appealing. It had been too long already.

Hiking his collar against the wind, he strode across the wet grass to his Bronco, parked near the pickup he'd used in the move. He climbed into the cab and shoved the rig into reverse, sending up a spray of gravel as he backed out of the driveway and headed north to the winking lights of Portland.

Kimberly. The thought that she had been Fisher's wife bothered Jake—much more than it should have. Although he shouldn't have been surprised. He'd known of Fisher's interest in younger, beautiful women. Kimberly Bennett was no exception.

Or was she?

Slowing for a red light, he snapped on the radio and tried to concentrate on the news. But his thoughts were already ahead, on the one woman who could help him bring down Robert Fisher.

He felt an unexpected pang of guilt for hiding the fact that he knew all about Fisher—knew of his cruelty the hard way. He should come clean with her, but he couldn't. Not yet. Kimberly Bennett, despite her beauty and obvious charm, had been involved with Fisher—had been the man's wife, for God's sake—and therefore she was fair game. Besides, he rationalized as he traveled in a path parallel to the dark waters of the Willamette River, this was a trade. Even up. He'd help her if she'd help him. Tit for tat.

So, why did his conscience twinge? And why did he feel as if he was using her?

"Because you're a fool," he said again, glancing at his eyes in the rearview mirror. "A damn fool."

Kimberly spent the remainder of the afternoon trying not to think about Jake McGowan. Instead she filled out reports, made phone calls, dictated letters and dealt with the investment department. She finally looked up from her desk at six and realized she'd be late again.

"Great," she mumbled, dialing her phone quickly and waiting impatiently until Arlene answered.

"Hello?"

"Hi," she said. "Take a guess where I am."

Arlene chuckled. "Oh, I don't know, trapped behind a stack of tax forms or files or whatever you've got down there."

"Right. Still at the bank. But I'll be home in twenty minutes."

"Don't worry about it." Arlene's voice was full of mirth, and Kimberly sent up a silent prayer for her good nature. "I'll just take Lindsay home with me. She can help with dinner for Lyle. He'd love it if you let her stay and eat with us."

"No, really, I couldn't."

"He doesn't see her very often," Arlene added. "You know she's the granddaughter he never had."

Kimberly sighed. "I shouldn't do this."

"Sure you should. Slow down and enjoy life a little," Arlene advised. "Go out with a friend tonight. Leave Lindsay to me."

"I don't have any plans—"

"So make some. Don't you have a friend or two down at that bank?"

"I suppose."

"Then go on. We'll be fine."

"Okay, but I'll pick her up by seven-thirty," Kimberly promised, thanking her and ringing off. She did have a couple of errands to run, she remembered, snatching up her purse, briefcase and cape as she headed out of her office. After she'd run to the pharmacy, dry cleaner's and grocery, she would collect Lindsay.

She slapped the call button on the elevator and rode down to the basement parking lot. A few other employees straggled to their cars as she crossed the dimly lit lot and headed for her Mercedes. Just as she reached the car, she stopped short. There, one hip resting insolently against a sleek black fender, was Jake McGowan.

He'd replaced his faded jeans and work shirt with a pair of gray cords, a cream-colored sweater and beat-up leather jacket. His hair, though still a little on the wild side, wasn't quite so rumpled, and some of the antagonism had left his face. Nonetheless he still possessed that earthy sensuality she'd noticed when she'd first met him.

She ignored his male charms and walked quickly to the car. "What're you doing here?"

"Waiting for you."

She lifted a brow. "Why?"

"I thought we should talk. About your case."

Tossing her briefcase and purse inside the Mercedes, she said, "We talked this afternoon. You made it perfectly clear you weren't interested in helping me or my daughter." For effect, she planted her hands on her hips and stared him down. "So I don't see that we have anything further to discuss."

His eyes didn't flicker. "Maybe you're right," he agreed, "but I've done a lot of thinking this afternoon and I read your file."

Bully for you! "You shouldn't have bothered."

His jaw clenched. "Look, I'm just here trying to help, that's all. I thought we could talk things out a little. It's no big commitment. But I told Diane I'd help you."

"Listen, Mr. McGowan—"

"Jake."

"Jake, then. You don't owe me any favors. As far as I'm concerned, you're off the hook. As for whatever obligation you have toward Diane, just forget it. I'll tell her it didn't work out and I found someone else."

"Who?"

Good question. She tossed her hair over her shoulder. "I don't know yet. But when I find her, I'll tell Diane."

"*Her?* Find her?" he repeated.

"Yes, her. I think I'd work better with a woman."

He smiled at that, and she couldn't figure out what he found so damn amusing. What kind of a game was he playing, telling her to go jump in a lake this afternoon and chasing her down tonight? The man was a bastard.

"It might look better to the judge if a man represented you," he thought aloud.

"I doubt it." Why was she even bothering with him?

"Your ex might insinuate you can't get along with men...."

She felt the blood surge to her face. "No judge would buy anything so ridiculous."

"Maybe. Maybe not. Your husband—"

"*Ex*-husband," she corrected.

"—is a very powerful man. You already said he knows just about every attorney in town. What about judges? Does he have any 'friends' on the bench?"

Her legs felt suddenly shaky, but she tilted her chin up and stared him down. "And I suppose you know who'll be assigned?" she baited. What was it about this man that got her back up?

"No."

"Of course not. No one does."

"But Robert—I have the feeling he'd like to tilt the odds in his favor a little."

"How would you know?"

His jaw clenched. "I read the papers."

Of course. Robert had more than his share of trouble with the law lately—or at least his name had been linked to a couple of police cases.

"It wouldn't surprise me if Fisher somehow ended up with a judge who was lenient where fathers' rights are concerned."

She swallowed hard and leaned against the car. She knew that Robert had friends in high places, including the courts. "You don't have much faith in our judicial system."

"I just know there are flaws."

"Surely no one who knows Robert would accept the case...." Her voice trailed off. She'd thought of it before, of course, had considered the possibility of Robert buying a judge, but it seemed so bizarre and unlikely, something out of a made-for-television movie.

"All I'm saying," Jake said, his expression suddenly kind, "is that there's a chance I can help you—or at the very least find someone who can do the best job."

"That's quite a turnaround. Why would you bother?"

"Because I do owe Diane Welby a lot and because I know a little about Robert Fisher."

"Oh, I remember. The papers, right?"

He grimaced. "Right."

She looked into his eyes. McGowan. Had Robert ever said that name before? She couldn't remember. But there was something about Jake McGowan that touched her. Beneath his crusty, cynical exterior, she saw an honesty in his flinty gray eyes that drew her like a magnet. So, what would it hurt to find out what he had to say? She still didn't have to hire him.

"It goes without saying that Fisher isn't one of my favorite people," Jake was saying, "and if Ben Kesler's going to represent him, then you'd better get cracking."

"Tonight?"

"Tonight." His smile was hard. "I'm going out of town for a few days."

"So it's now or never, right?" she asked, feeling more than a little prickly.

His eyes flashed in the darkened lot. "No, it's now or late next week."

She almost smiled. He was clever, and that was good. She was tempted to listen to what he had to say, but she had to clear the air first. "Look, McGowan, let's be honest, okay? I don't like the way you treated me this afternoon. I came to you for help, and you immediately started baiting me."

"That's what'll happen in court," Jake replied.

"Fine. But I don't need it from my attorney."

His sensual lips tightened. "Let's just get one thing straight. If we come to some sort of agreement and I take your case, we'll play this my way."

She bit back a sharp response. This new side of Jake McGowan, slightly threatening and authoritative, caused her temper to flare, but maybe his arrogance was an attribute. She certainly didn't want a wimp representing her, and right now, glaring at her in the shadowy parking lot, McGowan looked far from wimpy. In fact he was downright imposing. He'd be perfect against a sleaze like Kesler. For the first time since she'd met him, she felt a ray of hope.

She checked her watch. "I promised my baby-sitter I'd be home by seven-thirty."

"We could start there—at your place."

The thought of him inside her home was more than a tad threatening. It made her feel naked and vulnerable. But what choice did she have? She needed a lawyer, McGowan might just be the best man for the job and she wanted to get home to Lindsay. "My place will be fine," she said with more calm than she felt. "I live—"

"I know your address," he cut in. "Remember, I read your file this afternoon."

"Oh." For the first time since meeting him, Kimberly was tongue-tied. The thought of his going through her private life, reading between the lines as he reviewed her relationship with Robert, was unnerving. She hated the thought of baring her soul to him, of sharing her innermost feelings.

And yet she didn't have much of a choice. If he was going to represent her, he'd have to know everything.

"I'll meet you there later," he suggested.

"Right." She watched as he climbed into a silver Bronco. Tall and slim, with dark hair and expressive eyes, he walked with an innate sensuality that caused her breath to stop somewhere between her lungs and lips. She noticed the casual movement of his hips, and when he unlocked the door of the Bronco and reached across the front seat, his sweater lifted, showing just the hint of tight skin across his abdomen.

Swallowing hard, Kimberly slid into her own car. She couldn't think of Jake McGowan as a man. He was her attorney—nothing more. And he wasn't even that, yet, she reminded herself as she jammed her key into the ignition. He hadn't said he'd take her case—just that he'd help her. And she wasn't all that convinced that he was the man for the job. Not yet.

But at least he was offering to help.

"Well, that's a step in the right direction," she told herself as she pulled out of the lot.

Jake drove to the nearest phone booth and placed another call—his third in the past two hours. On the fourth ring an answering machine clicked on, and Ron Koski's voice rasped in his ear, telling him to leave his name and number.

"It's McGowan again," Jake started, just as Ron picked up.

"I got your message earlier," Ron said, his voice gravelly from too few hours' sleep and too many cigarettes. "I thought you'd given up on Fisher."

Jake grimaced, turning up the collar of his coat against the cold. "I guess I can't."

"Maybe you should give it a rest, man. Nothin' you can do will bring Dan back."

Jake had told himself the same thing for the past few years. "I know, but I got caught in something else, and Fisher's name came up." He glanced over his shoulder to the dark night and the few people walking briskly along the wet streets, making sure no one was watching him.

"So you want me to reopen the investigation?"

"Immediately. And send me a copy of everything you have on Fisher."

Ron laughed. "It'll fill an encyclopedia. But nothing can be proved. There's no hard evidence."

"I know, but send it anyway—and that friend of yours in the police department?"

"Brecken?"

"Yeah. See what he knows about Fisher, his organization and his wife."

"His *wife*?"

"Yeah. Both wives, actually. The first one's name is Bennett—Kimberly Bennett. She's the mother of his only child. The current wife is a woman named Stella Cross Fisher."

"What do his wives have to do with anything?"

"Probably nothing," Jake admitted, surprised that he cared. He found himself hoping that Kimberly was just a naive innocent—a woman who really didn't know her husband was Portland's answer to the *Godfather*. "But check them out anyway."

"It's your money," Ron said.

No, Jake thought as he hung up, *it's Kimberly Bennett's money and it probably comes right from the source—Robert Fisher.* No doubt Kimberly made out like a bandit when she divorced Fisher, though nothing in her file suggested a huge settlement: just the house, which was a piece of rental property Fisher had owned, the car, college education for the kid and a few dollars a month in child support.

He hopped back into his Bronco and took off, threading the rig through the city traffic that still, though it was nearly seven, crawled at a snail's pace.

He felt the sting of guilt when he considered that he'd been less than honest with Ms. Bennett, but he rationalized his deception as a necessity. Until he knew just how far he could trust her, he'd keep some things close to the vest—especially anything to do with Daniel.

He headed south through the wet, shimmering streets and crossed the Sellwood Bridge. Lights from the houseboats on the east side of the river were reflected in the dark water. On the east side of the Willamette, he rounded several corners and wondered at her choice of neighborhoods. Sellwood had its points, but it was hardly prestigious enough to attract a woman of Kimberly's means.

But then much about Robert Fisher's beautiful ex-wife didn't make sense. The woman worked—held down a nine-to-five at First Cascade and had for a few years. No, he decided as he wheeled into the rutted driveway of the small cottage that was her home, there were things about Kimberly Bennett that just didn't fit the rich-bitch image.

He strode up a cracked concrete path that was littered with gold-and-brown maple leaves. On the front porch he punched the bell, and the door opened almost immediately.

Kimberly, dressed in a soft plum sweater and stone-washed jeans, looked nervous and younger than she had in her stark black cape and business suit. Her cheeks were flushed, her eyes wide. "Come on in," she invited, moving out of the doorway to let him pass. She leaned back against the door to shut it. "I think you should know that I'm not used to baring my soul to strangers."

He smiled. "No one is."

"I know, but I don't want you to get the wrong impression. I don't like talking about my marriage or my ex-husband. As far as I'm concerned, it's all ancient history. Dredging it up again is . . . difficult. And if it weren't for the fact that I'll do anything, I mean *anything*, to keep Lindsay, I wouldn't talk about my marriage—or the rest of my private life—at all."

"Fair enough."

She took in a deep breath and rubbed her hands together. "Well, now that that's over with, maybe we should start over. I'll take your coat. . . ."

"Thanks." He shrugged out of the jacket and watched as she hung it in a nearby closet.

She managed an anxious smile. "If you light the fire, I'll make coffee."

"It's a deal." He walked into a small room lighted only by table lamps placed strategically in the corners. An old sofa filled one wall opposite the fireplace, and an antique rocker swayed gently near the archway leading to the dining room. Wicker baskets filled with greenery and dried flowers added color to the rather Spartan room. A few sketches, drawn by a young child, were framed and hung on the walls.

"It's nothing fancy," she explained, "but it's home."

Jake tried to hide his surprise. The house was cozy, filled with the scents of spice, lemon and last night's fire, but it lacked the feel of wealth he'd expected. Aside from a few antiques and a faded Persian rug, nothing inside the small rooms seemed of any value.

Then he reminded himself of the sleek black Mercedes in the garage. And the expensive cape and boots—he hadn't imagined them.

So, what was it with Ms. Bennett?

Kimberly disappeared through the dining room and called over her shoulder, "There's kindling in a basket and matches on the mantelpiece."

Jake found the necessities, leaned over the grate, adjusted a few mossy oak logs and struck a match to cedar kindling. The fire caught and crackled, adding flickering light to the room.

He dusted his hands and rocked back on his heels, spreading his palms to the gentle warmth of the first few flames. Feeling someone's gaze on his back, he glanced over his shoulder and saw Kimberly standing in the doorway to the kitchen, her wary blue-green eyes transfixed on him. "Something wrong?"

She licked her lips, and something deep inside Jake stirred—something dangerous and very, very primal.

"No—yes...well, everything," she said with a small smile. "If things were going great, you wouldn't be here, would you?"

"I guess not."

"The coffee's about ready. Do you want sugar or cream?"

"Black's fine. I'm a purist."

"It's decaf."

His lips twisted. "Well, I've never claimed to be all that pure."

Kimberly knew then that she'd made a colossal mistake by inviting him into her home. He was too masculine, too irreverent, too damn sexy. Maybe it was just that she hadn't been with a man for years—hadn't dated much since the divorce, but Jake's presence seemed to fill the entire house.

Forcing a smile she didn't feel, she retreated to the kitchen and tried to calm her nerves. He was just a man—an attractive man, yes, but she met attractive men every day. Still, her hands shook a little as she poured the coffee, and she silently berated herself for being such a ninny.

By the time she returned to the living room, Jake had already opened his briefcase and withdrawn a pad, paper and tape recorder. He sat on a corner of the couch, the yellow pad resting on one knee.

He looked up as she entered. "I think we'd better get started. You ready?"

Never. "As ready as I'll ever be." She set both steaming mugs on the table.

"Okay, let's start at the beginning. How you met Fisher, how long you dated, when you got married and how it fell apart."

"Diane knows most of this," she said.

"I know. But I'd like to hear it from you."

She should have expected this, she supposed, but still it was difficult. "I was barely twenty, still going to school. I transferred up here from U.C.L.A.—"

"Why?"

"Why?"

"Why the transfer?"

"Scholarship. My mother didn't have any money to send me to school, and I worked part-time, but the scholarship up here was a godsend." She took a sip from her cup and frowned.

"And you met Fisher at school?"

She shook her head. "No. I was working part-time at First Cascade as a loan clerk. He met me there." With difficulty she went on to explain about those first few magic months when she'd dated one of the bank's wealthiest customers and how, because of Robert's sophistication, charm and money, he'd swept her off her feet. She glanced up at him. "I know this all sounds ridiculous now. But that's how I felt."

"So you didn't know about his reputation?"

Kimberly swallowed a sip of coffee. "I'd heard a few rumors while I was dating him, of course, but I'd chalked them up to office gossip and jealousy. When he asked me to marry him, I jumped at the chance."

"He's quite a bit older than you are."

"Fifteen years," she admitted.

"That didn't bother you?"

Kimberly sighed, but lifted her eyes to meet the questions in Jake's. "It bothered me a little. But not enough. I'd convinced myself that I loved him."

He quit writing. The fire burned softly. The clock on the mantel ticked. Shadows flickered across his face. "Did you?"

Compressing her lips, she struggled with an answer. "I— I, uh, don't think so. I don't know how I could have."

"Why not?"

"The rumors...well, I couldn't ignore them and all those lawsuits. I thought they were all a part of his business until a few years ago when a man was killed—or committed suicide." She shuddered and noticed that Jake's face had become tense, his eyes narrowing.

"Go on," he clipped.

"The man's name was...Daniel...Stevens, I think."

"You don't remember?"

She snapped her head up. "I try not to. Anyway, from that point on, things were worse, much worse. Robert became secretive, and he changed, grew colder." She bit her lip as painful, frightening memories enveloped her.

"What do you know about Daniel Stevens?"

"Nothing. Only what I read in the papers," she said.

"Robert never said anything?"

"We didn't discuss anything remotely connected with his business."

"And you think Stevens's death was connected to your husband's business?"

"I didn't say that. He was a police officer. And I understand he was investigating Robert. That's all I know." She took a sip of her coffee and asked, "What's this got to do with my divorce?"

Jake's eyes were dark. Tiny lines bracketed his mouth. "I just need to know all the facts."

"Well, I don't know anything more about Daniel Stevens."

He hesitated a second, his gaze hard and assessing. "So, even after all Robert's bad press, his shady business ties, the fact that he might have been involved in Daniel—"

"No—he wasn't. It was suicide, I think."

"Despite all that, you still stayed married to him?" he asked, his voice filled with disbelief.

"You have to understand that I grew up believing in marriage, in vows, in loyalty."

"Oh, until death do you part?" he said caustically.

"Yes!"

"And I—I didn't want the stigma of divorce."

"It's not a stigma."

"But it was to me. My parents had a wonderful marriage—never a fight until the day my father died. And I thought—I hoped—that Robert would...that he'd see that he was on the wrong path...."

"But he didn't?"

"No."

"So, what changed your mind about divorcing him?"

Kimberly frowned. "Robert was unfaithful—had been all along, I guess. But then he met a woman and he fell in love with her."

"Stella?"

"Yes." Kimberly let out a long sigh. Why Robert's affair with Stella hurt, she didn't know. She didn't love him, probably never had, but Robert's betrayal had cut deep into her pride. And then there were all those accusations . . . all those late nights. Had he been trysting with Stella—or had it been much worse? She shivered, then went on to explain that Robert was so anxious to be rid of her that he'd agreed to give her full custody of Lindsay. She demanded nothing else of him—the support she received she stuck into a trust fund for Lindsay. He'd given her the small house and car.

Jake asked a few more questions, less personal but difficult just the same. Kimberly answered as honestly as possible, but didn't meet his eyes. Instead she concentrated on her coffee, or watched the fire burn down and tried not to notice the scent of his after-shave.

Suddenly the front door burst open, sending in a blast of chill air. Lindsay, blond hair flying behind, bounced into the room. "Mommy!" she cried, stopping dead in her tracks when she spied Jake. "Who're you?"

Kimberly stood, held her arms open and was rewarded by Lindsay flinging herself against her. She swung her daughter up into the air and squeezed her. "This is Mr. McGowan, he's a . . . friend of mine," she said as Arlene bustled inside.

"The name's Jake," he said, his face softening as he stared at the tiny blond bundle of energy.

"I told her to slow down," Arlene complained good-naturedly, sending Lindsay a knowing look, "but she was just too excited."

"It's all right," Kimberly said. Lindsay's chubby arms surrounded her neck, and she smelled of lilac soap.

"She's all ready for bed. Just take off her coat and boots," Arlene explained, though her gaze wandered to Jake.

Still holding Lindsay, Kimberly made quick introductions, and Arlene's dark eyes regarded Jake with more than a little interest. "Glad to meet you," she said, then added quickly, "I've got to run. Lyle will worry if I don't hightail it back." She adjusted her rain bonnet over her gray frizz.

"Thanks a bunch," Kimberly said.

"No problem." Arlene glanced again at Jake. "Any time. You know we love to have her." With a quick wave she hurried out the door.

Jake shoved his notes and pens inside his briefcase and snapped the leather case shut. "I think it's time I shoved off, too."

"Good." Lindsay regarded him suspiciously, her lower lip thrust out.

"I'll call you when I get back into town," he said, his lips twitching in response to Lindsay's outright hostility. "We'll get together and sort this all out."

Kimberly's heartbeat accelerated. Suddenly she wanted him as her attorney. She'd seen a hard edge to him, felt his intensity. She guessed that if he represented her, he'd give it his best shot. "Then you'll take my case?"

He rubbed the back of his neck and frowned. "I'll take it on two conditions. The first, you already know—we do things my way."

"And the second?"

"That you don't hold anything back from me," he said solemnly. "There are things you might not want to talk about, but if we're going to win the case, I'll need all the facts. Painful as they may be."

"Of course," she said quickly, though his gaze seemed to read her mind. She tilted her chin up and squared her shoulders. "I have a couple of conditions myself."

"Shoot."

"I want you to keep me abreast of the case at all times. No surprises."

"Fair enough."

"And if you ever think, even for a second, that Robert's got the upper hand, I want to know about it."

"Why?" he asked.

"I just want to know where I stand," she said, lying a little. Already she was beginning to trust Jake, and if he thought Robert had a chance of taking Lindsay away from her, then she'd do what she had to do to keep her daughter with her. Even if it meant running away from Robert—and from the law.

Chapter Four

Jake sat in the bar and glared out the window to the snow-covered slopes of Mt. Bachelor. Gray clouds hovered over the craggy peaks of the Cascades, and a fine, misting rain drizzled from the sky, melting the snow. The temperature was nearly forty degrees, and the extended forecast called for a warming trend.

"Wonderful," Jake muttered sarcastically, signaling to the bartender for another drink. He sipped his beer slowly, and his mood deteriorated with the weather. The raucous noise from the stereo didn't interest him, and he couldn't care less about the skiing exhibition on the big screen.

Other patrons of the bar, drenched skiers in wet jackets and sopping wool hats, seemed to find solace in grumbling together, drinking and even laughing about the rain.

Jake didn't. He'd spent too many weeks planning this trip. He was anxious and coiled tight as a spring. And, though he was loath to admit it, his thoughts kept turning to Kimberly.

Her image had been with him ever since he'd left her two nights before, lingering with him like the evocative scent of an expensive perfume. Try as he might, he couldn't forget her wise blue-green eyes, gently curving lips or the sweet seduction of her voice. He couldn't help feeling he should've stayed in Portland and started working on the mess with her ex-husband.

At the thought of Fisher, he pulled his eyebrows together. Glancing outside to the dismal day, he wondered if God were getting even with him and the rest of the noisy crowd in the smoky bar.

He swore pointedly under his breath, finished his drink, left some bills on the polished bar and strode through the throng as fast as his ski boots would allow.

Outside, the weather was miserable. Melting icicles dripped in tempo with the soft fall of the rain. Ignoring the conditions, he stomped into his ski bindings and jabbed his poles into the ground. His right ski caught in the slush, but he made it to the four-man lift and, without a word to the other souls braving the rain, let the rig carry him over the tops of the drooping pine trees to the summit.

Once there, he skied down the ramp and stopped, surveying the lower slopes. Partially hidden by low-hanging clouds, the run was wet and slushy.

Cold rain ran down his neck and settled into his bones. He blew on his wet gloves, but his fingers were frigid. Glowering furiously at the dark heavens, he found no relief in the ominous sky.

There was no reason on earth to stay here any longer. He thought again of Kimberly, shoved his poles into the snow and took off, nearly flying down the run. He may as well return to Portland, he decided fatalistically as he headed for the lodge. At least in the city he could do something worthwhile.

And he would see her again. For the first time all that miserable afternoon, Jake smiled.

Kimberly placed a set of statements for the Juniper account on the security cashier's desk in the operations section of the trust department. "If you could just double-check the dividends—make sure that everything was posted last quarter," she said to the woman in the cage, a glassed-in office where the actual bond and stock transfers took place.

"Anything wrong?" Charlene asked. Red-haired and quick, she hardly ever made a mistake.

"Nothing that I know of, but Mr. Juniper has some questions. He's sure that the dividends and interest were down for the quarter. I looked it over and it seems fine, but if you'd double-check it, I'd appreciate it."

"You got it," Charlene said as the phone in her office started ringing.

Kimberly headed back to the administrative offices and nearly bumped into Marcie. "Oh, good, I was looking for you," Marcie said. "Mr. Compton's scheduled a meeting for all the officers at four-thirty in the boardroom."

Checking her watch, Kimberly said, "I'll be there."

"Good. Oh, and that list of attorneys you wanted? The ones associated with this bank? I left it on your desk."

"Thanks, Marcie," Kimberly said as she turned the corner and came face to face with Robert. Her footsteps faltered, but she managed to keep walking.

Robert glanced lazily her way, then turned back to the cluster of men he was with. Tall and distinguished looking, he was surrounded by a group of bank bigwigs. Eric Compton, vice president for the trust department, Bill Zealander, Aaron Thorburn, president of the bank, and Earl Kellerman, adviser to the board, were gathered together near the elevator doors.

Robert's blue eyes flicked back to Kimberly quickly again before returning to Thorburn. A cold needle of dread stabbed her.

"I'll be in my office," she said to Marcie.

She'd just settled into her chair when Robert slid into the room and closed the door quietly behind him.

For the first time since the divorce, Kimberly was alone with him. "Hello, Kimberly." His voice was just as melodic as she remembered.

"What do you want?" she asked. She leaned back in her chair to stare up at him.

He slung one leg over the corner of her desk. "Now that's a silly question."

Her heart began to pound. "I mean, what're you doing here?"

"Oh—" he waved and frowned "—nothing important. Just a little bank business."

"And it's finished? Then you can leave."

"In a minute." He folded his hands over his knee. "I thought you and I should talk—and not through our attorneys." He smiled warmly, and Kimberly saw a little of the man she'd married—charming and sophisticated.

"Talk about what?"

"Our daughter."

Kimberly braced herself. "What about her?" she asked, feigning innocence.

"You know she's better off with me."

"I don't think so."

"Kimberly," he whispered in a way he thought was seductive. It made her furious.

"Just say what you have to say, Robert."

He looked perturbed. "I want my daughter, Kim. She needs a father."

"And a mother."

"Stella—"

"I don't want to hear about Stella. I'm Lindsay's mother."

His color began to rise, and he arched an imperious brow. "There comes a time when a man needs to know he's not . . . so mortal, I guess."

"You should have thought of that before."

His eyes blazed, and he bit out, "I won't rest until she's with me. Don't you know that?"

The arrogance of the man! "So, what is this—some kind of threat?"

"No," he said, his smooth brow creasing. "Threats don't seem to work with you."

"Then what?" Dear Lord, she hoped he couldn't hear her heart pounding.

"I want you to reconsider. Think what's best for the child. Stella and I can offer her anything money can buy."

"Maybe that's not enough."

"It's more than you're giving her."

"I give her love, Robert. I'm the one who wanted her, remember? You weren't too interested in having children. Especially a daughter."

"I know, I know," he said with maddening calm. "But things have changed."

"You mean since Stella can't give you a son?"

"That's a cold way of putting it."

"Too bad. It's the truth. And it doesn't change things. We had an agreement, Robert." She stood, hoping to gain some advantage from the added inches in height. "And I expect you to honor it. Lindsay stays with me."

"You know, Kimberly, you're too stubborn for your own good."

"I don't think so."

"I could make it worth your while."

"What's this?" she asked, incredulous. "A bribe? Oh, Robert, get real! I don't want your money. If I had, I would have made claims during the divorce."

He clucked his tongue. "Kimberly, Kimberly," he said, rising to his feet and towering over her. "You just don't get it, do you? I want my daughter."

"Do you? Well, why is it that never once have I heard you say you love her?"

His mouth clamped shut, and all the friendliness left his eyes. "You know, you might sing a different tune if you lose your job."

She thought about his influence with the bank. "I'd get another one."

"It might not be that easy," he said.

"Your scare tactics don't work with me, Robert. You said so yourself." She leaned across her desk, propping herself with her hands, and forced her features to remain calm while deep inside she was quaking to her very soul. "If you care anything for Lindsay, please don't do anything that might hurt her. Consider her first."

"Oh, like you've done."

"Yes!"

A sharp rap interrupted them, and Robert's bodyguard, a burly blond man with a ponytail, poked his head into the room. "You said to remind you of the meeting with Schuster," he said, almost bowing.

Kimberly wanted to get sick.

"I'll be right there," Robert told him. He glanced down at Kimberly's hands on the desktop, and for the first time she noticed the typed sheet on her desk pad—the list of attorneys connected to the bank and therefore to Robert.

She didn't even bother being sly; she just turned the page over before he could read too much.

His cold eyes held hers. "I guess I'll see you in court."

She didn't flinch. "I guess so."

"And you'll lose, you know. You'll lose big."

"I don't think so."

"We'll see."

She couldn't resist one parting shot. "At least I don't have to travel with a bodyguard."

"Maybe you should." With a tight smile he left the room.

The second the door closed, Kimberly collapsed into her chair. What was he planning? How could he be so self-assured? No court would grant him custody—or would it?

Biting her lip, she flipped the paper over and skimmed the list of names, searching for one. But Jake McGowan wasn't listed.

She felt a tiny sense of relief, but it was short-lived. She knew she'd heard Jake's name before. Diane had mentioned him, of course, but someone else had, as well. If she hadn't heard Jake's name from someone in the bank, then where? Certainly not from Robert. Or had she?

Her throat went dry with dread. She sensed that Jake had run across Robert before, though he hadn't said as much. He seemed to have a knowledge and interest in Robert that went beyond the usual curiosity derived from reading the paper. Had Jake been Robert's attorney? Had Robert double-crossed him?

"Oh, stop it!" she whispered, angry with herself. Shuddering, she rubbed her arms. Robert meant business. And she was scared. More scared than she'd ever been in her life.

The intercom buzzed. Marcie said, "It's Mr. Juniper on line two again. Should I, uh, tell him to call back?"

"No. . ." Kimberly shook her head as if Marcie could see through the walls. "I'll get it." She picked up the phone, glad for the distraction. "Hello?"

"She's at it again!" Henry Juniper exclaimed.

"Who's at what?"

"Carole. She's going for blood, I tell you. Going to contest the entire will—claim she needs an additional three hundred thousand for taking care of Dad during the last couple of years. And then she wants her legal fees paid on top of that! It's positively ludicrous."

"Please, slow down, Mr. Juniper," Kimberly said evenly, though she was still distracted. "Why don't you start at the beginning?"

As Henry Juniper launched into his tale of woe, she listened, but her gaze was fixed on the picture of Lindsay propped on the corner of her desk. Her fingers curled tightly around the telephone, and her jaw set. For the first time in his life, Robert wouldn't win. The stakes were just too damn high.

Hours later she'd calmed down. The evening with Lindsay had been special, and she'd tucked the child into bed later than usual, enjoying every waking moment with her.

Only when Lindsay had yawned and repeatedly rubbed her eyes had Kimberly done her motherly duty and turned out the lights in Lindsay's sleeping loft.

Now, her back propped against the couch, an old quilt tossed over her shoulders, Kimberly sat on the floor in front of the fire. She tried to concentrate on the magazine spread open on her lap but couldn't. Her mind was working overtime—with thoughts of Robert and Jake. Robert's threats kept pounding at her brain, and she kept them at bay by hoping that Jake could help her. At the thought of him she smiled, though the situation was far from happy.

"Mommy?" Lindsay's voice filtered down from the loft.

Kimberly was on her feet in an instant. "What is it, honey?" she called, climbing the stairs two at a time.

Sitting up in her bed and rubbing her eyes, Lindsay complained, "I had another bad dream."

"It's over now, sweetheart."

"But it was scary." Tears gathered in Lindsay's eyes.

"I know." Kimberly sat on the edge of Lindsay's twin mattress and smoothed her tousled hair. Wrapping her arms around Lindsay's shoulders, Kimberly whispered, "Just think happy thoughts like rainbows and dinosaurs and snow and puppies—"

"Can I have one?" Lindsay asked, her tears forgotten.

The great debate, Kimberly thought. "Someday."

"When?"

"I don't know. When you're older."

"Like tomorrow?"

"Like in a few years when you're old enough to feed it, walk it and clean up after it."

"I just want to love it," Lindsay argued, her lower lip protruding in a tired pout. "Daddy said he'd give me a puppy."

Kimberly's heart froze. Every muscle in her body went rigid. "He did?"

"Umm." Lindsay was nodding off again. "When he called me."

"He called you? Here? Again?" Kimberly repeated, trying not to sound alarmed, though cold panic was taking hold. All of his threats echoed through her head. Would he try something as foolish as kidnapping his own daughter? Certainly not unless the custody battle went against him. Her throat was suddenly tight, the words hard to form. "Did—did Arlene talk to him?"

Lindsay scooted lower under the covers. "No. She was in the basement." Turning her face into her pillow, Lindsay yawned.

"Has Daddy called before when I'm not here?"

But Lindsay didn't answer. Breathing softly, she snuggled deeper between the sheets and drifted to sleep. Kimberly stared at the sleeping child and wanted to cry. She'd always wanted children, but even that overpowering desire to become a mother hadn't prepared her for the depth of her feelings for this sometimes spoiled, often precocious, but always precious daughter.

After dropping a kiss on Lindsay's tangled crown, she silently walked downstairs. So Robert had called. So what? He had every right to talk to his daughter. There was no need to panic. But the memory of her own conversation with Robert left her chilled to the bone.

She poured herself a glass of water, then set the teakettle on the stove. Gazing out the window, she wondered if she should just give up the fight, grab Lindsay and a few of her belongings and flee. And run where? California? Canada? Mexico? Her head began to throb. She pressed the cold glass to her forehead.

The kettle shrilled loudly, and Kimberly switched off the stove and reached for it just as the doorbell rang.

She glanced at the clock. It was after nine. Who would be braving the rain and wind at this time of night?

Robert!

And his entourage of bodyguards!

Her heart dropped like a stone, then she managed to pull herself together. Robert was in for the fight of his life! Steeling herself, she set the kettle down and marched back through the living room, ready to lambast the man.

She peeked through the arched window carved into the front door, and her knees threatened to collapse as she saw

Jake standing in the protection of the porch, his breath fogging in the cold air. Dressed in faded denim jeans, a steel-gray sweater and blue ski jacket, Jake reached for the bell again, then glanced at the window, where his gaze touched hers.

A smile as warm as a southern breeze slashed across his chin.

Kimberly fumbled with the lock, then threw the door open. "Thank God it's you," she said, clinging to the knob so she wouldn't impulsively rush into his arms like an idiot.

He actually chuckled. "You missed me?"

"A little," she lied. "Well, maybe more than a little." Her throat grew thick, and she felt hot tears of relief well in the corners of her eyes.

Jake's smile faded. "Hey, what is it?"

For a second she didn't trust her voice. She closed the door and leaned heavily against the cool wood panels. "It's Robert," she admitted, clearing her throat. "I saw him to-day—he was . . . pretty determined."

"To get his daughter back?"

"Right." Her throat swelled again. "He wasn't too sub-tle."

"He *threatened* you?" Jake demanded. His face became a hard mask.

"Warned me, I think, would be more like it. Look, I thought you might be he, and I'd even gone so far as to think he'd just bulldoze his way in here, grab Lindsay and disappear in the night, so . . ." She glanced up at him and managed a tremulous smile. "Just give me a minute to pull myself together, okay?"

"Sure." To her surprise, he reached forward and sur-rounded her with his arms, drawing her close against his wet jacket. His strength and warmth seemed to permeate his clothes and flow into her. She didn't think twice, just rested her cheek against the steadying wall of his chest. His scent enveloped her, an earthy smell that reminded her of pine forests and clean skin.

Listening to the steadying sound of his breathing, she wouldn't acknowledge that he interested her as a man. Being attracted to him was just too complicated. And dangerous. Still, being held and comforted, feeling his breath stir her hair, caused her skin to tingle.

"You okay?" he asked gently.

She nodded against his jacket, wondering why she saw this roguish, cynical man as some kind of knight in shining armor. The fantasy made her smile. He'd die a thousand deaths if he knew.

She lifted her head and slowly stepped out of his embrace. "I, uh, thought you were out of town," she said, embarrassed that she'd let down her reserve, that he'd caught sight of a vulnerable side of her.

"I'm back."

"Obviously," she said dryly. "Look, I didn't mean to fall apart on you—"

"You didn't."

"Yeah, I did." She nodded.

He grinned again, and she felt the stupid urge to smile back at him. "Okay, you did. Now, tell me what happened."

"Can we wait a little on the heavy stuff?" she said, still trying to calm down. "I'll be okay, but I need a few minutes."

"Sure." He turned his palms up. "Whatever you want."

For the first time, she really looked at him, noticing the water spots on his shoulders and his wet hair. "No umbrella?"

His grin twisted. "I can't stand those things. Besides, I'm getting used to the rain. I just spent a couple of days wiping it off my goggles at Mt. Bachelor."

"Oh, so you're a skier?"

His eyes flashed devilishly. "You wouldn't have guessed it this week." He glanced around the room and shoved his hands in the pockets of his jeans. "When the weather report said 'more of the same,' I decided to pack it in. I have plenty of work, and I thought we could pick up where we left off."

"Now?"

"No time like the present." Bending one knee against the hearth, he rubbed his hands together, then placed his palms near the flames. Firelight caught in his hair, reflecting on the dark strands and casting golden shadows over his angular features. Glancing over his shoulder, he said, "Relax, I won't bite."

"Is that a promise?"

"Yes." His eyes twinkled. "Are you sure you're all right?"

"I think so."

"Can we get started?"

She nodded, rubbing her hands together. "It's going to be difficult, you know. Telling you my life story."

He snorted. "You'd better get used to the idea. We'll be spending a lot of time together."

Somehow that was comforting.

"I'll have to know about you—and Robert—and anything you think is important, no matter how 'difficult' it is to talk about."

"I see."

"You want to back out?"

"No!" she said sharply. "We've got a deal. Remember?"

"Right."

Despite her uneasiness, she felt the corners of her mouth lift. There was something about him that made her want to smile, and yet there was a part of him, a dark, sensual side that touched her deep inside. "So... would you like something warm—a cup of coffee or tea, or maybe something stronger? I think I've got... I don't really know," she said with a shrug. "Maybe vodka."

"Anything."

He followed her down the short, scarred wooden floor of a hallway leading to a tiny kitchen.

"Is Lindsay already in bed?" he asked as she poured hot water into mugs.

"For the second time." She told him about Lindsay's nightmares and sighed. "They began last summer, a couple of months before she started kindergarten. Coffee or tea?"

"Coffee—does she go to school every day?" he asked.

"Half days. Arlene picks Lindsay up after lunch and brings her home for her nap. They spend their time here unless Arlene decides to run errands or take Lindsay to the park to feed the ducks."

"And Lindsay likes Arlene."

"Adores her."

"You're sure?"

"Umm."

"And school. Does she like it?"

"Yes—and her teacher is a dream. What is this—the third degree?" she asked as she handed him a steaming mug.

"Not yet. Just the preliminaries." He took an experimental sip from the cup. "Believe me, it gets worse."

"That's what I was afraid of," she murmured, motioning toward a small round table with two chairs. "Please, sit down."

Jake twisted a cane-backed chair around and straddled it, leaning forward. "So, tell me about Arlene."

"Why?"

"She's Lindsay's baby-sitter. That might be a sore point with Robert. He might bring up something about your working and leaving his daughter in the care of an elderly woman."

Kimberly sipped her tea. "I wouldn't call Arlene elderly to her face if I valued my life," she said.

Jake grinned. "I'll remember that. You trust her?"

Kimberly almost laughed. "Implicitly. I've known her all my life. She's a friend of my mother's. They grew up together in the Midwest before Mom and Dad moved to California."

"She's married?"

Nodding, Kimberly set her tea bag in a saucer. "Lyle's her husband. He was a longshoreman, but he retired a couple of years ago when he hurt his back."

"So Arlene watches Lindsay for the money?"

Kimberly bristled at the implication. "The money really doesn't matter. Arlene loves my daughter. Lindsay is the granddaughter she never had." She set her cup on the table and forced her eyes to Jake's. "You met her the other night—what do you think?"

"Just showing you a preview of what the courtroom will be like," he said, his face growing sober. "If it gets that far. Believe me. It's not going to be a picnic. Not for you. Or Lindsay."

"I know." She felt the same nervous jitters in her stomach she always did when she thought about the court date looming ahead. "I wish I could avoid it. I don't like the thought of fighting over Lindsay, of hanging my dirty laundry out where everyone can see it. Robert's name is in the papers enough."

A dark cloud seemed to shadow Jake's eyes. But it passed quickly. "Maybe we can avoid that," he suggested.

"How?"

"If we can convince Robert to drop the case—"

Kimberly laughed brittlely. "Impossible. I've tried. When it comes to Lindsay, we don't see eye to eye."

"But he gave you custody once."

"Oh, yes," she said, sighing. "When he wanted the divorce so that he could marry Stella. That was before he knew that she couldn't bear children. It's ironic, I suppose," she added sadly. "He didn't want a child, and the fact that Lindsay was a girl only made it worse. But suddenly, now that Stella can't conceive, he's interested in Lindsay again." Though it was difficult, she explained about seeing Robert at the bank. As she repeated the conversation, Jake didn't move. His coffee sat barely touched on the table, and Kimberly saw the tensing of his muscles, the wariness in his eyes.

"Wonderful man," he said finally.

"I thought so once," she admitted, wondering how she could have been so naive. Feeling suddenly cold, she rubbed her arms and asked, "Have you ever been married?"

He frowned into his cup. His jaw tightened. "For a while. It didn't last long. Probably a mistake from the beginning."

Surprised, she glanced up and saw pain flicker in his eyes. A cold spot settled in her heart. Jake obviously loved his wife very much.

"She's gone now," he said, clipping the words out, his voice husky. "Killed in a car accident a few years ago. It happened not long after the divorce."

Her heart went out to him. "I'm sorry," she whispered.

"Don't be. It wasn't your fault."

"I know, but—"

"I'd rather not talk about it," he said darkly. Shifting uncomfortably in his chair, he added, "Besides, I didn't come here to discuss my personal life."

"No, you're here for mine."

"Right. So, what about yours? Let's start with Robert."

Kimberly's stomach twisted.

"Do you still love him?"

Her gaze flew to his. "What kind of a question is that? He's remarried and—"

"Do you still love him?"

"Of course not!"

He lifted a dark brow.

Instantly outraged, she said, "Would I be fighting him so hard if I still cared about him?"

"I don't know. Sometimes relationships are complicated. I just thought we should start with the basics."

"And I thought I told you I'm not sure I ever loved him."

His gaze didn't falter. "Okay. Now, the other side of the coin. Do you hate him?"

"No."

"Why not?"

"He's Lindsay's father—I can't forget that."

Jake snorted. "A man comes by and threatens to take your child away and you can't forget he's the kid's father."

Her fists clenched impotently.

"This isn't going to be a walk in the park, you know," he said kindly. "It could get pretty bloody."

"I realize that."

"Then tell me, what kind of a man is Fisher?"

"Relentless," she said quickly, "and single-minded. When he wants something, he goes after it."

He tented his fingers under his chin. "Tell me about him—this relentless side to his nature."

Her hands shook a little as she picked up her cup. She sipped her tea, found it tepid and set the cup back on the table. "For example, if he wanted your law practice, he'd find a way to get it. He's incredibly patient, and he'd do whatever he had to do, wait however long it took to make you see that it was in *your* best interests to sell to him, whether you wanted to or not."

The lines near the corners of Jake's mouth tightened.

"So, now that he's zeroed in on having Lindsay come live with him, he won't back down. Diane already told me that he doesn't have a chance, and yet I don't believe it. Robert's like a cat—he always lands on his feet." She bit her lower lip. "And sometimes his claws are extended."

Jake surveyed her thoughtfully. "What was it like being married to him?"

She frowned, feeling all the old pain. "At first it was wonderful—at least I thought it was—but that all changed fairly quickly."

"Why?"

She lifted a shoulder. "I don't know. I suppose I began to bore him."

One side of his mouth lifted, and his gaze softened. "I find it hard to think of you as boring."

"Well, he lost interest, and then there were all those stories about him. You know, the rumors tying him to everything that's rotten in the city."

Jake's stare grew sharp. "You don't believe he's part of organized crime in Portland."

"No!"

"But you're not sure."

"He's Lindsay's father!" she said automatically.

"That doesn't answer my question."

Kimberly tossed her hair away from her face and thought long and hard. For years she'd heard the rumors about

Robert, but never would she believe he was as horrible as he had been painted. "Maybe I'm incredibly naive, but I lived with the man. I won't dispute he walked a thin line with the law, and he probably even bent it on occasion. But I can't believe he's a part of anything as sinister as the mob."

Jake scowled. "You're right on one count. You *are* incredibly naive."

She bit at the inside of her lip. "Well, it's hard to think that the man you married..." She shuddered.

"Go on."

"As I said, I don't know what all he's involved in, but he did change about the time of that police investigation."

"Change? How?"

She couldn't really explain it. "He grew more secretive, and some of his business acquaintances changed."

Jake was staring at her so hard that his gaze seemed to cut through to her soul. She rubbed her fingers together nervously.

"What acquaintances?" he asked so quietly she barely heard the question.

"I didn't know them, never really met them, but I got the feeling..." She lifted her eyes to his. "The feeling that Robert's business interests had shifted. Maybe it was all in my mind, but, I tell you, he changed."

Jake rubbed his chin. "You never heard any new names?"

"No—he didn't confide in me."

The seconds ticked by, and Jake didn't take his eyes off her. The fire popping and the hum of the furnace provided the only sounds.

"You know, Kimberly, if we could prove Fisher is a part of something—anything—illegal, it will weaken his case considerably."

"I know."

He touched her lightly on the arm. "Would you be willing to testify against him?"

She remembered the cold fury in Robert's eyes that afternoon. Taking a bracing breath, she nodded. "I would, but believe me, I don't know anything."

"Just think about it." Then, as if dismissing the subject, he waved and glanced at his watch. "It's late. I'd better shove off." Standing, he returned his chair to the table. "I'll call you next week after I've talked with Kesler. There's a chance he and I can work something out that you and Robert will both agree to."

"I doubt it."

He flashed a cocky smile as they started down the hall to the living room. He grabbed his coat off the back of the couch. "You never know until you try."

She shook her head. "Obviously you haven't come up against Robert."

His features tightened almost imperceptibly. "There's always a way," he said calmly, his voice turning strangely dangerous as he slipped his arms through the sleeves of his jacket. "I'll call you next week."

As he opened the door, a rush of damp air filled the room, billowing the curtains and causing the dying flames within the grate to leap brilliantly. Running quickly down the steps, Jake disappeared into the night. A few seconds later, the interior light of his Bronco flickered, and Kimberly watched him slide easily behind the steering wheel.

She shut the front door and wondered why the house seemed so suddenly empty without him. "Don't be a fool," she said, but smiled nonetheless.

In the kitchen she poured herself a fresh cup of hot tea and had just sat down with a magazine when the phone rang. Smiling, she picked it up on the third ring. "Hello?"

"Hi!" Diane Welby's voice sounded over the wire.

Kimberly glanced out the window. "Well, how's the bride-to-be? Cold feet yet?"

"Never! In fact I'm not even nervous."

"Sure."

From the window, she could see the shimmering dark streets. Beneath a street lamp, she noticed a man lingering, drawing deeply on his cigarette as he gazed steadily at her house. Her heart began to pump.

Diane was saying, "I just called to see how things were going with Jake. He is taking your case, isn't he?"

"Why—oh, yes."

"Good."

Kimberly snapped off the kitchen light so that she could watch the man, but it was too dark to see his features. He was tall, wore a raincoat and hat—nothing out of the ordinary. She thought about confiding in Diane, but what could she say? It wasn't against the law to smoke on the street corner.

"And are you two getting along?"

The man on the street started walking away, around the corner and out of her line of vision.

"Kimberly?" Diane said again.

"Oh, yes. Well, we got off to a pretty rough start," she admitted, still looking out the window as she filled Diane in on the particulars. " . . . he just left about fifteen minutes ago."

"Good, good. I'm not kidding about the fact that he's the best."

"Best or not, he wasn't all that crazy about representing me," Kimberly said, coiling the cord around her fingers. "But he won't say why."

There was a long silence on the other end of the line, and finally she heard Diane let out her breath. "Jake had a difficult time a few years back. A messy divorce."

"He mentioned it."

"Did he?" Diane sounded delighted.

"He didn't go into it much."

"He wouldn't," Diane said, but didn't elaborate.

There was a click on the line, and Diane muttered, "Damn. I've got another call. I just wanted to know that everything's okay and that you'll be coming to the wedding."

"I'll be there," Kimberly promised. "See you then." She hung up and stared out the window. But other than the normal evening traffic, nothing seemed out of the ordinary. "You're losing it, Bennett," she told herself as she snapped the shade shut. "Definitely losing it."

Nonetheless, she looked in on Lindsay again, double-checked the dead bolts and window latchings and knew she wouldn't get much sleep.

Jake paid little attention to the speed limit. Putting his Bronco through its paces, he steered through the puddled streets of Sellwood, across the Willamette River and on to Lake Oswego. His house, a bungalow that had once been a cabin retreat for wealthy Portlanders in the early nineteen hundreds, was located on the south side of the lake.

The drive home took twenty minutes. Jake didn't remember any of it. His thoughts hadn't strayed from Kimberly.

In the driveway, he braked to a gravel-spinning stop and switched off the engine. Rain continued to beat on the roof as the cooling engine ticked in counterpoint. Jake stared through the blurred windshield and wrestled with his conscience.

Inwardly he sensed that Kimberly Bennett was a woman with whom he could enjoy a lasting relationship. But now, because he'd agreed to see her professionally, she was, at least in the broadest sense of the word, his client. And she'd been married to the man who Jake was sure had been responsible for Daniel's death. Getting involved with Kimberly would only spell trouble. And then there was her daughter—charming as hell, but Jake didn't want to get too close to a kid. Nope, he'd had enough pain to last him a lifetime, and if he could help Kimberly out and put Fisher away at the same time, that's all he could ask for. So, why couldn't he forget her?

His fingers curled over the steering wheel, and he had to beat down the urge to drive back to her home and offer to take her out. Or to bed, he silently added, furious with himself for a physical attraction that was so damn compelling he couldn't think straight.

"Get real," he muttered to himself as he climbed out of his car and slammed the door shut. Lupus, his white shepherd, barked loudly. Tail whipping his behind at a furious tempo, Lupus leaped from beneath the dewy branches of a rhododendron. Jake bent down and scratched the old dog's wet ears. But his mind hadn't left Kimberly.

Starting an affair with Kimberly Bennett was out of the question, he told himself for the hundredth time as he headed to the door. He couldn't see her socially, and there was no point in even thinking about it. She was his client, Robert Fisher's ex, and that was that.

Why, then, he wondered, kicking angrily at a stone in his path, was making love to her lodged so firmly in his mind?

Chapter Five

Two nights later Jake stood and stretched. His back ached from sitting at the old rolltop desk in his living room, where he'd been reading everything he could on the most current custody cases.

Lupus, curled on the rug near the window, growled low in his throat. His snow-white hair bristled at the sound of footsteps on the porch.

"Relax," Jake chided the dog as he opened the door. "It's only Ron."

Ron Koski grinned, displaying slightly yellowed teeth. "*Only* Ron. Well, I like that a lot! Especially after what I went through for you." He wiped his ratty old Nikes on the mat and stepped inside. A draft of cold winter air seeped in with him. "As a matter of fact, you owe me a beer. It's *definitely* Miller time."

"You're on."

Lupus curled up beside the fire, and Ron took a chair at the small table in Jake's dining alcove.

"So, you got something on Fisher," Jake called over his shoulder as he wandered into the kitchen, opened the refrigerator and yanked out two bottles.

"I don't know if you'd call it 'something.' You know how slippery Fisher is."

"Yeah, I know." Probably better than most people, he thought, twisting off the caps and thinking of Daniel.

Returning to the dining alcove, he found Ron with one foot propped on another chair and a thick file folder spread on the table. A cigarette burned in a nearby ashtray. "Here's what I got on Fisher," he said, accepting the offered bottle with a grin. "Mostly news clippings, a couple of police reports I managed to get from Brecken and some information from the surveillance job I did on him a few years ago."

"I remember." Jake pulled up a chair and eyed the neatly typed reports, yellowed newspaper articles and snapshots. Robert Fisher always seemed to photograph well. A large man with thick, jet-black hair, intelligent brown eyes and a heavy-boned face, he cut an imposing figure—even in yellowed black-and-white. Jake skimmed the report on Daniel's suicide, and his stomach tightened. Daniel had been an investigator for the Portland Police. He'd been assigned to the narcotics detail and had eventually followed a lead to Robert Fisher.

From what Jake learned later, Daniel had hoped to make a huge drug bust and expose Fisher, but it hadn't worked out. Daniel had been found dead, from what appeared to be a self-inflicted overdose. Several kilos of cocaine, stolen from the police department's evidence warehouse, had been found in his apartment along with a typed suicide note.

The ensuing scandal had rocked the very foundation of the police department.

Jake stared at the copy of the note included in Ron's file, and hot rage burned in his gut. Daniel was clean. He'd never used drugs in his life. His body was clean—no other needle marks. On top of all that, he wouldn't have taken his own life.

There had been an investigation, of course, but it had been short and inconclusive and swept under the rug with the rest of the dirt that couldn't be explained.

Jake had never bought the suicide theory. It just didn't wash.

Ron ran a hand through his short blond hair. "There's no reason to dredge all this up again. It's over, man."

"Maybe not." Jake flipped through the first few reports, his eyes scanning the sheets.

"What're you on to?"

"Nothing as sordid as all this," he replied, disgusted at the pile of dead ends that should have led to Fisher. "It's a custody case. Fisher's daughter."

"What about her?"

"He's making noise about wanting custody. His ex-wife doesn't like the idea."

"Don't blame her." He finished his beer, then took a final drag of his cigarette and crushed it in the ashtray. "Fisher doesn't seem like the fatherly type," he said in a cloud of blue smoke.

"He wasn't. But for some reason he's changed his mind."

"Can he do that?"

Jake's mouth turned into a thin, determined line. "Not if I can help it," he said, sifting through the documents. The opportunity to thwart Robert Fisher was a stroke of luck, and the chance to help Kimberly made it all the more tantalizing.

He started to smile at the thought of her. Though he barely knew her, he hadn't been able to get her out of his mind for the past couple of days.

"So, what's she like?" Ron asked, lighting another cigarette and letting it burn neglected in the ashtray.

"Who?"

"Fisher's ex." Ron's eyebrows elevated a fraction. "Young? Beautiful? Built?"

Jake's gut tightened. "I suppose," he evaded, refusing to think about Kimberly with the likes of Robert Fisher.

"Probably took him to the cleaners—if that's possible."

"Maybe." But he was starting to doubt it. Though her car and some of her clothes were expensive, her house was little more than a cottage, vintage 1920 or so. And any of the documents he'd seen indicated that she hadn't stiffed Fisher for half his vast property holdings or alimony. No, it appeared as if Kimberly had wanted out of the marriage—period. Unless she had a Swiss bank account or a stock portfolio hidden away somewhere, she seemed relatively middle-class.

Jake rolled his sleeves over his forearms, aware that he'd been lost in thought, and Ron was staring at him curiously. "She seems to think that Fisher was clean until Daniel started poking around."

"No way." Koski narrowed his eyes a fraction. "But it does seem that until then, he wasn't in quite so deep. It's been since Dan's death that Fisher's risen in the organization."

"How do you figure that?"

Koski thought. "My guess is that someone did Daniel, and Fisher owed some big favors to keep his name out of it." He glanced sharply at his friend. "I doubt that Fisher did the dirty work. He likes to keep his hands clean."

Jake's chest grew tight, and his mind wandered back to dangerous territory. "Doesn't matter," he said without much conviction. "Daniel's dead."

"And now you're helping out Fisher's wife."

"Ex," Jake reminded him. "There's a big difference."

Ron shrugged. "Have you met the kid?"

Jake nodded. "Five-year-old girl."

"Too bad she's caught up in all this."

"Yeah," Jake said, thinking of Lindsay's laughing blue eyes and pixieish expression. She was beguiling, no doubt about it, but he wasn't about to get too close to Robert Fisher's child. Nor his ex-wife. "Come on," he said gruffly. "Let's get to work."

"Some of us already have been," Ron said with a good-natured chuckle. "You know, when I talked to Brecken at the department, I got this feeling that he wasn't telling me everything."

"He's supposed to be discreet."

Ron drew thoughtfully on his cigarette. "No, it was more than that," he said. "I think he was being evasive."

Jake's head snapped up. "Meaning?"

Ron grinned. "I've known Brecken a long time. When he clams up, something's going down. And I'll bet you it has to do with our friend here." He tapped a thick finger on the picture of Robert. "Ten to one, the police are on to him again."

"You think he's about to be nabbed?"

"Nah." Ron stubbed out his cigarette. "I bet the police think they're going to nail him again. There's a big difference."

Amen, Jake thought. Scowling, he sorted the information into stacks. It would take days to sift through everything, but he'd take the time. He owed it to himself and to Daniel.

And to Kimberly, he told himself, surprised at the turn in his thoughts.

"You may kiss the bride!" The preacher's words rang happily through the little chapel.

From the back pew Kimberly swallowed a thick lump in her throat. She watched Scott Donaldson lift the ivory-colored veil, uncovering Diane's flushed face. Diane's eyes were bright and blue, her cheeks rosy as she tilted her head back. Scott entwined his fingers in her blond, lace-covered hair and lowered his head, taking her lips possessively with his.

A whisper of approval swept through the tiny chapel, and teary-eyed guests smiled.

Kimberly felt close to tears herself. It was obvious these people loved each other—Diane, nearly angelic in ivory silk, and Scott, tall and lean in his black tuxedo.

Jake sat at the far end of a pew in the back. He looked the part of a courtroom attorney in his stiff white shirt and dark tie.

His gaze shifted, and his steely eyes clashed with hers.

Then he smiled—a lazy, off-center grin that caused her heart to beat a quick double-time.

The organist pounded on the keys, and the bridal march filled the chapel. The bride and groom strolled from the pulpit down a long wine-colored runner and through the exterior doors. The guests followed suit.

Outside, mist gathered in the cool air, clinging to the blackened branches of the bare oak and maple trees that flanked the church.

Diane and Scott received guests on the chapel steps. Kimberly stood in line, waiting, and saw Jake, detached from the crowd, hands in his pockets, on the brick path leading to an ancient cemetery. He was studying her intently, not bothering to hide the fact that he was staring. One cocky black brow raised in expectation as she moved closer. Kimberly met his gaze, forced a thin smile and hoped to God that her accelerated pulse wasn't visible in the hollow of her throat.

Storm clouds gathered overhead, and the wind picked up, catching in her skirts. Kimberly barely noticed. Her attention was solely on Jake.

Suddenly she felt Diane's hand on hers and forced her gaze back to the laughing eyes of her friend. "Congratulations," Kimberly whispered, hugging her. "It was a wonderful ceremony."

"Then you forgive me for bailing out on you?" Diane teased.

"No, but I've learned to live with it." Kimberly felt her cheeks dimple. "But if there's any way I can talk you and Scott into staying..."

The groom, overhearing her, laughed. "Not a prayer."

"What can I say?" Diane rolled her eyes. "L.A. born and bred."

Kimberly sighed. "Well, if you ever get tired of the warm weather, sunshine and beaches..."

"Don't count on it," Scott said with a chuckle.

"So, how're things with you?" Diane asked, her smile replaced by sudden concern.

"Same as ever."

"And Jake?" she motioned to the path where Jake was standing.

"He's very concerned," Kimberly allowed. "I think he'll do a good job."

"I know he will," Diane said, squeezing her arm. Then she smiled again. "And admit it, he's not too hard on the eyes."

"Who isn't? Me?" Scott asked, picking up on the tail end of the conversation.

"Only you, darling," Diane deadpanned.

"Come on, you've got to meet Frankie and Paul...."

Thunder rumbled over the hills, and Kimberly moved on, allowing other guests access to the bride and groom.

Kimberly glanced back to the path, but Jake had moved, had walked farther up the cracked old bricks to the cemetery. He stood, shoulder propped against the rough bark of an ancient cedar, his face trained toward the sea of weathered white tombstones. Hesitating only a second, she took off up the path, gathering her skirt in one hand so that it wouldn't drag in the pools of standing water and mud.

His back to her, Jake shoved a hand through his hair. The wind played havoc with the branches overhead and tossed his hair back across his face.

Kimberly stopped behind him. "The rest of the party's going inside," she said.

"What?" He turned quickly, and his expression was grim, his eyes dark and remote, as if he were caught in some private hell.

"I'm sorry—I didn't mean to intrude—"

"You didn't." He forced a smile. His lips, thin and sensual, curved wryly, and his eyes glinted with silvery interest. Lightning sizzled across the dark sky.

"It's not safe out here." With a large hand on her shoulder, he drew her away from the protection of the lacy branches of a cedar tree until they stood beneath a weathered arbor, where rose vines, now only skeletal brambles, still clung to the latticework.

"Maybe we should go inside," she whispered, suddenly breathless. She was all too aware of that warm palm against her shoulder, the tips of his fingers leaving hot impressions on her bare skin.

He glanced to the heavens as thunder rumbled again and electricity charged the air. Though late afternoon, the day had turned suddenly dark as midnight. Rain started to fall, thick drops splattering against the ground. Instinctively he held her closer. One arm slid around her waist, offering the slight protection of his jacket. She was pressed against his body, hard and lean, and the scent of after-shave mingled with the fresh, rain-washed air.

His expression grew tender, absurdly protective, and his eyes turned to quicksilver. Intuitively she knew he was about to kiss her, and she swallowed hard. Her hammering heart nearly fell to the rain-spattered bricks, and her breath was lost somewhere between her throat and lungs. She could see her own reflection in his eyes as he lowered his head, pulling her to him, crushing her against him. His lips slanted over hers with such possession, she couldn't think, could do nothing but feel—the strength of him, the warmth of his mouth on hers, the sensual touch of his hands splayed across her back.

Her pulse skyrocketed. She closed her eyes and kissed him back. A few solitary raindrops slid down her neck to tingle already electrified skin.

Her lips parted willingly, and he licked them, causing a shudder to pass through her. Her knees went weak.

Groaning, he lifted his head. His heavy-lidded gaze delved deep into hers. "Oh, God, Kimberly," he whispered against her hair. "I shouldn't have—"

"No, don't!" She couldn't stand an apology. Not now. She didn't want to think about a kiss filled with so much passion that her fingers still trembled in its aftermath. She forced a smile. "A few nights ago, you helped me."

His mouth quirked. "So it's payback time?"

"You looked like you could use a friend."

"Thank you." The sadness in his eyes disappeared. "I do." He asked, "Is this how you treat all your friends, Ms. Bennett?"

Laughing, she shook her head. "Only very special friends."

Thunder cracked again, and the rain began in earnest, slanting persistently downward. Jake grabbed her hand and started back to the reception hall just off the chapel. Half-running to keep up with him, her skirts bunched in one hand, she dashed down the brick path to the reception hall.

Inside, the party was in full swing. Most of the guests had already convened in the softly lighted room. Candles, their flames quivering, graced long linen-clad tables, and flowers filled the hall with the delicate fragrances of rose and carnation. Floor-to-ceiling windows glowed with the reflection of the candlelight as bejeweled guests clustered in small groups.

Jake poured them each some champagne. She watched the raindrops bead in his hair. She couldn't deny the physical attraction she felt for him and wondered what she could do about it. She wasn't in the market for a man, and this man, the one who was going to represent her, was the last person she could get involved with. Whatever happened, it was important that Jake keep his objectivity in the custody case.

He offered her a glass. "To Diane and Scott?" he said, holding his glass aloft.

Kimberly nodded, glad he hadn't said "to us." There could be no "us." She clinked the rim of her tall glass to his, then stared through the paned windows to the murky Willamette River as it rolled slowly northward.

The door burst open, and Diane and Scott stepped into the room. Laughing gaily, they shook rain from their hair and suffered good-naturedly through the rites of the newly married. Together they managed to slice the three-tiered cake, feed each other a gooey, frosting-laden piece and, with arms entwined, drink champagne from engraved silver cups.

"Barbaric ritual, isn't it?" Jake joked.

Kimberly laughed, relaxing a little as Diane tossed her bouquet of roses, baby's breath and carnations high into the air. The beribboned flowers landed squarely in a young girl's hands, and she squealed in delight.

"You should have tried to catch it," Jake said. "Maybe you would have got lucky."

"Or unlucky, depending on how you look at it," Kimberly replied.

"Uh-oh, that sounds a little cynical, Ms. Bennett."

"Just judging from experience."

"So, don't tell me you've given up on the institution of marriage."

"Not for everyone," she replied. "Just for me." She eyed him over the rim of her champagne glass. "And what about you?"

"Once is more than enough," he agreed.

"No need to have a wife serve your every whim—wash your floors, scratch your back, clean your Porsche?"

His eyes flashed. "You applying for the job?"

"No."

"Good, 'cause I don't have a Porsche. But I think you deserve a consolation prize."

"For what?"

"Not catching the bouquet. Here..." Reaching with his free hand, he plucked a long-stemmed white rose from a basket overflowing with blue and white flowers. "For you," he said, his voice husky, his eyes bright.

"Don't you think Diane will mind?"

"Diane owes me."

"Funny, that's what she says about you."

"Oh, but I'm paying off my debt." His eyes glinted. "Besides, I think Diane's too wrapped up in Scott to notice one flower."

Kimberly accepted the fragile bud and sipped her champagne.

From a corner near a broad bank of windows, tuxedoed musicians tuned up. As the soft notes of the anniversary waltz filled the room, Mr. and Mrs. Scott Donaldson danced together for the first time as man and wife.

"Shall we join them?" Jake asked, cocking his head toward the dance floor. Flickering candlelight reflected in his sable-brown hair.

She glanced at her watch. "I really should be going. . . ." But she felt the glass being lifted from her fingers, and then she was swung gracefully onto the shiny patina of the dance floor, joining Scott and Diane and a few of the braver guests.

She hadn't danced in years, but Jake made following the strains of the waltz easy. His strong arms wrapped comfortably around her waist, and his body, hard and lean, pressed intimately against hers.

He gazed down at her, his eyes sparkling from the candlelight, his breath whispering through her hair.

Though the room was filled with guests, she didn't notice anyone or anything but Jake and the sensual power of his embrace. He pulled her even closer, so close that her breasts were crushed against his chest and her thighs pressed intimately against his. One of his hands splayed possessively across the small of her back.

The fragrance of roses and carnations filled her nostrils as she closed her eyes to sway still closer to him. Though a thousand voices in her mind screamed "beware," she didn't heed one of them.

His gaze, dark with passion, drove deep into hers, and she shivered, not from cold, but from the tingle of electricity that swept up her spine.

This couldn't be happening. It *couldn't*. She was feeling like a teenager again, thrilling to this man's touch when he was the last man in the world she should be attracted to.

The dance ended and she stepped out of his arms. "I really have to go," she said, reaffirming the notion to herself.

"The party's just begun, and I think we could have fun," he persuaded.

She was tempted, but knew in her heart she could get entangled with him. "Really. I have to get back. Arlene's got Lindsay and she's probably already waiting for me." Forcing a smile and still holding the single white rose, she turned to leave before she changed her mind and decided to stay with him.

His brow knit in frustration, Jake stared after her, watching her escape—for that's what it seemed to be. Her mahogany-colored hair billowed away from her face, and her silky gown shimmered as she dashed through the door.

Just like Cinderella at the stroke of midnight, he thought furiously, his fists clenched as he shoved them into his pockets.

He wanted to follow her. There was something about her that challenged him—something that touched him in a way he'd never been touched before. "You're imagining it," he told himself as the band started playing a lively pop tune.

He stared through the windows, saw her sidestep the puddles of the parking lot, her slim legs moving quickly, the wind catching in her hair. A jagged flash of lightning illuminated her face—a beautiful face that was fierce with determination one second, only to melt into sensual invitation the next.

He wondered if there was another man in her life, but discarded the idea. He'd felt her respond when he'd kissed her so impulsively. That was a decided mistake. Kissing Robert Fisher's ex-wife, for God's sake. What's gotten into you, McGowan?

She drove out of the lot, and another car, a white station wagon, pulled away from the curb at the same time. Jake caught only a glance of the driver when Diane nudged him on the shoulder.

"So—I see you're getting along well with your new client?" She tried to hide a smile and failed. Her blue eyes danced, and Jake felt as if he'd been conned.

A waiter carrying a silver tray passed by, and Jake reached for another glass of champagne. "Don't tell me this is another one of your feeble attempts at matchmaking, Dr. Welby."

"It's Donaldson now—remember that," she warned. "And it didn't look so feeble to me. Besides, she needs your help."

"So you and she keep saying."

Diane's eyes lost their mischievous sparkle, and she grew serious. "I shouldn't have to explain to you about the fear of losing a child."

Jake stiffened as if to protect himself.

"And you could help her, you know, and get back at Robert Fisher at the same time. Kill two birds with one stone."

Jake's head snapped up. "You told her about Daniel?"

Diane shook her head. "Of course not. It's not my business." Her blue eyes clouded, and she touched the side of his face. "But I wish there were a way you could lay him to rest."

I will, Jake vowed as Diane, spying Scott across the room, threaded her way back to her groom.

Eventually, he supposed, he'd have to tell Kimberly about his relationship with Daniel. And he'd have to do it before he lost his head and got involved with her.

He took a long swallow of champagne and stared out the window, wondering what to do about her. If he were scrupulous, he'd lay his cards on the table, tell her everything that was going on, admit that he was Daniel Stevens's half brother and that he didn't want to get involved emotionally with any woman—especially a woman who had a child and had once been married to Robert Fisher. He'd also tell her that he wanted her.

Unfortunately it seemed lately that scruples weren't his long suit.

Chapter Six

Kimberly hardly dared breathe until she had driven several blocks away from Pioneer Chapel and Jake McGowan. Why had she followed him to the cemetery? Why had she let his bleak look disturb her? And why, dear God, had she let him kiss her?

Sighing, she glanced at the single white rose, now dewy with rainwater, lying on the passenger seat.

Smiling wryly at the bedraggled flower, she flicked on the wipers, then licked her lips anxiously, only to be reminded of Jake and his overpowering kiss. Deep inside her there was a yearning—a yearning she didn't want to acknowledge.

"Get a grip on yourself," she warned, glancing at her reflection in the rearview mirror. Her hair was a mess, her cheeks flushed, her eyes unnaturally bright. "Oh, Kimberly, you *are* an idiot," she whispered, barely noticing the car trailing after her.

Compressing her lips, imagining the feel of Jake's mouth against hers, she cranked on the steering wheel and veered her car into the puddle-strewn driveway of her cottage near the park.

Steadfastly Kimberly pushed aside her fantasies of Jake. They were out of the question. He was her lawyer, for God's sake! He had to remain objective in order to help her keep Lindsay!

Scooping up her purse and the rose, she climbed out of the car and ducked under the dripping clematis clinging to the eaves of the back porch.

The door banged shut behind her.

"Mommy!" Footsteps echoed in the hallway, and Lindsay, her cheeks rosy, her blond hair streaming behind her, nearly slipped as she ran across the kitchen floor and threw herself into Kimberly's waiting arms.

"Hi, honey!" Kimberly hugged her daughter fiercely, as if in so doing she could erase the black cloud that hung over them.

Lindsay squirmed, squealing happily in her arms. "Oooh. You look beautiful!" Round blue eyes studied Kimberly's dress and the single strand of pearls encircling her throat. "Where'd you go?"

"To a wedding. And look—here's something for you!" Kimberly handed Lindsay the white bud.

"I wanted to go, too." Lindsay pouted, her lower lip protruding in vexation as she took the flower and contemplated the ivory-colored petals.

Kimberly kissed her daughter's forehead. "Maybe next time," she promised as she heard Arlene's brisk footsteps in the hall.

"How was the wedding?" Arlene asked, entering the kitchen.

"Just like the ending of a fairy tale. Diane was working her way past cloud nine and headed for ten."

"Good for her. You could take a lesson, you know."

"On love?"

"Yes—on love. All men aren't the same," she said meaningfully as she untied her apron.

Don't I know it, Kimberly thought. Lindsay climbed away from her mother and headed down the hall.

Kimberly shook the rain from her hair. "So, how'd it go today? How was Lindsay?"

"An angel, as usual."

"Sure." Kimberly laughed.

"Well, maybe her halo tilts once in a while, but she wouldn't be normal if it didn't."

"I suppose you're right." Kimberly found a cup in the cupboard and poured coffee from the glass pot in the coffee maker. She held up the pot to Arlene, but the older woman shook her head.

"Had enough. My back teeth are already floating. Now, tell me every last detail of the wedding."

Kimberly went through the entire ceremony, and Arlene's eyes twinkled. "Well, I'm glad you went. You need to go out and have yourself a good time once in a while."

"I don't know if I'd call a wedding a 'good time.'"

"You know what I mean. You need to live a little and kick up your heels. And going out sure beats sitting around here and worrying about what that—" Arlene glanced nervously at Lindsay, but the little girl was already in the living room searching for her blanket "—that ex-husband of yours has up his sleeve. I tell you, if I ever see him face-to-face..." She let her warning trail off, but her sharp birdlike eyes blazed with indignation.

Despite her fears, Kimberly laughed at Arlene's militancy. "If Robert only knew, he'd be shaking in his boots!"

"He'd better be! Now, listen, I made a big pot of lentil soup. It's on the stove. And there are fresh chocolate ka-doodles in the cookie jar."

"Oh, thanks. But take some home to Lyle," Kimberly insisted, thinking of Arlene's crippled husband.

"Another time, maybe, but not tonight. The last thing we need is something more to nibble on." She reached for a plaid jacket hanging on a peg near the back door. "I'll be back in the morning. If the weather clears up, I'll take Lindsay over to the park—just to see if there are any ducks who haven't figured out that they should be in Palm Beach." With a wave she stepped outside.

Kimberly watched her leave, then lifted the lid of the soup kettle. Tangy, spice-laden steam curled upward in a soft cloud.

"Hey—lookie at me!" Lindsay stumbled into the kitchen. She was wearing a rhinestone tiara in her hair, a long strand of pop beads, one of Kimberly's lace slips and a pair of Kimberly's satin pumps. "I'm a bride," she proclaimed proudly, her large eyes meeting her mother's.

"And a beautiful one," Kimberly said, laughing as she twirled her daughter off her feet. One of the high heels dropped with a clunk to the floor. "So, who's the lucky guy?"

"Guy?"

Kimberly couldn't help grinning. "You know—the man you're gonna marry."

"No one!" Lindsay said emphatically. "Like you."

"Like me," Kimberly said as she held Lindsay close. "Well, pumpkin, it's hard to have a wedding without a groom—but if that's the way you want it, it's okay by me."

"Good." Lindsay smiled slyly and eyed the ceramic teddy bear jar on the counter just out of her reach. "Now can I have a cookie?"

"Later. First, we'll have some soup."

Lindsay made a face, crinkling up her nose. "I like ka-doodles better."

"Most of us do," Kimberly admitted as she placed her daughter on the floor. Lindsay concentrated on balancing in the spiked heels again.

Kimberly patted Lindsay's pale curls. "I've got to get changed, and then we'll have dinner."

She hurried down the short hall to her bedroom, and Lindsay followed, the shoes clomping noisily.

"Who was the bride today?" Lindsay asked.

"Diane—remember?"

"Oh."

Kimberly tugged the dress over her head and stared at her reflection in the oval mirror above her bureau. Small creases lined her brow, but her blue-green eyes sparkled. Thoughts of Jake skittered through her mind.

She felt an annoying flush climb slowly from the swell of her breasts to her throat. Smiling to herself, she brushed the tangles from her wet, bedraggled hair. Her feelings concerning Jake McGowan were in a jumble. Professionalism had to overcome this ludicrous joy she felt at the mere thought of him. Suddenly annoyed, she flung her brush onto the bureau and kicked off her shoes.

She should never have followed him to the cemetery, should never have allowed herself to be charmed by Jake McGowan. Glancing at the mirror again, she frowned. "You've made a mess of things this time," she chided her reflection. Wearing only her lace slip, her hair shining from the recent brushing, she sank onto the mattress of her double bed.

No matter what had happened, she still had to approach Jake as a professional. Damn it all, she needed him. "You've got no choice," she whispered into the empty room. With that, she leaned back against the pillows and closed her eyes, only to see the mocking image of Jake's face.

His thoughts all tangled in Kimberly, Jake drove home from the wedding reception. His senses still reeled, and he wondered what kind of fool he'd been, kissing Kimberly impulsively, then dancing so close to her. Caught in the fragrant cloud of her perfume and the yielding warmth of her body pressed tantalizingly to his, he hadn't been able to think clearly.

Even now his palms began to sweat around the steering wheel as he remembered looking down at her when they'd danced. She'd tossed her head back, her hair brushing his arm, her gaze touching a forbidden part of his soul.

She hadn't seemed to mind that her dress was stained by the rain, nor that her hair had been tossed in the wind. He'd wanted to bury himself in those long, rain-darkened strands, and he'd had trouble dragging his gaze away from the pink pout of her lips.

Overwhelmed, Jake had felt a crazy desire to sweep her off her feet and steal her away so that he could get lost in her body and soul. But he hadn't. Common sense had prevailed.

Staring at the dark streets, he realized he hadn't been so fascinated with a woman in years. Though his mind screamed that he was making an irrevocable mistake, he couldn't fight the jolt of possession that ripped through him.

That she had been Robert Fisher's wife was unthinkable. She was warm and soft, and erotic thoughts still fired his blood, pounding with the same driving beat of his heart.

Taillights glowed in front of him, and he stomped on the brakes. The Bronco fishtailed.

"Forget her," he growled at himself. But as the words passed his lips, he knew he never would.

Two days later Jake winced against the morning sunlight. His eyes burned from too little sleep and too many hours poring over every scrap of information in the Robert Fisher file. He'd hoped to come up with something he could pin on Fisher, something concrete that he could use as a bargaining tool to get him to drop the custody case.

Of course, he'd hoped for even more than that—a shred of overlooked evidence that would put Fisher away for good. No such luck.

He climbed out of his Bronco and told himself that his bad mood had nothing to do with the fact that he hadn't seen Kimberly since the wedding. What could it matter?

But early this morning, when he'd finally given up and closed the Fisher file, he'd dropped onto the bed, only to stare at the clock and listen to the sounds of the night while his mind wandered back to Kimberly—over and over again. No matter how many times he forced his thoughts away from her, they always crept back to her soft smile and dark-fringed eyes.

Muttering an oath to himself, he shoved open the office door and was greeted by the sound of classical music and the smell of warm coffee.

Sarah, the plump secretary he'd inherited from Diane, was at her desk, diligently typing on a word processor keyboard, her fingers moving skillfully.

She glanced up at him and smiled. "Good morning, Mr. McGowan."

"It's Jake. Remember? Unless we're dealing with stuffy clients, let's keep things informal."

"You got it. Coffee's on. You want a cup?"

He forced a smile. "I can get it myself."

"I'd be glad to—"

He held up a palm. "Relax, Sarah. This isn't the Dark Ages. You're liberated now, remember?"

She snorted, but smiled and went back to her work.

Jake headed down the hall. In the kitchen he poured a mug of dark coffee and warmed his hands on the side of the cup. He had several client appointments this morning, but his concentration wasn't on property line disputes, patent infringement or tax loopholes—or anything other than Robert Fisher.

And Kimberly Bennett.

"You're obsessed," he muttered, crossing through the reception area again and picking up a stack of phone messages from the corner of Sarah's desk. He flipped through them quickly, hoping to spot Kimberly's name, but stopped at the final note. Ben Kesler had finally returned his call.

Jake McGowan's mood improved. "Now we're getting somewhere," he said as he kicked his office door closed and plopped down in his chair.

He hadn't noticed that Sarah had rearranged his desk, not until he picked up the receiver and saw the picture. His hand paused in midair as he stared into the face of a small, two-year-old boy. A boy with dark hair and blue eyes. A boy holding a stuffed yellow duck and wearing a wide smile. A boy he'd loved with all his heart. A boy he'd called his son.

Jake let the telephone receiver drop. His throat knotted, and he picked up the picture, staring at the lifeless photograph. Steeling himself as he always did, he took the framed photo and placed it behind him on the credenza.

His forehead creased, and he waited until he was composed again. Then he reached for the phone and punched out Kesler's number.

Kesler was in a meeting and would call back. Without really thinking, Jake dialed Ron Koski's number and left a message. Ron called back half an hour later.

"How are you doing?" he asked, his gravelly voice needing no introduction.

Jake got right to the point. "I didn't find much in the Fisher file," he said, "in fact just about nothing I didn't know already. So I want you to get back to Brecken. See if you can find out anything."

"What's up?"

"Nothing, probably," Jake thought aloud, leaning back in his chair. "But if the police are getting close to Fisher, he'll know it. Someone will leak the information to him for the right price. If that's the case, maybe he's getting ready for a long vacation."

Koski let out a low whistle. "You think that's why he's interested in his kid all of a sudden."

"I don't know," Jake admitted, hating to think what would happen to Kimberly if she lost her child. "I just want to cover our bases. See what you can dig up."

"Will do. But Brecken's become pretty tight-lipped."

"I know," Jake said, rubbing his jaw. "That's what worries me."

At five o'clock Bill Zealander stormed into Kimberly's office. His ruddy face was set in a scowl, and his eyes, behind wire-rimmed glasses, were nearly black. "What's the meaning of this?" he demanded, slapping down a file folder with a memo clipped to it.

"Of what?"

His eyes narrowed as she read the memo. "Eric's reassigned the Juniper trust to you. Why?"

"Because the heirs requested me."

His nostrils flared. "Which heirs?"

"Henry and Carole—the children."

"That's preposterous! Do you know them?" he challenged.

"Not personally, no," she said calmly. "But I helped Henry secure a building loan when I worked in mortgage trust, and I helped Carole set up a custodial account."

"And that's all?" he asked, sneering his disbelief.

"Other than the couple of weeks I've worked with them on the estate. Why?"

"You know why." He leaned over her desk. "The Juniper trust is well over five million dollars—one of the largest in the department." His mouth set in a tight grimace. "Don't think I won't talk to Eric about this!"

Kimberly smiled, but her eyes met his levelly. "I wouldn't dream of it, Bill. Go right ahead. Talk all you want."

"I will." Snapping the folder up, he strode out the door as quickly as he'd marched in. Kimberly dropped her forehead into her hands. "Men," she muttered under her breath.

"Ms. Bennett?" Marcie's voice buzzed over the intercom. "Call for you on line two. Mr. McGowan."

Kimberly's heart jumped. "Thanks," she said into the intercom as she picked up the phone. "Kimberly Bennett."

Jake got right to the point. "I'd like to meet with you. As soon as possible. I just got off the phone with Kesler."

Kimberly's breath stilled. "And?"

"And it looks like you were right. Robert is hell-bent to gain full custody."

She closed her eyes, and her fingers tightened around the receiver, holding it in a death grip. "I knew it!" she said, furious. "I just knew it!"

"I think we'd better get together."

"Absolutely!"

"I'll pick you up at the bank right after closing. We'll go to dinner, then get down to brass tacks."

She didn't even think about arguing. She was too shaken. So, Robert was going through with it. Just as he threatened. "Can he take her away from me?" she asked, bracing herself.

"Not if I can help it."

Still numb, she hung up the phone. At least she had Jake on her side. That was good. Jake McGowan, she decided, thinking back to the jut of his chin and the anger that could spark in his flinty eyes, would be a dangerous enemy.

True to his word, Jake arrived less than forty-five minutes later. Marcie, who showed him in, winked at Kimberly from behind his back, then made a quick escape.

Kimberly glanced up from her desk, saw the concern in his eyes and felt her heart flutter uncontrollably.

"What did Kesler say?" she demanded, shutting the door behind him.

"You want to talk here?" he asked.

She glanced around the cherry-paneled walls and bit her lip. "Probably not. This might sound paranoid, but there's too much of Robert here. He's a major client with the bank."

"And the walls have ears?" One side of his mouth tilted upward.

"I just don't like to take chances." Kimberly licked her lips. "I'm scared, Jake," she admitted. "Really scared."

"Don't be. Nothing's happened yet."

"I can't lose her. I can't." His arms surrounded her, and she leaned against him. The strength of his body felt so right—so natural. She didn't even consider pulling out of his embrace, but clung to him. The soft texture of his jacket rubbed against her cheek, and the smell of leather and after-shave filled her nostrils. "Lindsay—"

"Shh. Didn't I tell you I wouldn't let that happen?"

She nodded, her crown brushing his chin. "But you don't know Robert."

His muscles tensed. "I know him."

"He can be so..."

"Ruthless?"

"Yes," she admitted, shivering. "Ruthless."

He tilted her chin up with one finger and forced her frightened gaze to meet the calm gray depths of his. "Then I guess I'll just have to be more ruthless, won't I?"

"You'd stoop to his level?"

His mouth twisted sardonically. "Let's just say I'll do whatever's necessary. Now, come on, let's go."

She didn't argue. Slipping reluctantly from the security of his embrace, she stuffed some files into her briefcase, snapped the leather case closed and grabbed her cape. "Where to?"

"Someplace close?"

"No." The after-work crowd hung out during happy hour in some of the local bars and restaurants nearby, and Kimberly didn't want to risk being overheard by anyone at the bank.

"Bollinger's, then?" he suggested.

Bollinger's was a restaurant perched high on the hills in northwest Portland. She couldn't suggest anywhere that was more out of the way. And, as far as she knew, Bollinger's wasn't one of Robert's regular haunts. "I'll meet you there."

"I could drive you."

She felt suddenly silly for the way she'd nearly fallen apart. Tossing her hair from her face, she said, "I can drive myself. Really. It's just easier that way."

"If that's the way you want it."

He walked with her to the elevators. In the parking garage she watched as he unlocked his Bronco, then she slid into her Mercedes and headed west.

Within twenty minutes she was seated across a small table from him. The restaurant was housed in an old Victorian structure, complete with turrets and gables. It clung to a forested hill in northwest Portland and had been remodeled several times since the turn of the century. Filled with paraphernalia of bygone years, Bollinger's was an eclectic blend of antiques—army recruiting posters from the World Wars I and II, artifacts from the forties and fifties, record jackets from the sixties, Tiffany lamps with hanging prisms and classic movie posters.

Kimberly barely noticed. "Tell me everything Ben Kesler said."

Jake sat on the other side of the small table. His knees nearly brushed hers, and candlelight flickered over the stern set of his features. "It's pretty simple, really. They're planning on trying to wrest custody from you because Robert's convinced that you're unfit."

"Oh, God."

"Saying it and proving it are two different matters," Jake pointed out.

A waiter dropped by the table, and Jake ordered them a bottle of wine. When she started to protest, he wouldn't hear of it and, without consulting her, ordered for them both.

Kimberly didn't care. She wasn't interested in food. She was only concerned about Lindsay.

The waiter returned with the wine, and Jake poured them each a glass. "Now, tell me about your life," he suggested.

"What about it?"

"What do you do all day?"

"You mean in my free time—between being a mother and a full-time bank officer."

His eyes twinkled in the reflection of the candles. "Right."

"I sleep—exercise a little. Watch some TV and read. Pretty interesting stuff, eh?" she asked, sipping from her glass.

The waiter deposited crisp salads and a crusty loaf of Viennese bread on their table.

"What about the men in your life?"

"Men? Plural?" she responded, feeling a little defensive.

"Okay, tell me about the *man* in your life."

She dropped her eyes and tried to stem the rage that boiled up by pronging a tomato slice on her salad plate. "I hate this, you know."

"What?"

"This—this—accountability. My life dissected under a microscope!"

"I know." He reached across the table, and his hand covered hers. "But I have to ask."

The tender gesture tore at her heart. She withdrew her hand and lifted her eyes to his. "There is no man." *Except maybe you.*

Jake stared at her for a second, then blinked and turned his attention to cutting the loaf of bread on the board between them. "Surely you've dated since the divorce."

He placed a thick slice onto her plate.

"Not much."

"So, tell me about the dates."

She wasn't used to sharing her personal life with a man—any man. And Jake was different. Baring her soul to him took courage. She had to remind herself that she'd hired him to probe into her personal life. "There's nothing much to tell," she said as the waiter removed the salad plates and placed steaming platters of pasta and vegetables on the table. "The first man was an old family friend—nothing romantic. And the second—well, it was a mistake."

"Why?"

"The man was Eric Compton. My boss at First Cascade. He's the vice president in charge of the trust department, only one step down from Aaron Thorburn, the president. It was only one date, but it caused all kinds of problems."

"Such as?"

"Other employees, one in particular, thought I was trying to sleep my way to the top."

He stared at her for a second. "Were you?"

Her mouth nearly dropped open, but she clamped it firmly shut. Did he think so little of her? "What do you think?"

His mouth curved into a lazy smile. "It doesn't seem your style."

"Thank you. It isn't. In fact I wish I'd never gone out with Eric. Things would've been much simpler." She frowned at the memory. Eric had hoped to start something that night, had expected her to fall at his feet. He'd even gone so far as to suggest she spend the night at his place, and she'd nearly choked on her drink. In many ways the evening had been a disaster.

"And you've never gone out with him again?"

"No." She sipped from her water glass.

"Why not?"

"No reason to fan the fires of gossip. I've got enough problems being the only woman trust officer without having to be known as the boss's 'woman.'"

"And Compton—he's accepted this?"

"He doesn't have much of a choice."

Jake stared at her. "Anyone else?"

"No one serious."

Silence stretched uncomfortably between them, and Kimberly wished she'd never agreed to meet him here. The small table was too intimate, and Jake was too close, his stare too intense. She could feel his gaze on her as he sipped his wine. She watched his throat work as he swallowed. That small motion, so natural, was sensual in the dark room. She dragged her gaze away from his throat and stared through the window. The lights of Portland twinkled in the distance.

"Tell me about Lindsay," Jake whispered.

Kimberly's head snapped up. "What about her?"

"Everything. She's what? Five?"

"Yes. Robert and I had been married a little over a year when she was born." Kimberly felt suddenly self-conscious. "When I found out I was pregnant, I was ecstatic."

"And Robert?"

"Suggested an abortion." That had been the start of the end, she knew now. "I wouldn't hear of it, and we argued a lot. During the last part of the pregnancy, he seemed to change his mind and became interested until she was born."

Jake's eyes were penetrating, the hard angles of his face illuminated by the single flickering candle. "What went wrong?"

"He wanted a boy." She smiled sourly. "Archaic, right?"

A shadow passed over his eyes. "Very."

She pushed the remains of her meal around on her plate, then let her fork drop. "He never seemed to care about her. Don't get me wrong—he was never cruel or anything, just inattentive. And he lost interest in me, too."

"So you wanted out—"

"Oh, no!" Surprised that it was so important he understand, Kimberly said, "He wanted the divorce. I fought it at first."

"Why?"

"Because we were parents. We had this wonderful baby between us, and I wanted to create this perfect little family unit." Her lips twisted cynically. "You know the image, right off the front pages of the old *Saturday Evening Post*."

"And he didn't feel that way?"

"By that time he'd found someone else," she said, the pain as real and cold as it had been the night he'd explained about Stella. "And then I started paying more attention to the rumors and innuendos in the papers."

"And believing them?"

"No—yes—I don't know. I believe that where there's smoke there's fire, but I never saw or heard anything that would confirm all the speculation about him."

She finished what she could of the dinner and pushed aside any lingering thoughts of Robert and their short, unhappy marriage. Jake turned the conversation away from the painful subject, and soon he had taken care of the bill and escorted her through the double doors.

"You know," he said once they were outside and darkness surrounded them, "we've got a problem."

"Just one?" she teased, flashing a smile in the clear night air.

"Believe me, it's enough." He took her hand in his, and his fingers were warm. A thrill raced up her arm.

Her heart began to beat against her ribs. "What is it?"

"You and me."

"What about us?"

"I'd like to see more of you, Kimberly," he said, the admission obviously difficult.

"I think we'll see a lot of each other in the next couple of weeks."

He plowed stiff fingers through his hair. "I know. But the trouble is, I want more. More than just a business relationship. I know it's crazy and off-limits, but that's the way it is." His eyes darkened with the night, and her pulse was pounding in her head.

"I don't think it's wise—"

"Hell, I *know* it isn't. But we can't deny what we feel."

"Oh, Jake, don't—"

But he cut her off. "Don't deny it, Kimberly."

Her throat tightened as he drew her close.

"I asked you those questions in the restaurant for two reasons. One was for the case. The other was for me."

Her pulse quickened. Unconsciously she licked her lips, and his gaze drifted down to her mouth. "I—I think we'd better keep this professional," she said, her voice unfamiliarly husky.

"I agree—but I don't think I can." He stared at her with such honesty, she nearly melted inside.

"I have a daughter to think about."

"I know."

"And . . ." She slowly pulled her hand from his. "And sometimes I feel that you're holding back from me, Jake. That you're not being completely honest."

His expression turned guarded. If he was going to share any secrets with her, it wouldn't be tonight.

Disappointed, she turned away, only to feel his fingers clamp on to her shoulders and turn her quickly. "I know it's crazy, but I can't help it," he ground out before his lips descended on hers and he kissed her with that same raging fire she'd felt before. She couldn't stop him, but kissed him back. Swept away in a rising storm of passion, she clung to him.

When at last he lifted his head, he stared at her with a hint of amusement. "Now, just how're we going to ignore this, Ms. Bennett?"

"We'll find a way," she teased back, her equilibrium shattered.

"You think so?" His grin slashed white in the night. "I wouldn't count on it if I were you." He dropped his arms to let her go, but she lingered a second.

"I just don't think I can get involved with anyone right now. Not until this is all over."

"I wonder if that's possible."

"I don't know," she whispered, but turned to her car. Not trusting herself alone with him another minute, she climbed into the Mercedes and took off.

She drove home automatically, guiding the car by instinct. Though she tried not to think of Jake's handsome face or enigmatic, off-center smile, his image seemed to loom in her mind's eye. He was her lawyer, for crying out loud. She'd convinced him to help her, and that was that. She touched her mouth softly, remembering the firm lines of Jake's lips as they had covered hers with a possession so demanding, so vibrant that she could still feel the pulsing desire that had swept from his body to hers.

"Stop it," she muttered, cranking on the wheel as she turned into the driveway. Angry with her wayward fantasies, she cut the engine and dashed up the back steps.

Stepping into the kitchen, she spied a pajama-clad Lindsay standing on a chair. Her heart wrenched at the thought of a future without Lindsay's precocious remarks and bright eyes.

A huge lump filled her throat. Lindsay was watching Arlene as the older woman bent over a boiling pot and stirred slowly. The scent of tart lemon filled the room.

"Baking again?" Kimberly asked as she dropped her purse onto the table.

"Mommy!" Lindsay scrambled out of her chair and dashed into Kimberly's waiting arms. "You're late!"

"I know and I'm sorry."

"I missed you!" Lindsay pouted.

Arlene clucked her tongue. "Don't you fuss," she warned, glancing fondly at Lindsay. "I told you she called." Without breaking rhythm in her stirring, Arlene nodded in Kimberly's direction. "Just give me a minute. Lindsay wanted lemon pie."

"But we still have cookies!"

"So eat 'em."

Kimberly slid out of her cape. "Really, Arlene, you didn't have to go to the trouble—"

"No trouble at all," Arlene said, chuckling. "It kept her busy, and lemon's my favorite, too."

"Arlene says I can stay overnight with her."

"Oh?" Still balancing her daughter on her hip, Kimberly crossed the kitchen and peeked into the kettle of simmering lemon pudding.

"Next weekend, if it's all right with you," Arlene verified.

"Are you sure?"

"Positive. Besides, it'll do Lyle a world of good to watch this little one."

Lindsay clapped her hands together. "We're going to make you a Christmas—"

"Shh!" Arlene said, grinning. "It's a surprise. Remember?"

"Oh!" The child looked positively stricken.

Kimberly touched her blond curls fondly. "Okay. You can spend the night, *if* you promise to be good, brush your teeth and go right to sleep when Mrs. Henderson tells you to."

"I'm always good!" Lindsay proclaimed, crossing her little arms over her flannel-covered chest.

"An absolute angel," Arlene said, smothering a smile. "Okay, here we go." She poured the lemon filling into a warm piecrust, then spooned thick globs of shiny meringue on top. Lindsay couldn't stand not being part of the action.

She squirmed from Kimberly's arms, climbed back on her chair and promptly stuck a finger in the cloudlike meringue.

Kimberly tried to stop her daughter. "Don't—"

"It's all right," Arlene said. "Half the fun of baking is testing, isn't it, sweetheart?"

Lindsay cast Kimberly an I-told-you-so look over her small shoulder. A dot of meringue stuck to the tip of her nose, and Kimberly had to laugh.

"I think we'd better wash you up and then get ready for bed."

"Not yet—"

"Come on," Kimberly insisted. "It's after eight."

"But I'm not tired!"

"Not much, you aren't," Kimberly remarked, noting the blue smudges beneath Lindsay's bright eyes and the fact that her thumb kept slipping between her small lips. "Come on, angel, I'll read you a story."

"But I want—"

"Shh." Kimberly carried her protesting daughter to the loft, which served as Lindsay's bedroom. Tucking the child between the covers, she lay beside her, opened a book of favorite nursery rhymes and began reading. Within minutes Lindsay drifted to sleep, her lips moving slightly, her blond head resting on a plump pillow, while she clutched her favorite stuffed animal, a fuzzy raccoon.

Kimberly's throat constricted as she stared at her sleeping child. No matter what, she couldn't lose Lindsay.

Listening to the sound of the rain droning against the roof, she placed her arm around her daughter's waist and closed her eyes. Somehow, she vowed silently, she'd find a way to keep Lindsay with her. And Jake McGowan would help.

Chapter Seven

Eric Compton knocked twice, then shoved open the door of Kimberly's office. A tall, striking man with thinning black hair, straight nose and brown eyes, he offered her his well-practiced smile. "Glad I caught you," he said, glancing at his watch. "I thought you might need the tax file on the Juniper estate." He dropped a manila folder onto the corner of her desk.

"Thanks." She took the file and tossed it into her In basket. "Have you got a minute?"

"For you? At least one—maybe even ten."

She grinned. "Good."

He dropped into a chair near the desk. "Shoot."

"Okay. I got a little flak about this one," she said, tapping the closed file with a fingernail.

"From Zealander. I heard." Eric frowned and ran his fingers through his receding hair. "Bill came flying into my office the other day, loaded for bear. He thinks I favor you.''

"Do you?"

Eric smiled. ''I'd like to. But not by giving you plums in the office. I've always tried to keep my private and professional lives separate.''

"Good. So have I," she said.

''I told Bill the same thing.'' He plucked at the crease of his slacks. ''However, I'm not sure he believed me. But—'' placing his hands on the arms of his chair, he pushed himself upright ''—that's his problem. Now, anything else?'' he asked without the usual double entendre.

"Not that I can think of."

His well-oiled smile faltered a little. ''Good. You know, Kim, I'd like to take you out. I've got tickets to the symphony next Friday.''

Kimberly sighed and shook her head. "I don't think so."

"Another time?"

''Maybe,'' she said, then winced when she recognized a gleam of hope in his eyes. ''But probably not. As long as I'm working here, I think it would be better not to date bank employees.''

"Even the boss?"

''Especially the boss,'' she said, offering him a dimpled smile.

He shrugged. ''Okay, but this is a warning. I'm not giving up, Kim. Just let me know when you change your mind.'' He started for the door, then paused and glanced over his shoulder. ''By the way, I saw a man hanging around the parking lot late last night. Be careful, will you? There'll be a memo sent to all the employees, but I'm telling everyone in my department personally.''

"You think he's dangerous?"

"Probably not, but we can't be too careful," Compton said as he closed the door firmly behind him.

Kimberly stared at the closed door. She thought about the man she'd seen lingering at the lamppost near her house and shivered. Though she'd nearly forgotten the incident, Eric's warning brought it all back into sharp focus.

She tapped her pencil on her desk as the intercom buzzed.

"Ms. Bennett? Mr. Juniper is here to see you," Marcie announced just as the door to her office burst open again and Henry Juniper, a small, round man with a red face, strode up to Kimberly's desk. She started to rise.

"My sister's trying to cut me out of the estate, isn't she?"

Kimberly was dumbstruck. "There's no way she could. I thought I explained all that."

"Oh, sure," Henry said, his blue eyes flaming. "Where there's a will, there's a way. Especially if you get a greedy lawyer involved."

"Why don't you slow down and tell me what you're talking about."

"It's Carole," he said in exasperation. "She's hired some hotshot attorney and now she wants more money! This guy—what's his name—Kesler—he's out to bleed me dry!"

Kimberly's heart dropped to the floor. "Ben Kesler?"

"The shark himself. I've heard he's a barracuda! That he never gives up. Just keeps biting at you!"

Kimberly, shaking inside, held up a hand. "The terms of your father's will were very clear. There's nothing Mr. Kesler can do to change that. Anything he tries will just be blue smoke and mirrors. The will is cut and dried."

He calmed a little and nearly fell into the chair recently vacated by Eric Compton. His fingers tapped nervously together. "You're sure about this?"

"Positive."

"And there's never been a case where one heir has been able to squeeze out a little more?"

"I didn't say that. It depends upon the circumstances, of course—"

"Aha! I knew it." His hands flew into the air. "Father lived with Carole for a while, you know, while he was convalescing after his hospital stay. I suggested a nursing home, but oh, no, she wouldn't hear of it. Wouldn't hear of it, I tell you!" He leaned closer. "Wanted to get on his good side, don't you know. I think she was trying to get him to change his will the entire time he was with her! It didn't work, and now she's going to charge the estate for his care—and then there's Kesler's attorney fees and God-only-knows-what else!"

"Slow down, Mr. Juniper," she said. "The head of our department, Mr. Compton, is an attorney himself, and he's worked very closely with the attorney for the estate. I assure you that everything's in order."

"Oh, great, just what we need! A couple more attorneys involved. That's what got us into this mess in the first place!"

She spent the next half hour going over the account and settling him down. By the time six o'clock rolled around, all she could think about was going home to dinner with Lindsay, a hot bath and a good book.

She tossed a few files into her briefcase and frowned at the pink memo in her In basket—the memo reminding everyone to be careful in the parking garage.

As she swiped her cape from the hall tree, the phone rang. Balancing purse, case and cape in one arm, she grabbed the receiver quickly. "Kimberly Bennett."

"Jake McGowan."

At the sound of his voice, her heart somersaulted.

"I know it's late, but I thought we could catch a movie, then have a late dinner."

"I thought we had an agreement."

"No, lady, you had an agreement."

"Jake, this isn't going to work—"

"What if I told you we have work to do?"

She smiled, forgetting about the hot bath and book. "I still can't go out. Arlene's busy tonight."

"You don't have another sitter?"

"None that I can count on." She was surprised at how her heart seemed to drop to the floor in disappointment.

"Then I guess we'll have to forego the movie and get right to it. I could drop by your place, and you could make me dinner."

She laughed and threw caution to the wind. What could one night hurt? "All right, counselor, you're on. I owe you that much."

There was a long, nerve-racking silence on the other end of the line. "You don't *owe* me anything." His tone was dead sober.

"Okay, don't consider it a debt. In fact you can bring the wine."

"White or red?"

"Surprise me."

"That, I'd love to do," he said silkily.

Kimberly's heart tripped.

"I'll see you between seven-thirty and eight."

Kimberly stood rooted to the spot until she heard him hang up. Then she dropped the receiver. Clutching her bag, briefcase and cape to her breast, she muttered, "You'd better get moving."

She took the elevator to the basement lot, which was as poorly lighted as ever. The hairs on the back of her neck raised a little and she felt as if unseen eyes were boring into her back. "Don't be paranoid," she chided herself, but nearly jumped out of her skin when she heard the scrape of a shoe behind her.

Her heart leaped to her throat as she remembered Eric Compton's warning. Spinning, she surveyed the lot, but saw nothing out of the ordinary. A few other employees straggled to their vehicles as she slid behind the wheel.

Her hands began to sweat, and she locked all the doors before pulling out of her parking space. As she drove through the gate, she caught a glimpse of a shadowy figure huddled behind a post, but it disappeared as quickly as it had appeared. "It's just your imagination," she said, hoping to calm her jittery nerves. "Nothing else." But she couldn't shake the feeling that she was being watched as she drove across the river to Sellwood.

The drive home, including a stop for groceries, took less than thirty minutes.

Kimberly juggled the two sacks as she unlocked the back door and hurried inside. Arlene and Lindsay were in the kitchen.

"Did you get anything for me?" Lindsay asked, eyeing the sacks from her vantage point under the table, where she was carefully stacking building blocks.

"Everything," Kimberly replied with a sly grin. "It's dinner. And we're having company."

Arlene's brows inched upward.

"What company?" Lindsay demanded. She scooted out of her hiding place to eye her mother. "Who's coming over here?"

"Jake—you met him earlier."

Lindsay's lower lip protruded, and her pudgy face clouded suspiciously. "I don't like him!"

"Why not?"

Lindsay shrugged. "He's too big!"

Arlene smothered a smile.

"Tell him to go home!"

"Wonderful," Kimberly whispered sarcastically. "This is shaping up to be a barrel of laughs!"

"Come on, you," Arlene said fondly, taking Lindsay's hand. "I'll help you get cleaned up."

While Arlene and Lindsay were upstairs, Kimberly unpacked the groceries she'd bought, put a kettle of water on the stove and raced into the bedroom. She changed into a pair of black jeans and an aqua-blue sweater, then hurried back to the kitchen and tossed lasagna noodles into the steaming kettle. After starting another pan of tomato paste simmering, she yanked out vegetables, cheese and the remains of a baked chicken, then started grating mozzarella cheese.

Arlene returned to the kitchen. "Lindsay wanted to finish dressing herself. She'll be down in a minute." She studied the boiling pot on the stove. "What're you making?"

"Chicken lasagna."

"Need some help?" Arlene snatched her favorite apron from a hook near the back door and tied the strings around her thin waist.

"I'll manage," Kimberly said wryly. She glanced nervously at the clock mounted over the stove and started working double-time on the cheese.

"Then let me bone the chicken," Arlene offered. Without waiting for a reply, she found a sharp knife and began expertly separating bones from meat. "Tell me about this McGowan character," she said, casting Kimberly a sly glance.

"Well, he's my lawyer."

"That much I know. I met him already. I assume he's single?"

"You assume correctly," Kimberly said, remembering how pained Jake had appeared when he'd talked of his marriage. "But he was married once. His wife is dead. They were divorced."

"What about children? Does he have any?"

"No." She filled Arlene in, surprised at how little she knew about Jake.

"Sounds like a bit of a mystery man to me," Arlene observed as she stripped off her apron.

"He is," she admitted, frowning. "I keep thinking I've heard of him before, but I don't know where."

"Does it matter?"

Kimberly lifted a shoulder. "Probably not." She layered the lasagna and stuffed it into the oven.

Lindsay barreled into the room. Wearing lavender stretch pants and a T-shirt with mint-green bears tumbling across its front, she handed her mother a wrinkled ribbon. "I did my ponytail myself!"

"So I see."

"But I can't tie the ribbon."

"I'll help."

"And I've got to scoot," Arlene said, pressing a kiss onto Lindsay's forehead. "I'll see you in the morning."

Lindsay cried, "What about the tree?"

"Tree?" Kimberly asked.

"The Christmas tree!"

Arlene's hand was poised over the doorknob, but she stopped. "Oh, right. Maybe tomorrow." She explained to Kimberly, "I've got a little Douglas fir I promised Lindsay. Lyle's brother brought us a couple of firs from his tree farm by Estacada. We only need one, so I left the other in a corner on your back porch."

"And we were s'posed to put the lights on it!" Lindsay said.

"Tomorrow—"

"Now!" Lindsay cried.

Rolling her eyes toward the ceiling, Arlene said, "I'll see you in the morning, angel. Don't forget you're staying overnight with me Friday night."

The tree momentarily forgotten, Lindsay grinned.

"And you," Arlene said to Kimberly as she opened the door, "take my advice and go out."

"I'll think about it," Kimberly said to the door as it banged shut.

"Go out where?" Lindsay demanded.

"I don't think it matters." Kimberly laughed, wiping her hands and then tying the ribbon around Lindsay's ponytail. "As long as I go. Come on, you can help me." She reached into the drawer and pulled out three settings of silver—part of a wedding gift from her grandmother. "Put these and the red place mats around the table in the dining room."

"And candles?" Lindsay asked, "and fancy glasses?"

"Silver, china, candles, the works," Kimberly said, laughing.

Lindsay's face brightened. She tore into the dining room and started her task with a vengeance.

Twenty minutes later the doorbell pealed, and Kimberly nearly jumped out of her skin.

"I'll get it!" Lindsay said, sprinting into the living room.

"Be sure to look out the window first—"

But Lindsay had already yanked the door wide open. Jake was standing on the threshold, two bottles of wine tucked under his arm. Cold air swept across the porch, swirling the few dry leaves that had collected near the railing.

At the sight of Jake, Kimberly's heart did an unexpected flip. But Lindsay eyed him suspiciously.

"Come in," Kimberly said, closing the door and taking Jake's jacket. "Dinner will be a while."

Inhaling dramatically, Jake said, "It smells great."

"Let's just hope it tastes as good as it smells."

"Here." He handed her the two bottles of wine, his fingers grazing hers. "Red or white—whichever you prefer."

"I want red!" Lindsay announced.

Kimberly laughed. "But you'll get white—the kind that comes from cows."

Jake uncorked the wine and poured them each a glass. "To success," he said, nodding in Lindsay's direction.

"Success," she agreed, wondering if it were possible as she touched her glass to his.

"Now, which do you want first—the good news or the bad?"

She froze. So this is why he wanted to go out. To prepare her. She felt her face pale a little. "I hate good news-bad news jokes," she said softly.

"This is no joke."

She sucked in her breath. "I was afraid of that. Okay, let's start with the good."

"Robert's attorney petitioned for a change of custody, and we have a court date. January twentieth."

"That's good news?" she asked, her heart nearly stopped.

"It gives us time to work."

"I hate to ask what the bad news is."

Jake touched her arm. "The judge assigned to the case is Ken Monaghan."

Kimberly nearly dropped her wineglass. "Monaghan? But he and Robert . . ."

Jake's lips thinned. ". . . have known each other for years."

"Surely he couldn't take the case."

"I objected and made a lot of noise at city hall, but Monaghan was assigned the case."

Kimberly rested a hip against the counter. All her fears settled in her heart. She'd been kidding herself, of course; there was no way to fight a man as powerful as Robert.

"Don't worry," Jake said, reaching forward, his hand cupping her shoulder.

"But he could take her away." Tears stung her eyes, and she had to fight from breaking down completely.

Jake drew her close. "Hey, I told you I wouldn't let that happen, didn't I?"

"But—"

"You asked me to keep you informed, to let you know everything that's going on. That's why I told you. But we've got to work fast."

"How—?"

"By proving that Robert isn't fit to be a father."

The room seemed to close in on her. Going to court against Robert was one thing; trying to publicly rebuke him was another. "But I couldn't—"

Jake's expression turned stern. "You promised," he reminded her, "that we would do this my way or no way. We both know that Fisher has been involved in a lot of shady deals, some of which have been downright illegal. You've suspected as much for a long time. All we have to do is connect him to the crimes."

Kimberly stiffened. "Crimes?" she repeated. It sounded so harsh. Her insides quaked.

"You don't have to play innocent, Kimberly," Jake said, all kindness gone from his features. His gaze drilled into hers. "You were his wife. You lived with the man. You saw things no policeman has ever seen."

"So you want me to play spy, is that it?" she asked bitterly.

"I want you to do everything possible to keep your child with you."

Kimberly leaned heavily against the counter. She knew it would come to this, of course. Jake had been dogged in leading up to Robert and his questionable connections. She sipped her wine but didn't taste it. Jake, like so many others, believed the worst of Robert. Not that she didn't think he had his faults. But a criminal? A crime lord? A man involved in drugs and prostitution and smuggling? She didn't believe it, though she'd noticed the change in him. "I just don't have any proof," she said. "I told you that already."

Jake face grew taut. "You're the only one who was close enough to him to know of anything incriminating."

"We've been over this before. He never discussed his business with me while we were married, and we've barely spoken since."

Jake's eyes grew cold and calculating. Kimberly shuddered as he insisted, "Maybe you saw or heard something you don't think is important," he prodded, pressuring her.

With a great amount of effort she concentrated, her thoughts returning to that bleak, lonely time that was her marriage to Robert Fisher. She remembered many things she'd rather forget, but nothing to do with his business.

"He—he was cold. Not interested much in the family. He spent a lot of nights away from the house."

"Did anyone visit him?"

"No." She chewed on her lower lip. "We had only a couple of parties while we were married, and most of the people who came were wealthy businessmen and their wives."

Jake's jaw slid to the side. "What about after Daniel Stevens's death?" he asked quietly.

She shook her head. "Nothing."

"Damn! It *wasn't* suicide, you know," Jake said, his gaze never leaving her.

"You don't know that."

"I do! Believe me, it just didn't happen that way!"

Kimberly finally understood. "You knew him, didn't you?" she asked gently.

"Yes."

"And you didn't tell me before?" she asked, staring at him as if he were a stranger—for in many ways he was. "Why not?"

"I didn't want to color your judgement."

"Or you didn't trust me with the truth." She felt anger swell up inside her. "That's it, isn't it? Even though you told me you'd tell me everything."

"Daniel's death doesn't have anything to do with your case!"

"Then why do you keep bringing it up? You lied to me."

He grabbed her wrist in an ironlike grip. "I did not lie to you. I just didn't mention my friend."

"Why not?"

"What would be the point?" They eyed each other for several seconds, and Kimberly was sure he could feel the quick beat of her pulse on his fingertips at her wrist.

"Let's just start out being honest with each other, okay?"

His mouth tightened. "Of course." Then, explaining, he said, "Daniel investigated a man who's been known to associate with the less desirable elements of society, including your ex-husband. And Dan ends up dead." Jake's nostrils flared slightly. "Now, Kimberly, just what conclusion would you draw from that?" His eyes were dark with an inner, raging fire.

"I don't know," she said, swallowing hard, unable to believe that Robert would be involved in drugs and murder. Her throat worked, and her voice was barely a whisper. "I—I'm sorry about your friend."

"So am I," he said, dropping his arm. He finished his wine and set his glass in the sink. "Let's not think about

Dan,'' he said under his breath. He shoved his fists into his pockets and closed his eyes. Slowly the tension in his features relaxed. "At least, let's not think about him tonight." He stared for a few long seconds through the kitchen window to the black night beyond. "Enough for now," he said quietly, "but if you think of anything—*anything*—that might tie your ex-husband to organized crime, you'll let me know."

"Organized crime?" she choked out, but his stern expression cut off any further protest.

"Yes."

"All right," she agreed, mentally crossing her fingers. Battling Robert for custody of Lindsay was one thing; trying to prove him a hardened criminal—perhaps a murderer—was beyond her comprehension. And she couldn't forget that Jake, if he hadn't actually lied to her, had kept the truth to himself.

The timer buzzed. Kimberly started, then getting a grip on herself, motioned toward the dining room. "Sit—and pour us each some more wine. The red. Lindsay and I'll serve."

Jake settled into the chair at the head of the table. The hard anger in his face disappeared, and he actually managed a thin smile. Oddly, despite his mood swings, Kimberly sensed that he belonged in this house, that his presence filled an empty void that she hadn't known existed until she'd met him.

With Lindsay's help he lighted the cream-colored tapers. Candlelight gleamed in his dark hair and in the ruby-red claret as he poured.

Kimberly placed the thick Portland phone book on a chair and hoisted Lindsay on top of it. Once Lindsay was settled, she set the platter of lasagna on the table and took the chair opposite Jake's. His gaze touched hers as she sat down. His sensual lips curved into a smile, and Kimberly's chest constricted against a wayward rush of emotion.

They could be friends, she thought, maybe even lovers, if circumstances were different. Jake McGowan was a fascinating, mysterious man and she liked him—more than liked him. That was the problem. Whether she wanted to admit it or not, she was falling in love with him. And yet there was so much she had yet to learn. Why hadn't he told her about Daniel Stevens being his friend? And why did she feel that he was still holding something back?

Later, after the dinner dishes had been cleared and Kimberly had tucked Lindsay into bed, Jake tried to tell himself to go home, that he had no business being here. He couldn't afford to fall for Kimberly, and he certainly didn't want to form any attachment to her daughter. Yet he lingered, watching Kimberly with a growing fascination that was dangerous and wanting to please the little blond girl.

"Coffee?" she asked, pouring water into the coffee maker.

"Maybe later." He motioned toward the back porch, where he'd seen what appeared to be a bedraggled fir tree. "Let's put up the tree and surprise Lindsay."

"You'd do that?" she asked. She set the plates in the sink.

He lifted a shoulder. "Why not?" Jake noticed the proud set of her spine, the graceful way her hair fell between her shoulder blades and the nip of her waist, visible when she reached into a high cupboard for the sugar jar. Her sweater slid up a bit, exposing creamy white skin. Jake felt a stirring deep within and glanced away, swallowing hard against a suddenly dry throat.

While he wrestled with the tree, Kimberly opened the closet under the stairs and began pulling out boxes of lights, tissue paper and ornaments. Finally she found the stand. After wiping off the dust and moving an old rocker, she

Here are your BIG WIN Game Tickets, worth from $5.00 to $1,000,000.00 each. Scratch off the PINK METALLIC STRIP on each of your sweepstakes tickets to see what you could win and mail your entry right away. (See official rules in back of book for details!)

This could be your lucky day – GOOD LUCK!

TICKET 1
Scratch PINK METALLIC STRIP to reveal potential value of this ticket if it is a winning ticket. Return all game tickets intact.

LUCKY NUMBER

1I 939281

TICKET 2
Scratch PINK METALLIC STRIP to reveal potential value of this ticket if it is a winning ticket. Return all game tickets intact.

LUCKY NUMBER

3Q 940923

TICKET 3
Scratch PINK METALLIC STRIP to reveal potential value of this ticket if it is a winning ticket. Return all game tickets intact.

LUCKY NUMBER

5N 939046

TICKET 4
Scratch PINK METALLIC STRIP to reveal potential value of this ticket if it is a winning ticket. Return all game tickets intact.

LUCKY NUMBER

9T 938429

TICKET 5
FREE BOOKS

We're giving away brand new books to selected individuals. Scratch PINK METALLIC STRIP for number of free books you will receive.

AUTHORIZATION CODE

130107-742

TICKET 6
FREE GIFT

We have an outstanding added gift for you if you are accepting our free books. Scratch PINK METALLIC STRIP to reveal gift.

AUTHORIZATION CODE

130107-742

YES!
Enter my Lucky Numbers in THE BIG WIN Sweepstakes and tell me if I've won any cash prize. If PINK METALLIC STRIP is scratched off on ticket #5, I will also receive one or more FREE Silhouette Special Edition® novels along with the FREE GIFT on ticket #6, as explained on the opposite page.

(U-SIL-SE 07/90) 235 CIS R1YS

NAME _____

ADDRESS _____ APT. _____

CITY _____ STATE _____ ZIP _____

Offer limited to one per household and not valid to current Silhouette Special Edition® subscribers.

©1990 HARLEQUIN ENTERPRISES LIMITED

PRINTED IN U.S.A

Carefully
detach card
along dotted
lines and
mail today!

Play
all your
BIG WIN
tickets
and get
everything
you're
entitled to-
including
FREE BOOKS
and a
FREE GIFT!

BUSINESS REPLY MAIL
FIRST CLASS MAIL   PERMIT NO. 717   BUFFALO, NY

POSTAGE WILL BE PAID BY ADDRESSEE

SILHOUETTE READER SERVICE

THE BIG WIN SWEEPSTAKES

901 FUHRMANN BLVD
PO BOX 1867
BUFFALO NY 14240-9952

NO POSTAGE
NECESSARY
IF MAILED
IN THE
UNITED STATES

placed the stand by the window and watched him struggle with the tree.

Dark needled branches swiped at Jake's face as he attempted to place the sawed-off trunk squarely in the stand. The house filled with the scent of fresh air and pitch. Unaware that needles caught his hair or that his muscles moved fluidly beneath his sweater, he adjusted the brace and asked Kimberly to hold the tree straight.

"I think it leans a little," Kimberly said, eyeing the listing Douglas fir.

"Which way?"

"Right—no, left."

Jake laughed. "Make up your mind."

"I will, when you quit moving it."

Swearing under his breath, Jake gave the tree a shake.

"That's better."

Jake's deep, rumbling chuckle erupted from beneath the lowest branches. "This could take all night."

Through the branches, he saw her grin. God, she was beautiful. Her hair was mussed, red-brown and framing her face in tangled curls, and her eyes, wide and intelligent, were the most seductive shade of blue he'd ever seen. She didn't want to get involved with him—she'd made no bones about it—and he knew getting romantically entangled with the ex-Mrs. Fisher was an irrevocable mistake. Yet he couldn't shake the hope that maybe she would change her mind.

"Okay—let's take a look!" he announced, climbing from beneath the branches and shoving his hair from his eyes. The poor tree was listing, fighting a losing battle with gravity. "Just a few minor adjustments," he said, delving beneath the lowest branches again. Extracting a pocketknife from his pants, he worked on the trunk, trimming off a few unnecessary limbs. His voice was muffled when he said, "How about a hand—can you straighten this thing?"

"I can try." Kimberly tugged on the tree, and it finally stood upright as Jake adjusted the brace.

"That's better," he said, leaning back on his heels to check the angle of the fir. Satisfied, he stood, dusting his hands.

He was so close to Kimberly she could see the streaks of darker gray in his eyes, feel his breath against her hair, smell the scent of some musky after-shave mingled with the odor of fresh fir boughs surrounding him.

"Now, the lights!"

She laughed. "You're as bad as Lindsay!"

"Doesn't everybody love Christmas?" he asked, grinning.

"Not everybody. Remember Scrooge and the Grinch and—"

Without a word he swept her into his arms so suddenly, her breath rushed out in a gasp. "Enough, already." His lips molded over hers so intimately that Kimberly's knees went weak.

"I—I thought we had an agreement," she rasped when he finally lifted his head.

"We do."

"Then what—?"

"Oh? Didn't I show you?" Eyes twinkling, he reached into his pocket and held up a sprig of mistletoe. "This cancels any rash promises we have made."

"That's not fair," she said, giggling. "Isn't it supposed to be dangling from the ceiling or something?"

"Something," he murmured, holding the sprig over her head and kissing her soundly again. This time Kimberly was ready, and despite the doubts crowding her thoughts, she returned the fever of his kiss, delighting in the feel of his lips, tasting the wine-flavored sweetness of forbidden passion.

His tongue prodded her lips, and she opened her mouth eagerly, her arms twining around his neck as his fingers gently scraped the bottom of her sweater, where the soft skin of her abdomen stretched enticingly.

Desire burned like wildfire in her veins. She felt his hips press intimately to hers, an erotic swelling beneath his slacks moving sensually against her. Slowly he lifted his head. "Sweet Jesus," he rasped.

Liquid inside, she opened her eyes. She was tingling all over, and she felt a bittersweet ache coiling deep within.

"This can't happen," he said as if trying to convince himself. "It can't!" Swearing loudly, he stepped away from her and forced stiff fingers through his hair. "God, woman, what you do to a man."

Bereft, Kimberly tried to slow the pounding of her heart, but hot desire still ran wantonly through her limbs. "That works two ways, counselor."

He smiled then, a self-mocking grin that lifted one corner of his mouth. "I hope to God it does," he said.

"Believe me." Taking deep breaths to steady herself, she found the string of lights and began untangling the green wires. "After we finish with these, maybe we should get back to business," she said, wishing she didn't have to bring up the custody hearing.

"What's the matter, Kimberly? Are you scared of what might happen if we don't keep things strictly business?"

She couldn't ignore his challenge. "No way."

He cocked a defiant dark brow. "You're worried that things might get out of hand."

She met the mockery in his gaze with her own. "Aren't you?"

"Hell, yes!" he whispered, stringing the lights.

Together they wound several strings of lights through the lacy branches. Jake shoved the plug into the socket. The tree sparkled in a blaze of red, green and gold.

Kimberly crossed her arms under her breasts and nodded. "Good job."

"Not bad, if I do say so myself," he admitted, observing the tree.

"I guess I'm in the majority that loves Christmas," she admitted.

"That doesn't surprise me." He stared straight at Kimberly, then brushed some needles from her hair. Kimberly's pulse jumped at the seductive glint in his eyes. "This year's going to be special."

"Oh, wow!" Lindsay chimed from the stairs. Her eyes were wide, and she flew down the stairs, her tattered blanket billowing behind her. "It's *beautiful*!" She clasped chubby hands together and dropped the blanket.

Kimberly grinned and picked her up. "What're you doing up?"

"Couldn't sleep," Lindsay said, then looked at Jake and added, "My daddy's giving me a puppy for Christmas!"

The magic of the moment shattered. Kimberly drew in a sharp breath, detesting Robert for his promise. "Oh, no, honey, I don't think—"

"He is, he told me." Lindsay folded her arms across her chest defiantly.

"We'll see."

"He is! He said so!"

Kimberly's brows drew together. "I just don't want you to be disappointed."

"Daddy doesn't do that."

"If you say so." Kimberly carried her daughter and the blanket up the stairs. Silently praying that Lindsay hadn't seen Jake kissing her, Kimberly said, "Come on, sweetheart, let's get you back in bed."

"Daddy promised!"

"He and I have to talk," Kimberly decided. "But right now it's time for bed."

"No—"

"Shh. It's late. Come on." She tucked Lindsay under the covers. "Good night, precious," Kimberly said as her daughter yawned and snuggled under the comforter. A few minutes later Lindsay was snoring softly. Kimberly kissed Lindsay's curly crown before sneaking quietly downstairs.

Jake was leaning over the fireplace, stacking chunks of fir in the grate. His shoulders bunched beneath his sweater as he worked, and Kimberly could imagine the rippling strength of his muscles hidden beneath the soft wool.

He glanced over his shoulder at the sound of her footsteps. "You don't mind, do you?" he asked.

"No, by all means—" she motioned toward the grate "—a fire would be nice." The room had become cozy, the colored lights of the tree glowing softly against raindrops drizzling on the windowpanes.

"I thought it might make things more comfortable before we begin."

"Begin . . . ?"

Then she noticed the coffee table. Mugs of coffee were steaming next to a yellow legal pad. Her heart sank. She didn't want to think about Robert any longer. Tired of his promises to Lindsay, his fight for custody, his dark business dealings and his damn lies, she wanted to block him out of her mind forever. But, of course, she couldn't. She sat on the arm of the couch, staring at the fire while twisting her fingers in her lap. "Let's get it over with."

He smiled, displaying the same crooked grin that touched her heart. "It's not an execution, you know." Stepping across the carpet until he was standing above her, he stared down at her, his gray eyes filled with kindness and understanding.

He lifted her chin with one finger. "Relax. This is gonna be a piece of cake."

"I hope so." But she forced a wobbly smile and tried not to concentrate on the warmth of his skin against hers. She swallowed hard, and, as if he'd seen her reaction, he quickly withdrew his hand, picking up his pen and snapping off the cap with his teeth.

Pressing a button on the recorder, he sat on the edge of the table, disturbingly close as he faced her. "Okay. We'll start out slow. Tell me about your family life as a child. Would you say it was happy?"

"Yes."

"How?"

She shrugged. "I don't know. We lived on a farm in Illinois before moving to California. Mom and Dad worked hard, and we never had a lot, but we didn't go without either. It was a...carefree existence. At least to me."

"What about your folks?"

"Well, they worried a lot. About the weather and the crops and the price of grain. That sort of thing. Mom gave piano lessons to some of the kids for extra money."

"So, all in all you were content?"

"As much as any kid is," she replied, surprised at how easily she explained her life on the farm. She entwined her fingers around one knee and thought back to the rolling hills of sweet-smelling hay, the apple trees in bloom, the sound of the windmill clicking as a breeze picked up. Telling him about helping with the haying in summer, harvesting and canning in the fall, she recounted her early years and smiled. The memories of life on the farm wrapped around her like a coat she'd outgrown but had missed. She went on to describe moving to California and eventually the loss of her father.

Jake brought the conversation back to Robert and her marriage. Folding her arms around herself as if against a sudden chill, she stared at the yellow flames of the fire. She could feel Jake's eyes on her and knew he was searching her face for some trace of her emotions, but she refused to look at him. Thinking about Robert and all the hope she'd foolishly held in her heart saddened her.

She couldn't tell him anything she hadn't already. And eventually Jake snapped off the recorder and leaned back on the couch.

"Is that it?" she asked, finding her voice. It sounded weak, and she knew her skin was pale.

"For now."

"Thank God." She was still caught in the storm of feelings that had surrounded her marriage, was still staring blindly at the fire when she felt his fingers surround her wrist.

"If it's any consolation," he said slowly, "I think your husband is the biggest fool I've ever heard of. He was crazy to let you get away." Grabbing her wrist, he drew her forward, off the arm of the couch, so that she fell against him. Her hair tumbled around her face, and her hands pressed against the soft fabric of his sweater.

His arms surrounded her. "And just for the record," he said, his voice low, "I think you're the prettiest, sexiest and most intelligent woman I've ever met."

Surprised, she had to suck in her breath.

Her face was only inches from his, and his eyes, a luminous gray, reflected the scarlet embers of the fire. "I also think you're the most intriguing woman I've known in a long time."

She could barely breathe.

The brackets near the corners of his sensual mouth deepened. His gaze shifted to her lips, lingering as if he were lost in their promise. His fingers spread lazily across the small of her back, moving gently.

"I—I don't think this is such a good idea," she whispered, but already her blood was throbbing through her veins.

"Neither do I." But he didn't release her. If anything, his grip seemed to tighten.

"Is this a test?" she wondered aloud, trying to think.

"A what?"

"You know—for the hearing—to see if I'm promiscuous?"

He chuckled. "If this is a test, it's a test of my self-control." His face was flushed, his eyes beginning to glaze.

Kimberly's heart was pounding so loudly she was sure he could hear it over the hiss of the fire, and she thought she heard a separate cadence, as if he, too, was having trouble slowing his heartbeat.

She knew he was going to kiss her again as she felt his fingers move lazily upward to tangle in her hair. She didn't stop him, because she couldn't. She wanted him as desperately as he wanted her.

All the reasons for her to get up, keep their relationship strictly business, crossed her mind, but still she didn't struggle for freedom. When his mouth finally caressed hers, she melted inside. Her lips parted of their own accord, and her arms wound around his neck.

She relished the delicate pressure of his tongue rimming her lips before slipping between her teeth and exploring the velvet-soft recess of her mouth. A feminine ache, starting deep in her soul and spreading outward, throbbed for release as the pressure of his lips increased. He sank deeper into the soft cushions of the couch, taking her with him.

Her fingers settled around his neck. She felt the fringe of his hair brush against the back of her hand.

Groaning, he kissed her harder, his lips molding over hers as one hand twisted in the fiery strands of her hair, pulling her head backward, exposing the creamy column of her throat.

"Kimberly," he whispered, pressing hot kisses against her skin, "Kimberly... why are you doing this to me?"

"I—I'm not doing anything," she murmured, barely able to think as his hot lips seared the length of her neck and lingered at the small circle of bones surrounding the base of her throat.

She felt his legs rub against hers as he held her closer still, until she was lying above him, her hair falling like a shimmering curtain to his shoulders, brushing against his chest.

"This shouldn't be happening," he groaned.

She stared into his eyes then and read the torment of conflicting emotions in his gaze.

"Then—then stop."

"I can't, dammit," he growled, swearing under his breath before cupping the back of her head with his hands. Pulling her forward, he forced her lips to crash against his in a kiss that tore the breath from her lungs and sent her dizzy mind reeling faster and faster until she couldn't think, couldn't reason, could only feel.

"Mommy?"

Kimberly froze. Swallowing hard, she heard Lindsay's feet hit the floor.

"Again?" Jake asked, dazed.

"I told you about the nightmares."

"Because of the custody battle?" Jake asked, his brows drawing down in concern.

"I don't know. I hope not." Kimberly sat up and combed her hair with her fingers as she heard the patter of feet.

Lindsay, blanket in tow, stood at the top step, rubbing her eyes.

"I had a bad dream."

"Oh, pumpkin." On her feet in an instant, Kimberly dashed up the stairs, scooped her daughter in her arms and held her close, glad that Lindsay wouldn't understand the flush climbing up her neck or the thud of her heart. "Let's get you a glass of water, hmm?"

Lindsay buried her face in Kimberly's neck. "I was scared."

"I know, sweetie, but nothing's wrong. I'm here with you and I always will be." Glancing down the stairs, she spied Jake staring up at her.

Still half-sprawled on the couch, his hair tousled over his eyes, he caught her gaze and winked suggestively. Kimberly's heart turned over as she carried Lindsay into the bathroom, gave her daughter a drink, then helped her back into bed.

"I'll leave the bathroom light on for you," she said softly. Pressing her swollen lips against Lindsay's blond curls, she asked, "Will you be all right?"

"You stay with me," Lindsay pleaded, and Kimberly couldn't resist.

"Okay." She climbed onto the bed, holding her daughter's head against her breast, stroking her baby-fine hair, and feeling the heat of Lindsay's breath as her daughter snuggled against her. "Go to sleep, honey," she whispered, watching the steady rise and fall of Lindsay's chest as she tried to calm her own breathing.

As Lindsay fell asleep, Kimberly thought about Jake and her violent reaction to him. Startled at the intensity of her feelings for a man she'd known only a few weeks, she cradled her daughter closer, shut her eyes and wondered how she would get through the coming court battle. She couldn't imagine being near Jake and still being able to keep her distance.

A quiet cough caught her attention. Her eyes flew open, and she found Jake leaning against the rail of the loft. He had already donned his jacket. He was leaving! Every emotion deep inside broke free, and she almost begged him to stay.

But before she could form a protest, he blew her a kiss and winked, letting her know he didn't begrudge her closeness with Lindsay. Then he disappeared from view. She heard the front door open and close and felt a gust of icy wind dance up the stairs. From the living room below, the glow of colored lights seeped into the loft, and Kimberly smiled to herself. No matter what the future brought, it included Jake, and that thought alone was comforting.

Chapter Eight

By the end of the week, Kimberly couldn't wait to leave the bank. She hadn't heard from Jake in two days, and she was surprised how often she thought of him, how much she longed to hear from him. And it wasn't only because of the custody hearing looming in her future.

Sighing, she slapped a few papers in her briefcase and snapped it closed.

Outside, winter had landed full force on Portland. A storm had dropped six inches of snow on the city, tangling traffic and causing delays. Electrical outages caused computer tie-ups and fender benders on the frozen streets. The bank's messenger service had been crippled, and everyone's nerves were at the breaking point.

Bill Zealander was the worst. Since the transfer of the Juniper account to Kimberly, he'd first complained loudly to Eric Compton, and when all his arguments hadn't budged Compton's decision, Zealander had begun to ignore her completely. Fortunately Kimberly had been kept busy dealing with Henry Juniper's paranoia, and she couldn't worry about Bill's fragile male ego. Not when Henry Juniper was convinced that sister Carole was getting into Daddy's funds.

She'd deal with Zealander next week, she decided, yanking her briefcase from the desk. Maybe he'd cool down over the weekend. Then again, maybe he'd only be worse.

"Don't borrow trouble," she told herself as she joined the exodus to the elevators. The doors parted, and Jake sauntered through. His warm gray gaze landed on her, and her heartbeat instantly quickened. "Well, counselor," she drawled with a smile, "what brings you here?"

"One guess," he teased.

"I give."

"You."

Her spirits soared. What was it about him that touched her so? Wearing a ski jacket, sweater, insulated pants and a Cheshire-cat grin, he took hold of her arm. "Taking off early?" he mocked.

"I pulled the early shift." She grinned up at him. "And it's been a l-o-n-g week."

"Good."

"I don't know what's 'good' about it."

He propelled her toward the elevators, along with the crush of other employees. "I have a proposition for you," he whispered in her ear as the elevator doors whispered shut.

"That sounds interesting," she murmured.

"It is, believe me."

The elevator groaned to a stop at the bottom floor, and the doors opened. Jostled by the tightly packed crowd, Kimberly let Jake guide her to the corner of the garage where his Bronco was parked next to her car.

"Okay, McGowan. Spill it," she said, her mood lightened just because she was with him. "What's the proposition?"

"How about going skiing with me?"

"Tonight?" Kimberly asked, shivering from the cold in the unheated garage.

"Why not?"

"Well, because it's dark and cold and a blizzard."

"Sounds perfect for night skiing to me," he said, a lazy smile slashing insolently across his face.

"I've never been night skiing in my life—"

"Time you tried. You do ski, don't you?"

"Once upon a time. But it's been years."

"You have gear—equipment?"

"Somewhere. But I really can't. Lindsay's—"

"Staying over at Arlene and Lyle's," he finished for her. "She said so the other night. So, unless you have any more excuses..."

She wanted to find some. But Arlene's advice rang in her ears as clearly as silver bells. *Kick up your heels—live a little.*

Glancing up at him, she asked, "And what's in it for me? You said a proposition, right? Both parties benefit."

"Why, you, Ms. Bennett, get my time and attention for the next six or eight hours."

"How can I say no?" she quipped sarcastically.

"You can't." His gray eyes caught in the dim light and fairly twinkled.

"I must be out of my mind," she muttered.

"I'll take that as a yes."

"A reluctant yes," she qualified.

"Then let's get going. I'll follow you to your place."

Wondering if she truly had lost her senses, Kimberly climbed behind the wheel of her Mercedes and watched as

Jake moved to his Bronco. Smiling, she started the engine of her car and backed out of her parking space, glancing toward the elevator shaft where Bill Zealander, *Wall Street Journal* and black umbrella tucked under his arm, stood glaring at her.

No doubt he'd watched the entire exchange. There was a chance he may have heard snatches of their conversation.

Kimberly shuddered. The expression on his big face was cruel and calculating.

You've done nothing wrong, she reminded herself as she put the car in gear, forced a smile and waved to Zealander, though he didn't acknowledge her wave.

The drive home was a nightmare. Added to the normal congestion of Friday afternoon rush hour was the anxiety caused by the snow and slush turning to ice as night fell. Cars crept along at a snail's pace. Though the houseboats on the river glowed with colorful Christmas lights that reflected on the inky water, the spirit of the coming season seemed lost in the chaos of traffic forcing its way across the Sellwood Bridge.

By the time Kimberly pulled into her driveway, she was a nervous wreck. She told herself it was because of the weather and didn't have anything to do with Jake McGowan or the fact that she'd agreed to spend the evening with him. But even as the thought drifted through her mind, she knew she was lying to herself. She was excited at the prospect of being alone with him.

As she turned off the engine, she heard his car roar down the street and saw the flash of headlights in her rearview mirror.

He climbed out of his car at the same moment she did, following her to the back door, their boots crunching in the heavy snow. The eaves were hung with icicles. Dead leaves of the clematis had been trapped in the crystallike prisons.

"This isn't a smart thing to do," Kimberly said, shivering as she unlocked the door.

"What isn't?"

"Driving in this mess. The road to the mountain must be treacherous."

"I called. It's been plowed and sanded."

"When?" She glanced pointedly at the shower of snowflakes still drifting to the ground before she shoved open the door and stepped into the relative warmth of the kitchen. "It's been snowing all day."

"No problem," he assured her, then eyed the cold coffee still sitting on a burner on the stove. "Don't worry, I've got four-wheel drive. This'll be a walk in the park."

"Sure."

His gaze scanned the kitchen. "Have you got a thermos?"

"Under the sink."

"You don't mind if I heat this up and bring it along?" he asked, lifting the pot. The cold coffee sloshed in the glass container.

"Be my guest." She hung her coat on the hall tree, then spied a large envelope with her name scrawled crudely across the white surface. Opening the envelope, she found a piece of tablet paper cut into the shape of a snowflake. Around the cutout diamonds and triangles Lindsay had written "I love you" in uneven, oversize letters. Kimberly's heart turned over. She reached for the phone and quickly punched out a number.

Arlene finally answered on the fifth ring. "Hello?"

"Hi. How's it going?"

"Just fine," Arlene said with a hearty chuckle. "We've already built a snowman, pulled out the Christmas candles and arranged the Nativity scene on the mantel. Now Lindsay's insisting we put up our tree."

"I know the feeling," Kimberly said, resting her hips against the hall table and staring at the paper snowflake.

"You want to talk to her?"

"For just a second."

"I'll see if I can wrestle her away from the tree."

Kimberly waited impatiently as Jake stepped into the hall. "Trouble?" he asked, suddenly concerned.

"No—"

"Mommy?" Lindsay sang over the wires.

Kimberly's heart melted. "Hi, honey."

"Did you get my surprise?" Lindsay asked, her voice lilting.

"I sure did. That's why I called—to thank you. I'm going to take it to work on Monday and hang it in my office."

"Are you *really*?"

"You bet. Now, are you being good?"

"Good as an angel," Lindsay said emphatically. "That's what they call me over here."

"So I've heard." She laughed. "I'll see you in the morning, then. I love you."

"Me, too."

"Let me talk to Arlene again."

"'Kay."

A few seconds later Arlene was back on the line. Kimberly explained that she was planning to go skiing and would pick up Lindsay the next morning at ten.

"Just don't rush over here," Arlene remarked. "Lindsay's doin' a world of good for Lyle."

"Thanks."

After hanging up, she found Jake still lounging in the doorway between the hallway and kitchen. "Everything okay?" he asked.

"Sounds like it." She dimpled. "I think I'll have to pry Lindsay out of there with a crowbar tomorrow."

Jake glanced down at the paper snowflake. "I doubt it," he whispered, and the timbre of his voice touched a special spot in her heart. "Seems as if your daughter's pretty stuck on you." His eyes turned introspective.

"I hope so." Kimberly met his eyes, was lost for a minute in his silvery gaze, then cleared her throat and passed him in the hallway. "It'll just take me a little while to find everything."

"No hurry. As long as you can manage it in fifteen minutes."

"Don't hold your breath," she said, grinning as she walked into her bedroom and closed the door. Then, to make up for lost time, she yanked off her leather boots and scrounged through her closet until she found the old ski bag. She'd shoved it into a dark corner years before. "How about that?" she murmured, tossing the bag onto the bed, then unzipping it. Inside were insulated bib ski pants in a deep violet color, goggles, hat, sweater and long underwear.

Stripping out of her black suit, blouse and stockings, she crossed her fingers and hoped her outfit would fit. She hadn't worn any of her ski clothes since long before Lindsay had been born. Though she weighed less than before her pregnancy, some of her weight seemed to have shifted.

However, a few minutes later she stood in front of the oval mirror on the bureau, noticing that her bibs and sweater were snug but not too tight.

Quickly she braided her hair away from her face and ignored the blush that colored her cheeks. Excited about the evening ahead, she couldn't hide the sparkle in her eyes or the smile that toyed at her lips.

By the time she'd found her ski boots and jacket in the front closet, Jake had reheated the coffee and filled her thermos. "My skis are in the garage," she said, a bag of dry clothes slung over her arm.

His gaze slid over her before landing on her eyes. "Then what're we waiting for?"

"A break in the storm? Reason to overcome insanity?"

"Trust me," he said.

And she did. Whether it was foolish or not, she trusted this man with his slashing, enigmatic smile, his wise-beyond-his-years expression and observant eyes.

They found her skis, snapped them into the rack on his vehicle, and, still brushing snow from their hair and shoulders, climbed into the Bronco.

Through the slushy streets, beneath bare trees, past houses glowing in rainbows of Christmas lights, Jake guided the rig, heading east to the slopes of Mt. Hood. The wipers slapped away the falling snow, and quiet strains of holiday music sounded over the grind of the engine.

While Jake drove the Bronco through the darkened roads, Kimberly poured them each a cup of coffee. Handing him a cup, she asked, "Have you lived in Portland long?"

"Most of my life."

"And your family?"

His jaw tightened a fraction as he switched lanes. "My folks died a few years ago."

"No sisters or brothers?"

"Nope."

She longed to ask him more, especially about his wife. She wanted to know so much about him, but he seemed to keep much of himself from her. Glancing through the foggy windshield, she wondered whether he had secrets he would ever share with her. "So, you've known Diane a long time?"

"Since law school."

"And then?"

"Then we worked together downtown in a big firm." A muscle pumped in his jaw. "She helped me through a few rough years. Got me into corporate law."

"Why?" she asked.

"Why what?"

"Why the move from domestic relations?"

He pressed his lips together hard and downshifted quickly. "It seemed the thing to do," he evaded, sliding her a glance. They headed out of the city, past rolling acres of farmland. Snow, adding quiet illumination to the night, drifted against fences and buildings.

"You were supposed to be one of the best family relations lawyers in the city," Kimberly persisted.

He lifted a shoulder. "That's a matter of opinion."

"And you weren't that crazy about taking my case."

He slid a glance her way. "What is this? Twenty questions?"

Leaning against the door, she eyed him, his handsome, chiseled features, large eyes, strong chin now covered with a faint dark shadow. "You seem to know just about everything about me."

"Not yet."

"But soon. I figured it was my turn, that I should know a little about you."

"Not much to know."

She thought for a minute, then asked the one question that had been on her mind for a long while. "Why haven't you ever remarried?"

"Does the statement 'I never met the right woman' sound too cliché?"

"Yes."

"Well, it's true. That, and the fact that I'm not sure the institution of marriage is such a good idea."

Kimberly's brows inched up. "Why not?"

"Probably for the same reason you've given up on it."

She had given up on marriage—that much was true. But since Jake had entered her life, she hadn't found the idea of tying herself to one man so difficult to accept. But then, she didn't allow herself to fantasize.

Jake continued. "Let's just say my experience wasn't so great. My wife wasn't happy with me, and it didn't last. As for my parents, they hung together, but it was a war zone most of the time." He glanced her way. "Surely you feel the same."

She shook her head and thought about the loving years she'd spent with her own family. "No, I think marriage can be perfect."

He snorted. "You've changed your tune since Diane's wedding."

"I guess I did sound a little cynical."

"A lot cynical."

"Well, obviously you have to find the right person." She frowned into her cup. "In my case, Robert wasn't the one."

"I'll buy that," he said dryly, but didn't comment further.

Had his ex-wife wounded him so badly? Had he loved her so much that she'd soured him on marriage when she'd wanted a divorce? They drove in silence for a while, and the snow-covered farmland gave way to steeper hills. The road began to climb, winding through the foothills of the Cascade Mountains, past small towns decorated with lights, tinsel and brightly lighted trees before the solitude of the forest closed around them.

Traffic slowed. The pavement was covered with packed snow and ice. Several cars pulled over, their drivers lying on their backs beneath axles as they chained up.

Though Kimberly was white-knuckled whenever the Bronco slid on the icy pavement, Jake remained calm, and before seven o'clock he pulled into the crowded parking lot near the lodge. "We made it," he said, patting her knee.

"Thank God." Ignoring the warmth of his hand on her leg, she gulped the rest of her coffee. Jake opened the Bronco's door and stepped into eight inches of powdery snow.

Following his lead, she donned ski boots, mask and goggles before tromping, skis balanced on her shoulders, to the lodge.

"You hungry?" Jake asked as they clipped on their lift tickets.

"A little."

"Want to eat now?"

She shook her head and surveyed the mountain. Stretched under the glow of colored lamps, the ski run gleamed in pristine invitation. "Let's take a couple of runs first."

"I won't argue with that."

They skied to the lift and after a short wait climbed onto icy chairs. Snowflakes caught in the few strands of hair that had escaped from Kimberly's hat and lingered against her cheeks.

"Warm enough?" Jake asked. He draped one arm around her shoulders, giving her a hug.

"Yes."

They were carried slowly up the hill, above the tops of majestic firs and hemlocks. Lacy branches, now laden with snow, moved slowly in the breeze. The sky was black, but lights illuminated the side of the mountain, showing off the white runs and craggy rocks of the higher elevations.

"It's beautiful up here," Kimberly breathed. "I'd forgotten."

"And quiet. Sometimes I think it's the solitude that is so special," he said. "Not many people here at night."

He was right. She'd remembered weekend skiing, when the lift lines had taken longer than the run. But tonight, a week before the holiday break, the mountain wasn't crowded. It seemed as if they were alone.

Jake's arm tightened around her, and she felt a warmth deep inside stretching itself throughout her body. Relaxed and content, she wondered how much time she could spend with Jake and still feel this fascination for him.

He was the first man who had interested her since her divorce, and the intensity of her feelings was overwhelming. She'd never expected to fall in love again, but here, swinging over the tree tops, feeling the serenity of the snow-draped forest, she felt a kinship with him that went far beyond the bounds of mere friendship or, she thought ruefully, a professional relationship with her lawyer. The thought that she was falling in love nagged at her, but she ignored it. She couldn't afford to fall in love. Not now. Not until Lindsay's future with her was secure.

"Here we go." Taking her gloved hand in his, he helped her ski down the ramp at the top of the run. "Ready?" he asked, stopping at a ridge.

"As I'll ever be."

"Okay. So show me your stuff."

Trying her best to muster some self-confidence, she plunged her poles into the powder and pushed forward, feeling the exhilaration of the frigid air against her face as she skied down the hill. At first her legs were uncomfortable and awkward, and she was careful. But slowly, as she made her way down a wide, tiered bowl, she became more confident.

She saw Jake ski past her, then wait at the next ridge near a rustic wooden structure with a huge stone fireplace. Smoke curled from the chimney, and lights glowed through the misty, paned windows.

Breathless, Kimberly caught up with him. She could feel the color in her cheeks.

"You're good," he said in admiration.

"I've taken more than my share of lessons—and spills."

"So, why'd you give it up?"

Kimberly wiped the snow from her goggles. "I got pregnant and didn't want to fall, then Lindsay came along and I was caught up in diapers, rattles and bottles." Thinking back to those years when her marriage had turned to ashes, she frowned and glanced toward the weathered, barnlike building. "What's this?" she asked.

"The warming hut," he said. "You can stop in here to get a drink or a doughnut and warm up."

"Clear up here?" She gazed down the hill, where skiers, gliding along the snow far below, were barely visible. Groups and pairs and singles wound around the mountain. One man, dressed in navy blue from ski mask to boots, slid to a stop beside them and bent over to adjust his bindings. Kimberly didn't pay much attention to him.

Jake was still explaining. "The warming hut can take the chill out of the lift ride. Sometimes it blizzards up here."

She believed him. Not far from the timberline above them, the ski run was long and steep. Smiling mischievously, she adjusted her goggles and said, "Come on, I'll race you to the bottom."

"You're joking...."

But she took off, flying down the hill, the wind screaming past her face as she sliced through the snow.

Jake caught her midway down, waved and left her to maneuver expertly down a narrow part of the run to the lift below. "You cheated," he exclaimed, laughing as she slid to a stop, spraying snow all over his pants.

She giggled. "Just a little head start. Besides, it didn't help. How about a rematch?"

"You're on."

The next run ended as the first, with Jake flying by her expertly, despite the fact that she was skiing better than she remembered. At the bottom of the hill, she flipped off her goggles and held up her hands in mock surrender. "I give up," she said, laughing and seeing her breath fog in the air.

Jake hugged her. "Just to prove that I'm not an obnoxious winner, I'll buy you dinner."

"You're on!" Kimberly agreed. Together they skied back to the lodge, and she was only vaguely aware of the tall, ski-masked figure in navy blue gliding effortlessly down the slopes.

Once inside, stripped of goggles and gloves, they found a table near a floor-to-ceiling stone fireplace. In a far corner stood a bushy Douglas fir decorated with silver bells, scarlet ribbons and winking lights.

"Until last night," Kimberly said, cradling a glass cup of Irish Coffee Jake had ordered, "I'd almost forgotten about Christmas."

"Is that possible with a five-year-old?"

"Not really. But I was so wrapped up in this custody thing that I hadn't really felt much Christmas spirit." Her eyes sparkled with the reflection of the lighted tree. "Thanks for bringing me up here."

"Believe me, it's been my pleasure." He toasted her before resting both elbows on the table, his coffee cup cradled between his palms. His eyes were warm and flinty, and when his gaze found hers, a spreading awareness—like an early-morning mist—filled every corner of her soul.

They ate in relative silence, devouring grilled salmon and wild rice until Kimberly was stuffed. "If I eat another bite," she groaned, motioning with her fork at the remains of the pink, flaky salmon on her plate, "I won't be able to ski anymore."

Jake's lips twitched. "You're not getting out of another run that easily."

"I wasn't trying to."

"Good. Let's do it again. Double or nothing." Reaching down, he snapped the buckles on his boots, then left some money on the table.

"Hey—whoa. What're you talking about?"

"Let's race again. The bet's double or nothing."

"But we didn't bet the first time!"

"So, let's bet now," he suggested, his eyes glinting like liquid silver as they walked outside.

"For what? A dollar? A drink?"

"Come on, you can be more imaginative than that."

She rolled her eyes. "Don't tell me—just like junior high, right? The one who loses is the other's slave for a week?"

Laughing, he shook his head. Snowflakes collected in his dark hair. "Now, *that* would be interesting."

"No bet!"

"How about something not quite that bizarre?"

"What?" she asked suspiciously.

"The one who loses has to spend one entire day helping the other one around his or her house."

"Meaning . . . ?"

"Well, for example, I've got some clothes that need mending, windows washed, that sort of thing."

"Oh, great," she murmured, but thought of the rusted back door lock, the paint peeling off the swing set, the faucet that wouldn't quit dripping and the rotten front step that had needed to be replaced for over a year.

"I'll give you a head start," he encouraged, eyes dancing.

"How far?"

"Two slopes. I won't take off until you pass the warming hut."

"But that's nearly a third of the way down."

"I know," he taunted, grinning with the self-assurance of one who assumes he'll win.

Kimberly thought she had an even chance and would have dearly loved to wipe that cocky smile right off his face. "You're on, counselor! But let's up the bet. Whoever wins gets two days of free labor!"

"And how many nights?" he asked.

She lifted a brow coyly. "That depends."

"On?"

"How much I win by."

His white teeth flashed in the night. "So, what're we waiting for?"

He won, of course.

Just when Kimberly had thought victory was within her grasp, Jake swooshed past her in a blinding spray of snow.

Awestruck and furious, she skied the remainder of the run, asking herself why she'd been so stupid as to go along with the bet. Even though she'd sped down the hill at the top of her form, he'd passed her as if she were standing still.

"Idiot," she chided herself under her breath as she struggled up the hill by the lodge. He'd already taken off his goggles and hat and was trying nobly to wipe the smirk from his face.

"I'd like to accuse you of cheating," she charged, "but I can't."

His teeth gleamed. "What about double or nothing now?"

"No way!" She caught the teasing glimmer in his eyes and tried to remain stern. But her traitorous heart began to pound, and she could feel a dimple creasing her cheek.

Laughing, he linked his arm with hers. "For starters, I need all my shirts ironed, and the curtains could be cleaned and pressed. Then there's dinner. I'll expect three courses, no leftovers—''

"I get the picture," she said dryly. "We are back to a slave-for-a-day."

"Two days," he corrected. "Starting tomorrow."

"*This* weekend?"

"Right."

Why not? she thought, glad for any excuse to spend more time with him. "Okay, then this weekend it is," she agreed, refusing to listen to the doubts crowding her mind, the doubts that reminded her he was her lawyer and that she should keep her relationship professional.

Laughing, they trudged back to the parking lot, and Kimberly noticed the solitary skier in navy blue carrying his skis to a white station wagon. He stopped at the car and wiped his goggles, but his back was to her and she couldn't get a glimpse of his face. She felt as if she should know the car—or the driver—but before she had a chance to say something, Jake clipped their skis into the rack and helped her climb into the Bronco.

Jake noticed Kimberly's fascination with the man in the white wagon, and it bothered him. Did she know him? Why didn't she stop and say hello? Thinking back, it seemed as if the man had been dogging them, following them down the slopes.

"Let's go," he said a trifle impatiently as he slid behind the steering wheel. Kimberly's expression was clouded, and he wondered what she was thinking.

"Someone you know?" he asked, nodding toward the car with its wheels spinning in the snow.

"No—at least I don't think so." She flashed a smile toward Jake that caught him unaware. Her fiery brown hair fell past her shoulders in tangled curls, and snowflakes, now melted, sparkled like tiny diamonds nestled in the vibrant strands.

The interior of the Bronco was foggy as the car idled, and the ice slowly began to melt on the windshield.

"Warm enough?" he asked.

"Mmm." She shivered, her cheeks rosy, her eyes luminous in the night. Damn, but she was the most fascinating woman he'd met in years.

"Coffee?" She held up the thermos.

"Great idea." He watched as she poured.

"You should take all the credit," she murmured, sipping from the red plastic mug, then made a face as if the coffee was hot and strong—too strong. "Here—if you want this, it's yours."

"I'll pass," he said, seeing her grimace.

She poured the dregs back into the thermos, then tightened the cap. Slanting a glance in his direction, she said, "Thanks for tonight. I've enjoyed myself."

"Me, too." God, her eyes were hypnotizing. They stared up at him through the sweep of dark, curling lashes, and seemed to cut right into his soul.

"We'll do it again," he promised, wondering why he would make such a rash statement. Knowing in his heart that he couldn't get involved with her, that she didn't want an emotional entanglement any more than he did, he rammed the Bronco into gear. He picked his way through the other cars, trying not to think ahead to the night stretching long before him.

Had the situation been different, he would have begun planning his seduction right now. He couldn't help it. Desire had flared hotly as the hours with Kimberly had passed.

Lapsing into silence, he tried to ignore the gentle curve of her knee so close to his hand on the gearshift, willed himself not to notice the soft rise and fall of her breasts as she breathed or the soft pout of her lips.

She rested her head against the far window and closed her eyes, seeming all the more seductive with her hair falling over her cheek.

He felt a tenderness for her that went far beyond reason. Without thinking, he pushed the wayward lock of hair from her face with one finger.

Her eyes blinked open, and she smiled, a soft grin that bored quickly into his heart. "Are we home yet?" she asked, yawning.

"Just a few more miles. Go back to sleep," he whispered gently, touched by the slumber still clouding her gaze.

His throat felt raw, and the burning deep within him didn't let up. Swallowing with difficulty, he attempted to concentrate on the road before him and the lights of Portland stretching endlessly beneath the inky sky. The asphalt was icy. Snow still fell, but Jake had trouble keeping his eyes on the highway ahead. As if having a mind of its own, his gaze wandered back to her perfect face.

Never had he wanted a woman more. In all his years, including a stretch of regrettable lust during his teens, he had never burned with a passion so hot as when he burned for Kimberly Bennett.

The Bronco slid a little, and Kimberly moaned softly. Jake eased down on the brakes, forcing himself to concentrate on the road and the trip home.

Chapter Nine

Kimberly stretched and rubbed the crick from her neck. She wasn't yet ready to give up the dream—a dream that promised the happy family she had worked so hard for....

Opening her eyes, she watched as Jake slowed and wheeled into her driveway.

"Finally wake up?" he asked as he switched off the engine.

"I think so." She yawned. "Sorry I fell asleep."

"It must've been all my sparkling, intelligent conversation."

"Must've been," she repeated dryly as she shoved the door open and a blast of icy wind knifed through the Bronco's cozy interior.

Snow fell silently, and her yard was covered with a thick, white blanket. Street lamps cast an ethereal glow over the whiteness, and some houses still displayed colorful lights, brilliant points of green and red reflected in the icy white powder.

She grabbed her boots and bag from the back of the Bronco as Jake unstrapped her skis and shouldered them. "You want these back in the garage?"

"That would be great."

Hunched against the wind, she carried her bag to the back door, then stomped the snow from her boots on the porch.

Inside, the house was dark and cold. Kimberly fumbled with the switches, turning on the lights and adjusting the thermostat before plugging in the coffee maker.

She tossed her jacket over the foot of her bed, then, on impulse, dashed into the living room and flipped the switch that was connected to the Christmas tree. Red, yellow and green lights winked in the shadowy room.

It was suddenly important that Jake see this house as she saw it—warm and cheerful. *And seductive?* She swallowed hard and leaned over the grate, striking a match to the logs in the fireplace, unable to find suitable answers.

The dry kindling caught, popping and hissing. Flames licked the mossy chunks of oak. She heard the back door creak open, felt the chill of a breeze seep through the rooms. "Come on in," she called over her shoulder. "I'll make us something hot in a few minutes—but don't expect anything as fancy as the drinks up at the lodge."

Jake chuckled, a deep, throaty sound that filled an aching void within her—a void that had been empty for so very long.

"I don't care what it is," he said, his voice nearer. Her heart began to thud. "Just as long as it's warm and liquid."

"That, I can promise." She felt his arms circle her waist, his chin balance gently on her crown, his warmth invade her.

"You've been driving me crazy all night," he admitted with a heartfelt sigh. The fire crackled.

"Me? Drive you crazy?" But she, too, had felt a special warmth at his touch. And she'd seen the naked sensuality in his gaze.

"You know things have changed between us."

Her throat worked. "Have they?"

"Oh, Kimberly, God, yes!"

His hands splayed across her abdomen, one thumb tucked beneath her breasts, and his breath whispered through her hair. "I want you, Kimberly," he conceded, his voice low. "I want you more than I've wanted a woman in a long, long time. Maybe ever."

Her heart soared. It was pounding so loudly, it echoed in her ears. Or was that thundering the sound of his heart beating out of control? She tried to reason, to be calm and rational and clear thinking. But emotion clouded all her thoughts, and when his hands drew her closer still, surrounding her with his strength, all she could feel was the wonder of him, the sheer maleness emanating from him, the hard evidence of his desire planted firmly against her hips. A thrill of anticipation darted up her spine.

"Tell me this will never work," he whispered.

"It won't. We both know it." But she entwined her fingers in his and sighed dreamily when his lips brushed across her hair. The shadowed corners of the room closed in around them, and she felt that being with him could never be wrong.

"Tell me I should stop."

"You—you should."

His hands moved upward, one thumb tracing the weight of her breast as his lips hovered invitingly over her neck.

"Tell me you don't want me."

"I can't," she admitted, her throat catching. There was no need to lie. They both knew the power of desire, the galloping, thoughtless heat of passion stirring deep in their souls. Slowly he turned her so that she was forced to look into the depths of his silvery eyes. Lost in that erotic gaze, she wound her arms around his neck.

"I thought we had a deal."

A smile tugged at the corners of his mouth. "Nothing on paper," he murmured. "You're dealing with a lawyer here—if it isn't signed, it isn't valid."

"You should have warned me."

"No, Kimberly. You should have warned me. I wasn't ready for this."

"Neither was I."

He stared at her for a few heart-stopping seconds, then his lips claimed hers with a fire as hungry as the flames burning in the grate, a passion as hot as the red embers beginning to glow in the fireplace.

His tongue probed her lips, and she parted them willingly, unafraid. Despite her doubts, she responded, arching her back, pressing her breasts as close to him as possible. Her tongue embraced his, eagerly meeting the delicate thrusts and teasing retreats.

Her fingers ran through his hair, felt the drops of melting snow still lingering in the dark strands as slowly, with his weight, he pushed them both to the couch where they had nearly made love before.

Lying over her, his eyes delving deep into hers, he felt his throat constrict. "Don't say no," he whispered, his hands deftly removing her jacket and finding the hem of her sweater.

"Never," she promised, her voice as breathless as the soothing whisper of the fire.

He lifted her sweater over her head, and once the heavy garment was removed, stared down at her, gazing at her ripe breasts peeking delicately over the sculpted lace of her bra, her firm nipples straining through the sheer fabric, dark, dusky circles that invited him ... tantalized ...

"Kimberly," he whispered hoarsely, then, taking her lips in his, he kissed her with the fever burning deep in his heart. Her lips, full and red, parted in invitation.

As his hands moved upward, skimming over her ribs to toy with the edge of her bra, Kimberly's breath seemed to stop somewhere between her throat and lungs. Sensations as warm and seductive as a summer breeze enveloped her.

He kissed her breasts, his tongue lazily caressing first one nipple, then the other. Against the wet fabric, dark buds blossomed.

"Please..."

"Please what?" His breath fanned the wet lace, fueling fires of passion sweeping through her blood.

Love me, she thought wildly, but her words were trapped deep within as her fingers worked feverishly on his jacket, sweater and shirt to discard them on the floor. When his dark chest was exposed, gilded by the flickering light of the fire, he unclasped her bra, dropping the tiny scrap of lace onto his clothes.

"Make love to me, Kimberly," he whispered, his eyes locking with hers. "Make love to me and never stop."

She couldn't help herself. Lost in the wonder he created, she felt his fingertips skim beneath her ski pants, grazing the soft flesh of her abdomen. Moaning, she heard the rustle of her bibs as they glided easily down the length of her legs.

After kicking off his clothes, he lay over her, the soft down on his legs pressing intimately to hers. His lips found hers again, and his hand spread over her shoulders, lifting her up to meet him. A satiny glow spread across her skin.

"I don't want to hurt you," he whispered.

"You won't."

"And I don't want us to make any mistakes."

She tried to think, but his hands against her skin were playing havoc with her reason. "Mistakes?"

"I don't want to get you pregnant, Kimberly." The words sounded harsh, though he'd spoken gently.

She tried to think straight—tried to consider the days of the month, but they blurred together as he caressed her. Pregnancy was the last thing on her mind. "Y-you won't."

"You're sure?"

"It's a safe time," she said dreamily, mentally calculating the days, then gasping as his thumb toyed with her nipple.

"You're positive?" Deep creases lined his brow.

"Yes!" Would he never quit tormenting her? Kimberly was swimming in that timeless sea of passion. Lightly touching his shoulders and forearms, sleek back and buttocks, she tingled at each sensual curve of his body. She tasted him, too, the salt of his skin welcome on her lips.

She was rewarded with the sweetness of his tongue and lips, touching her in intimate places, kissing her behind the ears, across her shoulders, along the intimate curve of her spine. Moaning, she moved with him, allowing the tenderness of his mouth to set fire to her skin.

When his legs parted hers, she knew there was no turning back. Poised over her, every muscle rigid with restraint, he held her head between his hands, and with his gaze probing deep into hers, he entered her slowly.

She gasped at the warm sensations building inside her.

"Love me, Kimberly," he groaned.

"Oh, Jake," she cried, his first, soul-rocking thrust piercingly deep. Her fingers dug into his back as he withdrew, only to delve again, more deeply this time and faster.

She moved with him, willingly finding his tempo and feeling the earth shake beneath them. Every sense aware, she kissed his chest, watching as his muscles rippled fluidly before closing her eyes to the sweet dizziness that he enticed.

As they fused, she felt as if she were spinning, faster and faster, higher and higher, entrapped within a kaleidoscope of colored lights as brilliant as the brightest Christmas star, until in this spiraling surge of passion, the lights exploded, her body convulsed and she let out a primal cry as raw as any winter wind.

"Kimberly!" Jake rasped, shuddering over her before he fell onto her and his labored breathing filled the small room. "Oh, sweet, darling Kimberly." He kissed the dark tip of each breast before lying over her again, his face pressed against her breastbone, his breath warm on her skin.

Tears starred her lashes, tracking slowly from the corners of her eyes to the cushions of the couch. Ashamed of her emotional response, she swallowed and tried not to sniff.

He looked up then, touched one tear still lingering on her cheek.

"Regrets?" he asked gently.

"No—"

"Then, what?"

She sniffed, blinking rapidly. Self-conscious, she laughed nervously. "It's—it's been a long time," she said, and silently added, *and it's never been like this. I've never felt so turned inside out—so completely at someone else's mercy.*

"Don't you know that you can trust me?"

Smiling, she wiped away the last of her tears. "I do," she admitted. "That's the problem."

Jake's eyes were filled with compassion, and he pushed a burnished curl off her forehead before placing his lips against her brow. "Robert—did he hurt you so badly?"

"I let him," she admitted. "But it's over." She didn't want to think of Robert. Not tonight. Tonight she had only room for Jake, and he filled her very essence, her thoughts, her mind, her body.

"You're sure?" His gaze sought conviction in hers. A log in the fire split, falling into pieces.

"Positive."

"Good—because I intend to make you forget him." Jaw hard, lines of conviction surrounding his mouth, Jake twisted his fingers in her hair.

She sighed. "If only you could."

"Just let me try," he suggested, his voice low as he kissed her again with the same breathtaking passion of just a few minutes before. Then he lifted her off the couch and carried her into the bedroom.

"What—what are you doing?"

He cocked a jaunty dark brow and grinned devilishly. "Having my way with you."

"Wrong," Kimberly quipped, winding her arms around his neck. "I'm having *my* way with you."

He tossed his head back and laughed. "I'll try to remember that."

"Do." Caught up in the wonder of this man, Kimberly decided that come what may, she would have this one night to flirt with danger without a thought to the future.

He crossed the threshold to her room, kicked the door shut and dropped her onto the cool coverlet of her bed. He was on top of her in an instant, the mattress sagging with his weight. "So have your way," he growled against her ear. Delicious shivers raced up her spine as he took her hand in his and guided it to touch him intimately.

"You're wicked," she chuckled.

"Only with you, love," he whispered. "Only with you."

* * *

Stretching lazily, Kimberly rolled over in the bed. She opened her eyes slowly and felt a strong arm pin her to the sheets.

Jake grinned devilishly, his jaw shadowed. Propped on one elbow, his bare chest covered with a fine mat of dark hair, he stared down at her with silvery, erotic eyes. "Good morning, lazybones," he drawled.

Passionate images flashed through her mind. Their lovemaking had been glorious, crazy and perfect. "Lazybones?" she whispered, her cheeks coloring as she shoved a tangled handful of hair from her eyes and glanced at the clock. It was nearly ten. Groaning, she flopped back on the pillow. "I've got to pick up Lindsay."

"I already took care of it."

"You did *what*?" she cried, sitting bolt upright in the bed. Then, as his gaze drifted lower to her uncovered breasts, she clasped the sheets to her bosom.

His grin stretched. "I called Arlene—she's very nice, by the way, very understanding."

"I'll bet." Kimberly moaned. Arlene would be doing handsprings if she thought Kimberly was involved with a man, especially a man like Jake.

"Anyway, I told her that I was going to buy you brunch and that we would pick up Lindsay around noon."

"You had no right—"

"I know." Leaning forward, he pulled the sheet to expose one dark nipple. To his delight, it puckered prettily beneath his stare.

"Jake, really..."

Taking the dark bud in his lips, he slowly tugged.

Kimberly melted inside, and all her concentration centered on that one aching breast. "Don't you think...?"

But he obviously didn't. With a groan he rolled over her,
his lips finding hers, his tongue wetting the edges of her
mouth as he moved familiarly on top of her and spread her
legs apart. "Just one more time, love," he whispered against
her hair.

Already her heart was pounding, the blood rushing wantonly through her veins. "We—we really should be getting
up," she murmured, but his fingers caressed her, found that
spot that was so vulnerable, and then his mouth lowered
hungrily to suckle at her breasts.

She couldn't stop him. Her fingers coiled in the sheets of
her old four-poster as he wet each delicate nipple and
breathed across their dampened tautness.

Arching upward anxiously, a storm of desire raging in her
core, she welcomed him. He made love to her then. Slowly.
With studied laziness, he kissed and suckled, entered and
withdrew until she was writhing beneath him, begging him
to end her bittersweet torment, bringing her time and time
to the brink, until he could resist no longer.

As she cried his name hoarsely, his restraint fled. With a
primal groan, he made love to her as furiously as he had the
night before. Once again Kimberly was caught in a tempest
of desire so wild and consuming it was frightening.

Convulsing, she cried low in her throat, and his voice
joined hers, resounding in the tiny room, bouncing off the
ice-covered windowpanes and echoing in her heart.

He fell against her, and she clung to him, legs entwined,
bodies dewy with perspiration. Dear Lord, she'd fallen in
love with him, fallen so fast her head was spinning. Loving
Jake was crazy, ludicrous—the one emotion she couldn't
allow herself to feel. But there it was. Big as life.

His breath, ragged and shallow, fanned across her naked
breasts, and she sighed in contentment.

"As I said last night," Jake finally rasped, "you're driving me out of my mind." He thought about the night before and how he'd made love to her over and over again, as if in so doing he could satiate himself with her.

But the lovemaking had proved true just the opposite. The more he had her, the more he wanted, like a thirst that couldn't be quenched.

"I don't think we should talk about sanity," she said, her thoughts turning black as she considered the court battle in front of her. "At least not this morning."

"I agree," he said, a triumphant smile stretching mischievously over his jaw. "Because for the next two days, you're in my debt."

"Don't remind me," she groaned, then suddenly smelled the scent of coffee drifting through the rooms. Casting him a suspicious look, she asked, "How long have you been awake?"

"For hours," he drawled.

"I don't believe it."

"How about long enough to make coffee and a phone call?"

"That's more like it." She reached to the foot of her bed, where her robe usually lay. During the night it had slipped to the floor unnoticed. With a wry grin, she scooped it up and slid her arms through the sleeves. "I'll start working off my indebtedness by making you breakfast."

"I like my eggs over-easy with waffles and homemade peach jam," he said.

"Dreamer," she tossed back at him as she scrambled off the bed.

"You know, I could get used to this," he teased. His gray eyes sparkled, and Kimberly couldn't help but notice the way his shoulder muscles rippled as he shifted.

"I don't think that's such a good idea," she said, but she didn't mean it. Waking up in Jake's arms, sharing breakfast with him, spending every day with him sounded like heaven. As she walked out the door, she felt a pillow land with a thump against her rear end.

Laughing, still thinking about what it would be like to be married to him, she made her way down the hall. "You're fantasizing again, Bennett," she told herself as she breezed into the kitchen, the linoleum cold beneath her bare feet.

"What's that?" Jake asked, walking up behind her.

"Nothing—maybe you'd like to fetch the paper."

"Oh, yeah, that's just what I'd like." Grumbling good-naturedly, he slid into his ski pants and sweater, then walked outside.

Kimberly watched through the frosted window as he broke a path in the six inches of snow.

The sun was high in a winter-blue sky, and golden rays reflected off of December's thick white mantle.

If not for the custody hearing and Robert's threats, Kimberly thought, her life would be perfect. But those were a couple of pretty big ifs.

She watched as Jake reached into the paper's box. He glanced back. Catching sight of her in the window, he smiled and gave her a crisp military salute. She laughed, and her stupid heart soared. Just the sight of him caused a thickening in her throat that she couldn't explain.

He stopped at his car, took out a huge bag and returned, stomping his boots on the back porch. "Mind if I change?" he asked as he passed through the kitchen and pressed cool lips to the back of her neck.

She was breaking eggs into a skillet as one strong arm surrounded her waist and he pressed his face into her hair. "Be my guest."

She turned back to the stove. So he'd packed a change of clothes. Doubts crowded her thoughts, and she pinched her lip in her teeth.

And what about you? her mind nagged. *With the soft lights, fire and zero resistance. Just who was seducing whom?*

A few minutes later she heard water running in the bathroom and the muffled sound of his off-key singing. Kimberly tried to convince herself that being with Jake was a mistake, that spending any time with him other than in his office was dangerous, but she couldn't believe it. How could anything that felt so right be wrong? she wondered as she scrambled eggs and prodded sizzling strips of bacon with her fork.

She heard the shower spray stop. Her heart began to pound all over again, and a few seconds later Jake, wearing only faded jeans slung low over his hips, a white towel draped around his neck and a knowing smile, entered the kitchen. "This smells great, and to think I'd suggested eating out," he said, winking and talking as if to himself. "Not only beautiful, but she can cook, too. You're a lucky man, McGowan."

"Sit down and eat," she ordered, but felt the compliment warm her cheeks.

They ate and talked, read the paper and sipped coffee, even cleared the table together. It was strange, Kimberly thought, as she stacked the dishes in the dishwasher, how easily she could slip into a life with him.

After she'd showered and changed, they walked together to Arlene's house and found Lindsay already shaping the third in a family of snow people. "Hi, Mommy," Lindsay called gaily, waving a mittened hand. "Wanna help?"

"Sure," Kimberly said, bending on one knee to sculpt the rotund sides of the snowman.

"That's Daddy," Lindsay said proudly, finding two sticks and stuffing them into the snowman's sides.

Kimberly's throat went raw.

"And that's you, and this is me." She indicated the other two snow people. "Now all we have to do is make a puppy!"

"Then what?" Kimberly asked, glancing up at Jake. His expression was unreadable as he leaned over and rolled another snowball.

"Then the family's done," Lindsay answered.

"I see." Kimberly's heart ached. Though Lindsay stated everything in a matter-of-fact voice, Kimberly wondered just how much pain the divorce had already caused her child. What would happen to Lindsay if there was a court battle?

"Here we go," Jake said, shaping a lumpy snowball.

"What's that?" Lindsay asked.

"The dog."

She eyed his four-legged sculpture suspiciously. "What kind?"

"A mutt."

If he felt uncomfortable about working on the perfect family, Jake didn't show it. Kimberly, despite her worries, almost laughed at his pathetic attempt.

"I've never seen a dog like that before," Lindsay said, wrinkling her nose and eyeing the creature that looked more like a Saturday-morning cartoon character than anything remotely canine.

Jake glanced at the statue of the rotund snow-woman. "Well, if it won't do, we'll start over. Because that—" he pointed to the icy figure "—is the spitting image of your mother."

"Oooh!" Kimberly cried, grinning. "I believe you just insulted me, counselor." She scooped up a handful of snow and hurled it at him. It smashed against his jacket, and he let out a whoop. "Those are fighting words."

Jake's silvery eyes gleamed. "Oh, yeah? Come on, Lindsay, let's teach your mom a lesson!"

Before she could duck behind a nearby tree, Jake pelted her with three snowballs and Lindsay tossed another that landed at her feet.

Giggling, Lindsay grabbed another handful of snow before Jake lifted the child to his shoulders and they chased Kimberly around the yard. Laughing and breathing hard, Kimberly finally had to beg for mercy near the front steps.

"Give?" Jake asked, his smile a satisfied slash.

"Yes—I give," she gasped, her eyes sparkling.

"More, more!" Lindsay insisted just as the front door opened with a bang.

"Lindsay—what's going on out here?" Arlene asked. Still wearing an oversize terry robe and slippers, she chuckled as she saw Lindsay riding on Jake's broad shoulders.

"They're trying to kill me!" Kimberly mocked.

"Exact our punishment," Jake corrected.

"You started it, Mommy," Lindsay rejoined, and giggled when Jake nodded in agreement.

"Good point," he drawled.

"Details, details," Kimberly murmured.

"Well, come on in and have a cup of coffee before all three of you catch your death!" Arlene's eyes were bright behind her glasses. She stood back from the door to let them pass.

Kimberly stomped the snow from her boots and followed Jake and Lindsay inside. She introduced Jake to Lyle, then hung her coat on the hall tree.

"We made you a surprise!" Lindsay announced.

They were sitting around a small maple table in Arlene's roomy kitchen, warming their frozen fingers around steaming cups of coffee and cocoa.

"What is it?" Kimberly asked.

Lindsay's face clouded. "I can't tell—otherwise it won't be a surprise. It's for Christmas!" She glanced at Lyle for support. "That's right, isn't it?"

Lyle nodded from his wheelchair. "That's right, angel. Maybe you'd better leave it over here for safekeeping until Christmas. Your mom might sneak a peek otherwise."

Lindsay's eyes rounded. "Would you?"

"Of course not," Kimberly laughed, tousling her daughter's silky hair.

"Good." Lindsay scampered into the spare bedroom and returned, carrying a crudely wrapped bundle that was half as big as she was.

"This is for me?" Kimberly asked, astounded.

"At Christmastime."

"I can't wait," Kimberly murmured, eyeing the package and feeling as if her heart might burst.

After coffee and cinnamon rolls, Jake shoved his chair away from the table. "I've got to get going."

"But you just got here," Arlene protested.

Jake grinned. "I know, but I've got a dog who probably thinks I've abandoned him, and there's the matter of a bet that has to be settled."

Kimberly felt her cheeks flame. "I guess we'd better be on our way, too," she said hastily before anyone could question Jake about his bet.

"No reason to rush off," Lyle interjected, but his wife, as if reading the signals between Jake and Kimberly, put a hand on Lyle's arm.

"We'll see you later," she said, her bright eyes shining. "Monday morning."

After donning their coats and gloves, Jake, Kimberly and Lindsay, carrying her ungainly present, trudged past the melting snow family to Kimberly's house. Jake insisted on carrying Lindsay's overnight bag over one shoulder while he held tightly on to Kimberly's hand.

Lindsay slid on her boots down a small hill. She whooped with delight as she landed on her rear.

"Looks like she's a skier already," Jake remarked, laughing.

"Will you take me sometime?" Lindsay asked eagerly.

Jake glanced at Kimberly. "I suppose we could arrange that."

"At nighttime?"

"Maybe," Kimberly said cautiously.

"Arlene said you went night skiing," Lindsay explained.

"Oh, she did, did she?" Kimberly asked.

"Uh-hum."

"What else did she say?"

"Just that you and me and Jake would probably be doing a lot of skiing."

"Once a matchmaker, always a matchmaker," Kimberly murmured.

"She told me all about you, too," Lindsay said, eyeing Jake. "You're a...turn key."

Jake smothered a laugh.

"An attorney," her mother corrected.

Lindsay's eyes were filled with questions, her cheeks rosy from the cold. "What's that?"

Kimberly struggled for the right words. "He's a man who's going to help us, honey," she said.

"We don't need help."

"Oh, yes," Kimberly replied, "sometimes everyone needs help."

"Not me!" Lindsay said, then squealed when Kimberly pulled her daughter to her and kissed her soundly on the cheek.

"Do it again!" Lindsay commanded, but Kimberly shook her head.

"That's enough for now."

Lindsay didn't seem convinced, but didn't argue.

Once they were all inside Kimberly's house and Lindsay had placed her package under the tree, Jake lingered near the door. "You're coming over, aren't you?" he asked.

"I promised, didn't I?" she quipped, though her stomach did a nervous flip. After the passion of the night before, she chided herself for her anxiety, but the thought of spending most of the weekend at his place was unnerving.

"You could catch a ride with me."

"I know, but I think I'll bring my own car. Most of the streets are plowed."

"Just so you don't renege," he said.

"No way."

"Good." He reached into his wallet, found a business card, then wrote his home address on the back side. "Call if you get lost."

"In Lake Oswego?"

"It can be confusing."

"Don't send the search party out for a while."

Flashing her a smile, he glanced at his watch. "You've got two hours."

"And if I'm late?"

Grinning wickedly, he slid a glance up her body that made her pulse leap. "Then I'll extract my punishment in ways too numerous to count."

"You *are* a dreamer," she retorted as he opened the door and strode briskly outside. A few minutes later she heard his Bronco roar down the driveway.

Still considering the night before and all the ramifications of a love affair with Jake McGowan, she carried Lindsay's overnight bag to the loft and unpacked.

She heard Lindsay's footsteps rushing up the stairs. A few minutes later, blue eyes gleaming, Lindsay peeked around the rail. She stared at her bag.

"Are we going somewhere?"

"To Jake's house."

Lindsay eyed the bag suspiciously. "Overnight?"

"Oh—no." Laughing, Kimberly tossed Lindsay's dirty clothes into a hamper. "I was just unpacking from *last* night."

"Oh." Lindsay worried her lower lip in her teeth. "I like him," she announced. "Even if he is a...whatever it's called."

Kimberly felt a surprising sense of relief. "I like him, too," she agreed. *I like him far too much.*

"Do you like him more than Daddy?"

Sighing, Kimberly sat on the edge of Lindsay's bed, hauled her daughter into her lap and hugged her close. "I like him differently than I liked your dad," she said slowly. "Your dad and I...we just don't get along."

"You don't love him."

That was true.

"And he doesn't love you," Lindsay said soberly.

Kimberly sighed again, surprised at the wisdom of her child. "No, he doesn't, not like he used to. But he loves you very much," she said, cringing as she considered her lie. She was certain Robert didn't know the meaning of the word "love," not even where his daughter was concerned. She squeezed Lindsay and planted a kiss on her forehead. "And I love you so much I could burst!"

"I know that."

Thank goodness!

"Do you love Jake?" Lindsay asked, twisting around so that she could stare straight into Kimberly's eyes.

"I like him a lot," Kimberly hedged.

"I know, but do you love him?"

"Can't I just like him—you know, as a special friend?"

Lindsay frowned as she considered. Finally she shook her blond curls. "I don't think so," she murmured.

I don't, either, Kimberly silently agreed.

"So—do you love him or not?"

"Yes, I guess I do," Kimberly admitted, not wanting to lie again. "I love him, but it's a different kind of love."

"Oh, I know. All that mushy stuff."

Kimberly rolled her eyes as she set Lindsay back on the floor. "Let's just think of him as a good friend. And keep this to yourself, will you?"

Wrinkling her nose, Lindsay grinned. "I won't tell anybody!"

Kimberly hoped her daughter could keep a secret. "Good, I'll hold you to it."

"I promise," Lindsay vowed. "Are you gonna marry him?"

"No!" she nearly shouted, then seeing Lindsay's vexed expression, added, "Love is complicated."

"No, it isn't. If you love someone, you marry them. That's what Shawna Briggs says."

"Oh, she does, does she?" Kimberly said with a smile as she thought of Kimberly's friend in kindergarten.

"Yep. And she loves Josh Barton and she's gonna marry him."

"Well, I hope you get invited to the wedding."

"I will," Lindsay announced with all the self-confidence of her five years.

As Kimberly unpacked, she tried not to think of anything as foolish as marriage to Jake, yet the idea refused to go away. Jake wasn't the marrying kind, she told herself. He'd gone as far as saying so. And there was still so much to learn about him.

"Come on, let's get changed," she said to Lindsay when the last of her clothes were placed in the drawer. "Then, if you want, we can go visit Jake at his place. Would that be all right?"

Lindsay grinned from ear to ear. "He has a puppy, doesn't he?"

Jake did indeed have a dog. A big, bounding, white wolflike creature that barked and whined as Kimberly eased her car down the slippery drive.

Jake's house was small, little more than a cottage. Pearl gray and nestled in a thicket of tall Douglas fir trees, his home looked like the vacation cabin it had originally been. Snow was piled in drifts against the windowpanes. A blanket of white weighted the drooping fir boughs and covered the ground.

Smoke curled from a river-rock chimney, dispersing in a cloudless blue sky.

"Oh, look!" Lindsay cried happily as Lupus placed his paws on the passenger side of the Mercedes, his nose against the glass.

"Lupus!" Jake was standing in the doorway, waving.

Kimberly's heart soared at the sight of him. He'd changed into a plaid wool shirt, tan cords and running shoes. Without a thought to jacket or boots, he loped down a path that had been broken through the snow.

"I'd about given up," he said, helping Kimberly out of the car.

"You said two hours."

"And you pushed it."

"It took us a while."

Lindsay scrambled over the hand brake and out the door on the driver's side. Lupus scurried around the car, discovered her, wiped her face with his tongue and barked excitedly. Lindsay squealed with delight, and the chase was on. Through the drifting unplowed powder, dog and child bounced, laughing and yipping.

"Soul mates," Jake observed dryly.

Kimberly was laughing so hard, tears sprang to her eyes.

"He's beautiful!" Lindsay called, and Kimberly laughed again.

"That's the first time he's ever heard that," Jake said, taking her hand. "Come on, I'll show you around."

While Lindsay and Lupus cavorted, Jake tugged on Kimberly's arm and led her down a snow-crusted path through the trees.

Behind the house, the ground sloped down to the shore of Lake Oswego. Icicles clung to the docking, and the icy water of the lake lapped against the bleached wood. The water was calm and stretched far to the opposite bank.

"It's gorgeous here," Kimberly said, her breath misting in the cold air. The privacy of Jake's backyard was ensured by the trees, a fence and, of course, the lake.

"You should see it in the summer."

From the front of the house, Kimberly heard Lindsay's laugh and Lupus's loud yip.

Though the temperature was below freezing, she felt warm inside and didn't protest when he folded his arms around her and pressed chilled lips to hers. She responded immediately. The banked fires within her needed little stoking. The pressure of his mouth moving sensually over hers was all it took to turn her liquid inside.

Willingly she wound her arms around his neck and felt his hands, bare and cold, slip beneath her jacket to rub anxiously against her sweater.

"I missed you." His voice was low and rough, and though he whispered, the words seemed to ring in the still air.

"It only took me a couple of hours to get here."

"Too long," he groaned, his mouth fitting perfectly over hers. She felt the pads of his fingers through her sweater, his warmth permeating the thick weave.

Lifting his head with a ragged sigh, he stared into her eyes. His hands slid from under her jacket to entwine in her hair. "Promise me when this is all over, you'll go away with me."

"What?" She didn't understand, but stared deep into his eyes, mesmerized by his gaze.

"When the custody battle's over, I want to take you away from here. Maybe we'll go to Mexico, or the Caribbean. Someplace where we can be alone for a long time."

"And . . . what about Lindsay?"

"She can come, too."

"So much for being alone," she said, but her voice sounded breathless. He was moving too fast. Kimberly couldn't think straight. "I don't know. Maybe that's not such a good idea."

"Think about it."

Lindsay and Lupus plowed through the snow toward them.

"Come on inside," Jake offered. "I've got a surprise for you."

Lindsay, already flushed in the face, positively beamed. "What is it?"

"You'll see."

She raced to the back door.

"Take off your boots—" But it was too late. Kimberly's command was lost in the winter air as the screen door banged shut. Lindsay let out a cry of delight, and Lupus whined pitifully at the back door.

"You didn't!" Kimberly cried, glancing at Jake as if he'd lost his mind. But he was grinning from ear to ear as they mounted the back steps and walked into the kitchen. "Look, she can keep it here, if you'd prefer."

"And you'll keep it for her?"

Kimberly was prepared to see Lindsay clinging to the neck of a puppy and was ready to give Jake a piece of her mind. But instead Lindsay was entranced with a furry brown-and-white guinea pig huddled in one corner of the cage.

"Can I pick him up?" Lindsay asked, her eyes as bright as the frightened rodent's.

"If you're careful."

"Oh, I will be." She reached into the cage, scooped up the nervous animal and held him close to her.

"A guinea pig? You bought her a guinea pig?" Kimberly couldn't believe it. "Why?"

"It was cheaper than a cocker spaniel," he deadpanned.

"Thank God."

"Every kid needs a pet."

"I suppose."

Lupus was whining and scratching at the back door. Once the guinea pig could be pried from Lindsay's hands and was safely back in his cage, Jake let the dog inside. He scrambled across the linoleum and leaped up, trying to lick Lindsay's face.

"He's jealous," Jake said with a laugh. "Now, how about some mint cocoa?"

A few minutes later, while Lindsay was dividing her time between dog and rodent, Jake and Kimberly sipped hot chocolate in front of the fire. Leaning next to him on the couch, her stockinged feet stretched out to the warmth of the flames, she felt as if she'd finally come home.

"So, when do I start paying?" she asked.

"You are," he said, and slipped one arm comfortably around her shoulders.

She leaned her head into the crook of his neck and closed her eyes. Being with Jake was perfect. Listening to the sound of Lindsay's muted chatter, soft Christmas music, the crackling fire and the steady beat of Jake's heart, she felt more content and safe than she had in a long, long while.

Chapter Ten

Lindsay fell asleep on a blanket near the fire. Her thumb slid between her lips, and she sighed.

The guinea pig came to life, digging in the shavings in his cage on the desk, and Lupus, ever vigilant, kept his eyes trained on the furry little creature.

"I think I'd better take my daughter home," Kimberly said quietly. "She's had a long day."

Jake grinned. "Very long."

Snuggled with Jake on the couch, sipping the last of mulled wine, she didn't want to move, couldn't imagine returning to her cold house without him.

He brushed his lips across her cheek. Touching the underside of her chin, he forced her to look at him. "Stay," he whispered, and his silvery eyes wouldn't let her go. "Spend the night with me. I mean, that was part of our bargain—two days and…as many nights as you want." His voice was low and velvety. "I'll make it worth your while."

She giggled. "Has anyone ever told you that you have an incredible ego, Mr. McGowan?"

"Too many to count," he said with a teasing grin. "Come on, Kimberly, live a little."

"I—shouldn't."

"Sure you should." His eyes gleamed. "I've got plenty of room for both of you."

"You mean all three of us," Kimberly teased, motioning to Lindsay's new pet. The guinea pig found his exercise wheel and started running.

Jake chuckled. But he wouldn't take no for an answer. He disappeared into the back bedrooms, only to return with a quilted baby blanket in which he gently wrapped a sleeping Lindsay.

Bemused, Kimberly followed him down the hall to a small bedroom where L-shaped bunk beds fitted into one corner and a matching dresser was pushed against the wall. The room, painted white, was stark and bare except for the two pieces of furniture, and Kimberly guessed no one had ever occupied it. And yet it stood ready for a child. What child? Certainly not Lindsay.

Tenderly Jake laid Lindsay on the bottom bunk, brushing a strand of hair from her face and tugging the blanket close around her chin. Kimberly's heart turned over. Never had she seen Robert deal with Lindsay with such care—such obvious love. And yet this man treated her as if she were his own. If only... she thought, projecting ahead. But she couldn't let herself think of a future in which she and Jake and Lindsay became a family. There were too many hurdles to vault first. And there were things about Jake, secrets he hadn't confided to her.

Jake reached to the dresser and snapped off the light. "See," he said, standing, his voice husky. "She'll be fine." Lupus trotted into the room, curled in a ball near the foot of the bed and, placing his nose between his front paws, sighed loudly. Jake chuckled. "She's even got a guard dog." He patted the white shepherd fondly, and Lupus's tail thumped the floor.

Kimberly smiled inwardly as they walked back to the living room in silence. The fire had nearly died. Jake busied himself rearranging logs in the grate while Kimberly stared for the first time at the bookshelves lining the wall. Law books, textbooks, computer manuals and a collection of science fiction and mystery paperbacks filled the shelves to overflowing.

In frames on the walls were copies of Jake's diploma and a graduation picture. But the photograph that caught her eye was a small snapshot in a hand-tooled frame on a corner of the mantel. A dark-haired boy, around three years old and dressed in a blue jogging suit, a football tucked under his chubby arm, smiled back at her. His blue eyes were serious, his grin a little forced. She didn't have to be told he was related to Jake.

Jake had stopped fiddling with the fire. Still squatting, he'd rocked back on his heels and stared up at her with an expression that could only be described as bleak. "That's Sam," he said gruffly. "My son." His eyes grew distant and unreadable.

"He's very good-looking," she said, slightly bewildered. Hadn't Jake said he was childless?

"Yes."

Standing, Jake shoved his hands into the back pockets of his jeans, and pain lingered in his eyes. "I told you I didn't have any children, but that wasn't the truth. I had a child for nearly three years. Sam was killed shortly after that picture was taken." Jake's throat worked, and he had to clear it.

Kimberly felt numb inside. To lose a child! Her heart went out to him. "Oh, Jake . . ."

He held up a palm and shook his head. "Don't say you're sorry, okay. I just don't want to hear it."

She bit her lower lip and wished there were some words of comfort, some tender endearment that she could whisper to ease his pain. Of course, there was none. "I—I didn't know."

He picked up the picture and held it in his palm. Staring at the photograph, he blinked rapidly. "Some things just never go away," he said, "no matter how hard you try to forget them."

Taking a deep breath, he turned the picture facedown on the mantel, then stood near the window, bracing one hand against the casing as he gazed outside. "It happened years ago, but it's with me every day."

She ached to touch him—to offer some comfort. "Is Lindsay sleeping in his room?"

He shook his head but didn't look back at her. "No. His furniture. But not his room. I—we—lived in the city then, a big house in Dunthorpe." Turning, he tried to smile, failed and pursed his lips. "Lydia, Sam's mother, wasn't happy. Thought I should be working harder to become a partner in the firm. She expected me to climb the success ladder a little more quickly than I was. Anyway, after Sam was born, she was really dissatisfied—claimed that life was passing her by." He shoved a dark thatch of hair from his eyes. "So she found someone else, another attorney in town, a man really going places. A man with expensive cars, a boat, a private plane." His lips curled. "A man who had the right connections."

Kimberly felt cold to the center of her soul.

Jake's eyes narrowed, and he walked to the bar, where he poured himself a stiff shot of Scotch.

"Who?" Kimberly asked, shaking inside. She wasn't sure she wanted to know the answer.

He tossed back his drink. "Your friend and mine. Ben Kesler."

"Oh, God," she whispered, her fingers clenching together. Ben was more than Robert's attorney—they were partners in some business ventures. Even Ben's plane, which was hangared in Mulino, miles out of the city, was partially owned by Robert.

The seconds ticked by as Jake glared gloomily into his glass. "Yep. She intended to take Sam, make sure I never saw him again and marry Kesler." He glanced at Kimberly. His mouth twisted wryly. "Now, that was her side of the story, mind you. I don't know if Kesler had any intention of marching down the aisle with her. He was just her divorce attorney and lover at that point—but it doesn't matter. Right after the divorce was final, Lydia and Sam were in an automobile accident. Neither of them survived." He took in a long bracing breath, and Kimberly crossed the room and took his face between her hands.

"I *am* sorry," she said feeling him tremble beneath her touch. "And I won't say I know how you feel, because I don't. I can't imagine losing a child."

"It's hell," he whispered, his eyes dark with agony. "Pure hell. I swear to you here and now, I'll never go through it again. Never!"

"Even if it means not having children?"

"That's the only way to make sure it doesn't happen, isn't it?" he said coldly.

Her throat closed, and she had to whisper. "The joy of having a child is worth the risk."

He knocked her hands away and turned his back to her. "As you said, you can't know how I feel. No one can." He reached for the bottle of Scotch again, grabbed it by the neck, discovered it was nearly empty and, swearing under his breath, hurled it into the fire. The bottle crashed, splintering into a hundred shards, and flames roared and flared as alcohol splattered against the wood.

"Jake..."

He didn't answer her, wouldn't look her way.

"Don't shut me out," Kimberly whispered.

The muscles in his shoulders bunched.

Kimberly felt helpless. "Please, Jake. I care too much for you. Let me help."

When he turned to look at her, agony was in every line of his strained features.

Suddenly she understood far more than he'd admitted. His divorce and the loss of his child had happened while he'd worked with Diane. He didn't have to say it. Kimberly knew. Diane had helped pull him from the abyss his life had become after Sam's death. She'd pushed him in a new direction—into corporate law—when he couldn't stand to deal with custody or adoption or divorce cases any longer.

How difficult it must have been for Jake to take her case. Tears filled her eyes. "I'd like to help."

"It's too late for help," he whispered, but his eyes held hers. "No one can bring Sam back."

Her heart breaking, she reached for him and wrapped her arms around his waist. She settled her head against his chest and fought tears. Slowly she felt his strong, tense arms fold around her. She tilted her face to his and pressed wet, tear-stained kisses to his lips.

He groaned loudly, his tall body stretched against hers.

"Trust me, Jake," she whispered as his lips, hot and hungry, slanted over hers again. He was everywhere. His tall frame molded hard around hers, his hands moving anxiously against her skin, his mouth and tongue seeking solace in hers.

She opened up to him as a flower to the sun, hoping to ease his pain.

"Kimberly, Kimberly," he cried, and his voice was rough with emotions he'd buried for years.

His hands were tangled in her hair, and he pulled them both down to the thick carpet in front of the fire. He stripped them of their clothes and lay upon her, his long, hard muscles firm against her yielding flesh. Staring into her eyes, kissing her neck, cheeks, breasts and abdomen, Jake lost control.

In front of the fire, with golden shadows playing upon their skin, Kimberly helped him forget. If only for a little while.

The next morning Jake blinked rapidly. His head pounded, and he was disoriented. Finally his blurry eyes focused on the bright room—his room. Sunlight, reflecting on the snow outside, was streaming in blinding rays through the windows. He stretched lazily and stared down at the woman sharing his bed.

Her dark, red-brown hair, was mussed, tossed around her face in a fiery cloud. Dark lashes lay against creamy-white skin, and her expression was peaceful and still, her nostrils barely moving as she breathed.

The sheet, twisted and wrinkled, covered one of her breasts. The other was bare, the dark bud of her nipple protruding beguilingly upward. Memories of wild, savage lovemaking slipped into his conscience, and he grinned wickedly. He'd spent the night purging the past in fierce union with this beautiful woman, and she'd met his wild passion with a wanton abandon that he'd never before experienced.

He twisted a lock of her hair in his fingers and wondered about her. She was kind and caring, but could turn into a seductress so intense that he still ached for more of her.

His memory ablaze with desire, he stared again at her breast—so perfect, so enticing. Unable to stop himself, he leaned over to kiss that rosy seductive point. Immediately he felt a tightening inside and a heated response in his loins.

To his delight the nipple hardened, and Kimberly moaned softly, shifting closer. He threw a leg across her, and she sighed. Still kissing her breast, he reached under the covers, to the apex of her legs, to touch that sweet furry nest and delve his fingers within.

She was ready—moist and waiting.

His gut tightened, and the ache between his own legs begged for release. He nibbled at her nipple again and glanced up at her face as her eyes fluttered open. Two slumberous blue-green eyes looked up at him with such erotic adoration that he nearly stopped his lovemaking.

She smiled, and that did him in. Sliding up the length of her, he kissed her face, laid himself atop her and buried himself deep within that warm, inviting spot that tore his soul from his body.

"Wh-what are you doing, counselor?"

"Saying 'Good morning,'" he drawled.

"I like the way you say it...."

He thrust deep inside.

She opened her mouth, but couldn't speak.

With the flat of his hand he felt her heartbeat pound erratically, saw the shallow breathing in the rise and fall of her beautiful breasts. "You are gorgeous."

Slowly he moved, so lazily that she lifted up to meet him in frustration and he felt the imprint of her hands on his buttocks.

"Be patient," he whispered, kneading her breasts and gritting back the urge to claim her as fiercely and savagely as he had only hours past.

While last night he was lost to pure sexual abandon, his lovemaking furious, a cleansing of all the pain in his past, this morning he paced himself, giving and receiving, watching for her response, enjoying himself as she reached peak after peak until at last she, not he, was spent. "Oh, Jake," she sighed.

Only then did he satisfy himself, losing his self-control as he stared down into an angelic face relaxed in afterglow.

They lay together afterward, Jake holding her close. Her face was pressed to his bare chest, and the clean scent of her hair filled his nostrils.

"We failed, you know," she finally said, glancing up at him and offering an impish smile.

"Failed? And here I thought we'd scored perfect tens last night."

She blushed, then laughed. "I wasn't talking about making love."

"I hope not!"

"But we didn't manage to stay uninvolved."

"Amen," he agreed. How could he ever live without her? How had he survived such a lonely past?

She looked over to the bedside clock and groaned, throwing an arm over her forehead theatrically. "I'd better get up before Lindsay comes running in here with all kinds of questions."

Jake grinned boyishly. "You're ashamed of me."

"No, counselor," she said, rolling her tongue in the corner of her cheek, "but I'm not up to explaining the situation to a curious five-year-old. However, if you'd like to fill her in on the facts of life—" she waved the fingers of one hand "—be my guest."

"I'll pass, thank you very much."

"I thought so."

Stretching, he finally released her and watched as she slid out of bed, then snatched her clothes from the chair near the closet. He loved the length of her thigh, the round curve of her hips, the nip of her waist, the way her breasts swung free. Unconsciously seductive as she pulled her sweater over her head, shook her hair free and slid into her jeans, Kimberly finished dressing, and Jake finally closed his eyes so that he could resist the urge to jump out of bed, grab her and throw her back across the rumpled sheets again.

What was the matter with him? He'd been with more than his share of women in his life. But never had he felt this insatiable urge to claim again and again. He'd gotten bored before. He knew that this woman with her quick wit and dimpled smile would always interest him. And he realized, with a shock that rocked him to his bones, that he wanted to spend the rest of his life with her. With Robert Fisher's ex-wife.

Groaning, he covered his face with a pillow. What had gotten into him?

He tossed off the pillow just to catch the movement of her backside as she walked out of the room.

Springing from the bed, he headed straight for the cool, healing spray of the shower. He considered hauling her into the bathroom and stripping her beneath the misting rivulets of hot, running water, but discarded the idea. Though he could imagine her giggling with delight, he could also picture Lindsay waking up and walking in at just the wrong moment. Frowning, he twisted on the water.

Nope, he wasn't ready to explain his personal sexual fantasies to an inquisitive five-year-old. He stepped into the shower and felt the needles of water against his back.

And what about Lindsay? If he wanted Kimberly, he ended up with her daughter, as well. They were a package deal. He, who'd sworn never to become a parent again, he, who would do just about anything to avoid the inevitable pain of fatherhood, was considering changing all his convictions and opening himself up to being a husband and father again.

He swore, angry with himself. Maybe all these feelings would go away. When Fisher was caught and Lindsay was secure with Kimberly, Jake might have a chance to live his life the way he had before she'd shown up at his office, her black cape billowing around her, her gorgeous blue-green eyes searching for his very soul.

A few minutes later, while buckling his belt, he heard the sound of footsteps padding across the oak floor of the bedroom. Glancing over his bare shoulder, he spied Lindsay staring at him curiously from the doorway.

"Good morning," he said as she gave him the once-over.

"Mornin'."

"You hungry?"

"Why're we still here?"

"What?"

Her little brows drew together, and she stuck out her lower lip. "I thought we'd go home last night."

"It was too late."

She looked as if she didn't believe him, but she thought about it and changed the subject. "Why don't you have a Christmas tree?" she demanded.

Jake's jaw grew rock hard. He hadn't put up a tree in his house since Sam had died. The trappings and festivities associated with yuletide had seemed frivolous and pointless without Sam's bright eyes and laughter. "I guess I just haven't gotten around to it," he evaded.

She tilted her little chin upward. "I'll help."

"Will you?" Jake grinned, charmed despite his own warnings not to get too close to this little blond imp. "I'd like that. I'd like that very much."

"We can do it right now. Mommy's making breakfast."
With that, she took off down the hall, and Jake,
dumbfounded, wiped the remainder of the shaving cream
from his face.

Lindsay was right. Kimberly was making breakfast. Her
hair pulled back in a ponytail, she moved around his kitchen
as if she'd done it for years.

Jake crossed his arms over his chest, propped a shoulder
against the wall and watched her work. Waffles browned in
the waffle iron, coffee perked on the stove and sausage
simmered in a frying pan. The kitchen was filled with scents
that tantalized and brought back memories he'd tried to
keep in the back of his mind. As he stared at Kimberly
cracking eggs into another frying pan, he remembered his
wife.

There had been a time when Lydia had taken time for the
family and cooked a large Sunday breakfast. But that time,
when she'd loved him and wanted to deal with Sam, had
been brief.

"Come on!" Lindsay cried. She'd found her coat and
boots and was heading for the back door.

Kimberly smiled as she looked over her shoulder. "Don't
tell me," she said, "you've been drafted into hunting down
a tree."

"I already have one," Jake replied.

"Where?" Lindsay stared pointedly at the barren living
room.

"Out here." He opened the door to the back porch, and
Lupus dashed through, startling a cat creeping under the
rhododendron bushes flanking the house and giving loud
chase. The tabby sprinted to the nearest maple tree and
scrambled upward while Lupus lunged and barked at the
trunk, his tail whipping behind him, his paws sliding on the
rough bark.

"He's silly!" Lindsay proclaimed.

"Very," Jake agreed, calling to the dog. "Lupus, here!" He slapped his leg loudly, but the shepherd wouldn't be distracted and whined loudly. "He'll give up," Jake confided to Lindsay.

"When?"

Jake considered. "Probably by the spring thaw. Come on, let's tackle that tree."

While Kimberly finished making breakfast, Jake pulled the little potted pine tree from his back porch into the living room. He found an old string of lights with only a few burned-out bulbs and a box of ornaments, and though the decorations were a little worn, the tree did add a festive touch to the room.

Lindsay wasn't convinced that the tree would do. "You need new stuff," she said, eyeing a broken decoration. "Lots of it. And a bigger tree."

"Next year," he said, swinging her off her feet. She squealed happily, then slid to the floor.

"Arlene will get you one," Lindsay exclaimed.

"Maybe we should ask her before you go making promises," he said, moving back to the kitchen.

"Here, you deserve this," Kimberly said, handing him an enamel mug filled with coffee. Her eyes were the color of a tropical sea, and her lips puckered into a little grin.

He took a sip, nearly burned his tongue and asked, "So, what's gotten into you? Why are you Ms. Domesticity?"

"Merely paying off my debt, Mr. McGowan," she said. "Remember? This is the weekend I work for you. After that, it's all over."

Jake grinned wickedly. "In that case I'll have to see that you don't waste a second."

She laughed. "Go ahead. I'm sure I can handle anything you dish out."

His eyes sparked. "We'll see about that."

"Do—but now," she said, plucking a long pine needle from his freshly washed hair, "you and Lindsay better sit and eat before breakfast gets cold. Oh—and by the way—while you were in the shower?"

"Umm." He took a swallow from his cup.

"The phone rang and I answered it. Some man—Koski, I think his name was—wants you to call him back."

Jake's muscles tensed. "Ron Koski?"

"That was it," she said, nodding. "He seemed rather insistent. Said he might be taking off for a few days. I wrote the number down and left it on your desk."

Jake glanced at the wall phone. His fingers tightened over the handle of the cup. "I'll call him later," he said, hoping his expression didn't give him away. For the time being, he didn't want Kimberly to know about Ron or the investigation, if there was one, on Robert. He wasn't yet ready to explain completely about Daniel, though he felt guilty that he hadn't placed all his cards on the table.

In time, he told himself as he slid into the chair and watched her sit across from him, *when things have settled down.* Then we'll destroy all the ghosts from the past and concentrate on the future.

The weekend flew by. Kimberly spent every second with Jake and, true to her word, mended a couple of his shirts, organized his kitchen, did two loads of laundry and even dusted and vacuumed his house.

He protested vehemently, but she didn't slack off, and in the end he contented himself by helping out or amusing Lindsay.

Kimberly couldn't remember when she'd been happier, and that worried her as she walked into the offices of First Cascade on Monday morning. Christmas music murmured

through the speakers, and the lobby of the bank was decorated for the holidays with strings of lights. Red and green
letters spelling out Happy Holidays hung over the teller
windows.

In the trust department, Marcie was already busy at her
word processor. She looked up and smiled at Kimberly, but
her fingers never left the keyboard.

Kimberly hung up her cape, then walked back through the
reception area to the cafeteria, where she poured herself a
cup of hot water and dunked a tea bag into it. Several
women from the mortgage banking department were clustered around a couple of Formica-topped tables. They drank
coffee, smoked and nibbled on doughnuts as they talked and
laughed before they had to head downstairs.

Kimberly spoke to Kelly and Annie, women she'd worked
with in the mortgage department, then turned to head back
to her office. She didn't get far. Bill Zealander, his face
flushed, marched stiffly into the room. "I need to talk to
you," he announced.

Kimberly refused to be cowed. "So talk."

He glanced to the women gossiping at the round table.
"Not here."

"Why not?"

His lips compressed, and behind his glasses his eyes slitted. "Because this is private. Okay?"

"Fine, Bill, fine." Kimberly wasn't in the mood to argue. She left her tea cup, followed Bill out of the cafeteria,
explained where she'd be to Marcie, then strode through the
door of Bill's office. "Okay, what's up?" she asked, trying
to keep the irritation out of her voice. She didn't like his
high-handed attitude, and she didn't bother sitting down.
Instead she crossed her arms impatiently and waited for the
storm that was sure to hit.

Bill stood on the other side of the desk, his back to a bank of windows as he fiddled with the knot of his tie. "I want to know what's going on with the Juniper trust."

"I thought you said this was personal."

"It is." He slid her a glance that was meant to cut her to the quick. It didn't. "You and I both know that you're mishandling the account."

"I'm what?" she demanded, floored.

"Oh, for Pete's sake, Kimberly, admit it. You can't even handle the heirs. Every other day Henry Juniper is crying on your shoulder. And from what I understand, Carole is planning to contest the will. You've had to ask for extra help from operations to make sure all the dividends were paid. And you can barely keep your mind on business."

"What're you talking about?"

He yanked off his glasses and polished them with a tissue. "The custody hearing for your daughter."

Kimberly crossed the room and leaned over his desk. "What do *you* know about that?"

He gestured with the hand holding his wire-rims. "It's common knowledge, Kim. Robert Fisher is a biggie at this bank. And it's no secret that you've hired some has-been attorney with a vendetta to get to Fisher. If you ask me, you're playing with fire."

"No one's asking you anything," she said, stung. It took all of her strength to stay calm. "And what I do with my personal life is none of your business."

"I know. But you're obviously under a strain. You've got more important things to think about than business."

"You're way out of line, Bill," she said, and he shrugged, then polished the lenses of his glasses again. Seeing him in a dark suit, in relief against the windows, set off a memory of another tall man—a man dressed in dark blue, a man polishing his goggles after night skiing. She didn't move, couldn't believe that her mind was leaping to such conclusions. And yet . . . Her mouth went dry.

"Now, look, I'm just trying to help you out," he was saying. He smiled benignly and slipped the glasses onto his nose. "I could handle the Juniper trust, get Henry and Carole working together rather than at cross-purposes, at least for a while, until you get your personal life back on track."

"My life is on track."

"Get real, Kim."

"Do you ski, Bill?" she asked suddenly, deciding she'd had enough of his arrogant insinuations.

"Do I what?" he asked, taken aback.

"Ski."

"Yes, but what—" He stopped suddenly, and a red flush climbed steadily up his neck.

She couldn't believe his reaction. "Have you been following me?"

"Are you out of your mind?"

"I don't think so." So furious she was shaking, she said, "I've just had this feeling lately that someone was watching me. And I thought I saw you up on the mountain night skiing."

He laughed nervously and reached into his suit pocket for his cigarettes. "Now you've really gone off the deep end."

"Have I?"

"Kimberly—"

"I don't know what you're up to, Bill, but I don't like it. So just stay the hell out of my life!" Spinning on her heel, she strode straight into her office and resisted the urge to slam her door.

Her temples throbbed. Taking deep breaths, she tried to think straight. Had Bill Zealander, in his efforts to further himself, actually taken to following her? But why? And what were all those cracks about Robert's being an important client of the bank? She felt a cold lump settle in her heart. Did Zealander's spying have something to do with the custody hearing? "Oh, God," she whispered prayerfully.

Her headache pounded behind her eyes.

She thought about talking to Eric Compton, but discarded the idea. Compton hated office in-fighting and petty jealousy, and she didn't blame him. Besides, she had no proof. No, she'd keep this to herself. At least until she saw Jake again.

Jake. Zealander had known she'd hired an attorney—presumably Jake. So, why the remark about a has-been lawyer with a vendetta?

She went back to the cafeteria, found her now-tepid cup of tea and reheated it. Then she stormed back to her office, located a small bottle of aspirin in her purse and swallowed two of the bitter tablets.

"Forget about Zealander," she told herself as she clicked open her briefcase and pulled out several thick files. She didn't have time to deal with penny-ante personality problems.

The intercom buzzed, and Marcie announced that Henry Juniper was on line one. Kimberly smiled, grateful for once for the distraction. Things were back to normal.

Jake finally connected with Ron Koski Monday afternoon. He stopped by Ron's office, a small three-room suite tucked between a maid service and a travel agency in Oregon City.

Ron's furniture consisted of a desk, two chairs, a small table and a credenza. A plate-glass window offered a view of Willamette Falls, a railroad crossing and smokestacks from a nearby paper mill. White clouds of steam rose over the city, melding with the gray sky.

Ron, in need of a shave, looked up when Jake strode in. "About time you showed up." Seated at his desk, his blond crew cut on the longish side, he offered Jake his hand.

"I've called your machine three times since yesterday." Jake clasped Ron's hand and shook it firmly. They'd been friends since high school, and Ron was one of the few people Jake would trust with his life. Diane Welby was the other. And now, of course, there was Kimberly Bennett.

Ron waved him into one of the side chairs. "I've been on a stake-out. But I thought you'd want to know that the police are definitely on to Fisher." He reached behind him, found a thermos of coffee and poured two cups.

Jake took the cup he was offered and dropped into a chair near the desk. "The police have been on to him before."

"I know, and there's always the chance he'll get away." Ron shrugged. "But the D.A. won't go for anything less than an open-and-shut case. He can't afford to go after Fisher with anything else. Too much public embarrassment."

"How do you know all this?"

"I've got my sources." Ron grinned and reached onto the desk for a pack of cigarettes. The pack was empty. He crumpled it and tossed it into a nearby wastebasket, then fumbled in his top drawer, where a carton was stashed. Opening the new pack, he shook out a cigarette.

"Brecken? Is he talking again?" Jake took a sip of the coffee. Bitter and hot, it burned all the way down his throat.

Ron lighted up and clicked his lighter shut. "Nope," Ron said through a cloud of smoke. "Brecken's been tight-lipped, but trust me, the source is good."

"When will it go down?"

"Don't know."

Jake was worried. The timing and the set-up were all wrong. "Why hasn't Fisher gotten wind of it?"

Ron frowned. "Maybe he has."

"Will he run?"

"Your guess is as good as mine. He's got a lot of ties here in Portland—it would be hard to pull up stakes."

That it would, Jake thought gloomily. Especially if Fisher intended to hang around long enough to fight Kimberly in court. Unless, of course, Fisher took the law into his own hands.

Cold certainty settled in the small of his back. Of course Fisher would run. His gut twisted, and it took all his self-control not to run out of the office, grab Kimberly and Lindsay and hide them somewhere safe. Because if Robert Fisher was running scared and he really wanted his daughter with him, he'd just take her. "Give me all the details," he said to Ron, his voice sharp.

"I don't have many."

"What?"

"My source gave me a little information, but she didn't blow the whole operation."

"She?"

Ron smiled slyly. "Okay... this is what I know...."

The last person Kimberly expected to run into on her way out of the bank that night was Robert. But there he was, big as life, surrounded by bank bigwigs again. And Bill Zealander was in the group.

Dread crept up her spine.

She hadn't seen Robert in the offices of First Cascade for months, and now he seemed to be there every other day. He saw her approach, but didn't bother to smile. In fact his face seemed strained, his lips a little white, and his eyes were so cold she actually shivered.

Robert and entourage disappeared into the elevator. Marcie was wrapping a wool scarf around her neck and had already slung the strap of her purse over her shoulder. "Wait," Kimberly called as the elevator doors closed.

"Sorry, boss, I'm outta here," Marcie teased.

"No, I don't need anything, just some information."

Marcie grinned. "You've got five minutes. I'm meeting Glen downstairs."

Kimberly asked, "Do you know what's going on with Bill and Robert Fisher?"

Marcie, who always had an ear open to office gossip, shrugged and tucked her bangs under the red scarf. "Nothing specific, but I do know that Bill's been busy lately. A lot of closed-door meetings."

"With Robert?"

Marcie nodded. "Once in a while."

Kimberly gulped and tried not to panic.

"As for Fisher, I think he's moving some money around."

"Within the bank?"

"I guess. Or maybe he's transferring it to another branch or something." She pulled out her compact and checked her makeup, then brushed a fleck of mascara from her cheek.

Kimberly's mouth went dry. Something was going on. Something big. "How do you know this?"

Marcie grinned. "From Heather. She knows everything."

And Heather was Bill Zealander's secretary. Images flashed through Kimberly's mind, pictures of Bill trotting after Robert when he was in the bank, a lone skier watching her with Jake, a man lingering near the lamppost across her street.

"Is something wrong?" Marcie asked, staring at her as she clicked her compact shut and stuffed it back into her purse.

Kimberly forced a tight smile. "I don't know. But thanks."

"Any time. And I'll check with Heather, see if she knows anything else." She waved as she walked to the elevators.

Kimberly picked up the phone on Marcie's desk. With quaking fingers, she dialed home. The phone rang three times before Lindsay's voice called, "Hello?"

Kimberly's knees went weak. She sank against the desk. "Oh, hi, honey, how're you? Was school okay today?"

"It was crummy. Bobby Hendricks kicked me! I got him back, though. I pinched him in the neck!" Lindsay launched into a blow-by-blow account of her day at school while Kimberly battled against sudden tears.

"Well, you certainly had an interesting day," Kimberly said before Arlene took over the phone and assured her that nothing was out of the ordinary and she was, as usual, watching Lindsay like a hawk.

"Now, don't you change your plans," Arlene admonished. "You go along and do some shopping before you come home."

Christmas shopping! She'd forgotten all about it. "I think I'd better come straight home."

"Hogwash! Lindsay and I are knee-deep in a project here, anyway. We'll see you in a couple of hours."

"All right, just be careful," Kimberly replied.

"I always am."

After hanging up, she took the elevator downstairs to the lobby and walked out the main doors of the bank. Santas on every street corner rang bells, shoppers trooped along the ice-glazed streets and store windows glowed with elegant Christmas displays.

The night air was crisp and cold, and Kimberly determined that for the next few hours she'd get lost in the dizzying, lighthearted spirit of Christmas shopping and leave her worries behind.

She glanced over her shoulder twice, just to make sure that no one was following her, then she ducked into Hollis's department store and headed straight for the toy department.

Tonight she'd find the perfect gift for Lindsay and maybe something special for Jake, as well.

Jake. Thank God he was on her side.

Chapter Eleven

Ben Kesler's smile said it all: smug, self-confident and pleased with himself. Dressed in an expensive wool suit, he leaned back in his desk chair and tented his hands under the beginning of a double chin. A Rolex peeked from beneath his starched white cuff, while diamonds glittered in his tie clasp and cuff links. Yep, Ben had money and he wore it, Jake thought, eyeing the attorney with distaste.

Ben's hair was thick and blond, trimmed neatly, his skin copper brown and his eyes a watery shade of blue. He looked as if he worked with weights and spent his extra hours inside a tanning booth.

Jake didn't mince words. "You said you wanted to work out a deal," he said.

"That's right. On the Fisher case."

Jake crossed his arms over his chest and waited. He noticed the mirrored bar recessed behind teak doors, the thick gray carpet, the oiled paneling and various objets d'art placed strategically around the room on the twenty-eighth floor. The office smelled of interior design, and Jake's lips twisted at the thought of his tiny office in West Linn.

Ben leaned forward. "I don't have to tell you that Mr. Fisher wants custody of his daughter very badly. He's willing to go to great lengths to have her with him."

"What lengths?"

"Five hundred thousand dollars."

Jake raised an eyebrow. "Half a million dollars? He wants to *buy* custody?"

Ben sat up and grinned even wider. "Mr. Fisher knows that Ms. Bennett has had to struggle. Working long hours, hiring an elderly woman as a baby-sitter, making ends meet. He thinks now that he should have been fairer with her during the divorce." Ben spread beringed hands. "He's willing to make it up to her."

"As I understand it, he didn't want custody then."

"He's changed his mind." Ben lifted a palm, and his eyes grew sharp. "You know how it is, Jake. During a divorce emotions run high, tempers flare—sometimes the best or most equitable decisions are passed by."

"So I've heard," Jake admitted dryly as a secretary, tall and dark haired with a trim figure and green eyes, stepped into the room. Quietly she left a tray of coffee on the corner of Kesler's desk.

"Anything else?" she asked, glancing quickly at Jake before turning back to Kesler.

"Not now." He waved her away, and she slid obediently out of the room. Jake half expected her to bow in the doorway. He felt sick.

"Anyway," Kesler continued, offering Jake a cup and picking up a mug with his initials engraved on it, "Fisher thinks he was hasty. He wants Kimberly to have all the creature comforts she was used to when she was married to him.''

"And in exchange he'll get Lindsay.''

Ben smiled as if to say, "What could be fairer?''

"She won't go for it.''

"You don't know—''

"I know.''

"But half a million dollars is nothing to sneeze at.''

"Neither is a child.'' Jake got to his feet, looking down his nose at Kesler. The man, in his Rolex and gold rings, was pathetic. How had he ever been jealous of him?

"Robert Fisher isn't used to taking no for an answer,'' Ben reminded him.

"Maybe it's time he got used to it.'' Jake started for the door, and Kesler sighed heavily.

"Fisher will up the ante.''

"No dice.''

"But—''

"I'll see you in court, Kesler!'' Jake strode through the door and let it slam shut behind him. As he did, he heard Ben swear roundly—a stream of invective that would have made a truck driver blush. Maybe Kesler wasn't so bad after all. With a smile Jake sauntered down the hallway, nodded to the dark-haired secretary and took the elevator to the first floor. It felt good to get under Kesler's skin. Damn good. Now, if only he could best him at his own game.

On the first floor he zipped up his jacket and walked outside. The city was ablaze with light, though the sky was black and the wind, whistling down from the Columbia Gorge, was bitterly cold. Ice glazed the once-wet streets. Patches of snow, piled against the curb from the plow, contrasted with the black asphalt.

Jake's Bronco was parked two streets over. He stopped beneath a street lamp to pull on a pair of gloves when he noticed the silver Mercedes idling at the curb.

Robert Fisher climbed out of the black seat, straightened the lapels of his black overcoat and, head bent against the wind, started for the building.

Jake's diaphragm tightened. He didn't breathe for a minute as the older man made his way through the revolving doors. It was hard to imagine Robert Fisher as Kimberly's husband . . . her lover.

And now he was trying to buy Lindsay.

Jake stretched his gloves over his fingers and walked briskly to his Bronco. Obviously Fisher didn't understand Kimberly at all, or he wouldn't have made his ridiculous offer. Half a million dollars for a child.

Climbing into the cold interior of his Bronco, he thought of Sam. No amount of money could replace him. Nor could it buy Fisher custody of Kimberly's daughter.

He jammed his key into the ignition, and the Bronco's cold engine sputtered twice, finally firing on the third try. Shoving the rig into gear, he guided it through the thick evening traffic and turned south. He started for Sellwood, but changed his mind and headed home.

With a cold sense of certainty, Jake knew Fisher was beginning to panic. And there was a good chance that he would try to bolt—with Lindsay. Gritting his teeth, Jake suffered through the traffic delays and finally, nearly half an hour later, pulled into the driveway of his house in Lake Oswego.

With Lupus on his heels, he raced into the house, packed a bag and set his plan into motion by calling Ron Koski. Then, whistling to the dog, he headed back outside. "You've got a job to do," he said as Lupus bounded into the passenger side of the Bronco. He scratched the white shepherd behind the ears. "Be on your toes tonight, okay?"

The dog whined and pricked his ears forward.

Jaw set, Jake backed out of the drive. Tonight or tomorrow or whenever Fisher decided to strike, Jake intended to beat him at his own game.

Kimberly wheeled around the corner of her street and noticed Jake's Bronco parked at the curb near the house. Despite her long day at work and fighting the crowds at Hollis's, she smiled as she pulled into the driveway.

Stashing her packages—a small bike, two games, a book and a doll—in the garage beneath an old blanket, she tried to keep her heartbeat under control.

She hurried inside and found Jake, Arlene and Lindsay diligently packing cookies into tins. The kitchen was covered with cooling racks and cookies shaped like trees, dusted with sugar or decorated with green frosting and red cinnamon candies.

"Hi, Mommy," Lindsay said, looking up from her work. She and Jake were struggling with a red bow on a round tin decorated with a reprint of a Currier and Ives yuletide lithograph.

"We don't already have enough cookies? Or do we need another twenty dozen?" Kimberly deadpanned.

"These are for all Lyle's relatives," Arlene explained.

Kimberly surveyed the kitchen slowly. "He must have an incredible family tree."

"Oh, we give them to friends, too. And there's always the church bazaar and the nursing home."

"And a few left over?" Kimberly teased.

Jake swallowed a smile. "Many left over."

"A few," Arlene admitted, her eyes twinkling.

"Arlene says we can keep some!"

"But not many. What was it—ten or twelve dozen?" Jake asked, giving up on the bow and straightening. He grabbed Kimberly's hand and squeezed it.

"Very funny," Arlene remarked, but she chuckled. "You three just run along, and I'll finish up here."

"Run along?"

Lindsay tied the bow, but it slipped off the tin. She gave up and trotted over to her mother. "They're singing Christmas songs—"

"Carols," Arlene corrected.

"—carols in the park. Jake said he'd take us."

"When?"

Jake glanced at his watch. "Ten minutes ago. We were just about to give up on you."

Kimberly grinned. "So, what're we waiting for?" She helped Lindsay into her coat, boots and mittens, and prodded Arlene into joining them, but Arlene would have none of it.

"I'm too busy here. Besides, I don't want to go out and freeze my tail off just to hear some kids singin'. Now, go on—it'll just take me a few minutes to finish up."

Lindsay bounded for the front door and opened it. Lupus, waiting patiently outside, started to run in, but Jake caught him on the porch and snapped a leash on his collar.

Kimberly eyed the dog. "The whole family, eh?"

"It's almost Christmas," Jake explained. "I didn't want to leave him alone." He smiled, but his eyes didn't warm as they usually did, and for the first time, Kimberly noticed a small duffel bag in the corner of the porch. Jake's duffel bag. He intended to spend the night. One part of her thrilled, until she saw again the wariness in his eyes. "Come on, we're late."

They hustled across the street to the park. Lindsay, holding hands with both of them, skipped as they hurried along the snow-crusted path. Lupus strained against the leash, sniffing the ground and leading the way.

Evergreens, their branches drooping from the weight of the snow, flanked the walkway. Soft light from street lamps glistened against the white snow, and a few flakes fell from the sky. The sound of Christmas carols drifted through the trees, growing louder as Kimberly, Jake and Lindsay approached a clearing near the pond. *"God rest ye merry gentlemen, let nothing ye dismay . . ."*

The carolers, fourth-graders from a local church, sang from risers placed near the lake. A crowd had gathered nearby.

"I can't see," Lindsay said, frustrated by the tall people in front of her.

"We can take care of that." Jake handed Kimberly the leash, then swung the little girl onto his shoulders, giving her a bird's-eye view of the singers. "How's that?" he asked.

She held on to his head for dear life. Her mittened fingers clutched his hair. "It's good," she said, enthralled.

Kimberly's heart felt as if it had lodged permanently in her throat. Jake, the man who never wanted any more children, who wouldn't let himself get that emotionally strapped again, and Lindsay, a child whose father considered her a possession, something to own—together they were laughing and as happy as if they were father and daughter.

Stop it, she told herself, angry at the romantic turn of her thoughts. How could she even project to a future that was so uncertain?

Jake brushed a snowflake from her nose, and her heart twisted.

We all belong together, she thought, we do! Jake closed his fingers over her hand. He stared at her, and she wondered if he could read her mind. Did he know that she imagined them a perfect little family, without the problems of their pasts, with a future as silver lined as the moon-washed snow?

How ridiculous. But the vision wouldn't fade.

"Hark the herald angels sing . . ."

Lindsay giggled. "That's what Lyle calls me," she said. "An angel."

Jake, whose left hand was wrapped firmly around both of Lindsay's ankles, winked at Kimberly. "An angel, are you? So, where are your harp and wings?"

"Tell him they're at the cleaner's," Kimberly put in.

"That's silly!" Lindsay laughed gaily, and Kimberly thought she couldn't be happier. Snuggled close to Jake, listening to the sounds of Christmas music punctuated by Lindsay's childish giggles, she felt the magic of the season and the wonder of this one very special man.

"Silver bells. Silver bells. It's Christmastime in the city . . ."

Lupus's ears pricked forward. Restless, he pulled on the leash and walked behind her. "Come here," Kimberly whispered, but the white dog padded back and forth, sniffing the air, his eyes trained on the thicket of trees that buffered one edge of the park from the noise and traffic of the street.

"I see a car like Daddy's," Lindsay proclaimed from her perch. She stretched a chubby arm toward the street.

Kimberly tried not to panic. "It's probably just one that looks like his."

Shaking her head, Lindsay said, "I don't think so."

Jake's lips compressed, and his eyes narrowed as he stared over the heads in front of him, looking in the direction of Lindsay's outstretched arm, eyes squinting against the darkness and powdery falling flakes.

Kimberly's chest constricted. "Is it—"

"I don't see anything," he said.

Lupus whined, tugging on the leash.

"He must smell a squirrel," Kimberly said, trying to push all thoughts of Robert aside.

"Or a rat." Jake, too, was watching the dog. His fingers tightened around Lindsay's ankles.

The carolers broke into "We Wish You a Merry Christmas" and ended the program. Jake helped Lindsay to the ground, but didn't let go of her hand.

Kimberly shivered, but not from the cold. A chill settled in her bones. There was something Jake wasn't telling her, something he'd learned today, something about the custody hearing...something that wasn't good. That's why he'd shown up with Lupus and his overnight bag.

As the crowd splintered in different directions, Jake, Kimberly and Lindsay trudged back to the house. Inside, Lindsay demanded hot chocolate and popcorn, which they devoured along with several of Arlene's sugar-dusted cookies.

"Okay, kiddo, it's time for bed," Kimberly said, wiping the colored sugar crystals from Lindsay's cheek.

"Not yet." Lindsay protested loudly, but Kimberly managed to carry her upstairs, bathe her, read her a story and turn out the lights by nine-fifteen. "I love you, Mommy," Lindsay whispered as Kimberly kissed her cheek.

"I love you, too, sweetheart."

When Lindsay nestled deep between the covers, Kimberly padded quietly downstairs. She found Jake in the living room, staring out the front window. He snapped the blinds shut on all the windows as she reached the bottom step.

"There's something you should know," she said, taking a seat on the arm of the over-stuffed couch. "I think Bill Zealander, a man I work with, is involved with Robert."

Jake's jaw clenched. He leaned his back against the fireplace. "Go on."

She explained about her conversation with Zealander and the times she'd seen him with Robert.

Jake's face grew hard, his expression brooding. "Why didn't you tell me you thought you were being watched?"

"Because it sounded so paranoid." She shoved her hair out of her face. "I thought I was being overly sensitive, hysterical about nothing."

"And now?"

"Now I don't know," she admitted.

"Does Bill Zealander drive a white station wagon?"

"I—I don't know."

"I saw a wagon follow you out of the parking lot after Diane's wedding," he said, thinking aloud. "It could've been the same car up on the mountain."

Kimberly felt numb inside.

"Is there anything else?"

"I'm not sure," she admitted with a sigh. "But there's some gossip about Robert at the bank. He's moving money around."

"Where?"

"I don't know, but I'll find out."

"No!" He shoved himself upright and leaned over her, his face only inches from hers. "I don't think you should take the chance."

"What chance?"

"If Fisher's really going to blow town, he might try to grab Lindsay."

"Blow town?" she repeated, dumbstruck. "You think he's leaving?"

"I don't know." He strode into the bedroom, opened her closet and found her suitcase. He flung it on the bed and snapped it open. "You've got to leave."

"Leave?"

"Yes. I know a place—a beach house of a friend of mine. You and Lindsay will be safe there."

Her heart chilled, and she licked her lips nervously as she found her courage. "Okay, McGowan," she said softly, her hands clutching the bedpost in a death grip, "what happened today?"

Jake leaned one knee on the bed. "I saw Ben Kesler. He seems to think that Robert will go to any lengths to get his daughter."

"I already told you that." She eyed him closely, and a cold fear settled in the pit of her stomach. "There's something more, isn't there—something you're not telling me?"

He hesitated.

"Look, we had a deal. Remember? You keep me informed on everything, and I do what you say. So far I've kept my end of the bargain."

He straightened. "I've got a hunch that Fisher's not going to wait around for any court date to try to win his daughter."

She was shaking inside. "Why?"

Raking his fingers through his hair in frustration, he turned and faced her. "Because it's only a matter of time before the police link him to organized crime in Portland."

"I've heard this all before...." She started out the bedroom door, but Jake grabbed her arm and spun her around so quickly the breath escaped from her lungs in a gasp.

"Kimberly, I'm serious," he said calmly. "I don't think you should take any chances."

"You've talked to the police?" she said, guessing, her throat so dry it barely worked.

"No, but I know someone who has. And my guess is that Fisher knows what's going down, too." His jaw clenched tight. "I talked to Ben Kesler today. Robert's willing to pay you five hundred thousand dollars for custody."

"He what!"

"I told him you weren't interested."

"And?" she whispered.

"He said Fisher would up the ante."

Sick inside, she said, "But that doesn't mean—"

He grabbed hold of her arm. "You just told me that he's moving money around. The way I see it, there's a damn good chance he's gonna run. And if he does, my guess is he'll try to take Lindsay."

"No!"

His fingers dug deep into her arm. "He was your husband, Kimberly. You told me yourself that he'd stop at nothing to get what he wanted, and right now, for God-only-knows-what reason, he wants Lindsay!"

She didn't want to believe him, but she saw the earnestness on his features. "What did you mean when you said Robert knows what's going on?"

"That the police are going to bust him."

"You're sure?"

"No." But his eyes were cold and convincing.

She sagged against the bed, and he sat beside her, holding her shoulders, supporting her.

"Now, tell me more about Bill Zealander."

Heart pounding with dread, she told him everything she could think of, including Bill's jealousy over the Juniper account and her friendship with Eric Compton. "And I'm sure he was the man who was following us on the ski slopes that day," she said, rubbing her arms but feeling cold to the bone.

"Then you've got to go away."

"You mean hide out, don't you?" she tossed back at him.

"However you want to look at it."

She glanced through the bedroom door and down the hall to the Christmas tree shining brightly in the cozy little room. Tilting her chin up mutinously, she said, "I'm not going to run away," she said, realizing that as many times as she'd thought of it, she couldn't run, wouldn't hide. She wasn't going to let Robert or any other man force her into being a coward. "Lindsay's my daughter, and unless he goes to court for her, he has no claim—"

"But he might not have the option of waiting around for the courts or his friend Monaghan to make that decision." Jake clenched his teeth together. "Look, Kimberly, you said once you'd do anything to save your child."

"I will."

"And you promised to do things my way."

"But—"

He laced a finger to her lips. "Just listen, will you? Tonight we'll pack, and then tomorrow you'll pretend everything's normal. Head out for the bank as usual, have Arlene come over, but take Lindsay with you and go straight through Portland. About the time you should be at the bank, you'll stop and make a phone call, telling your boss that you're sick, then you'll drive on to the coast." He reached into the pocket of his jeans and extracted a key. "I'll meet you there later."

"You've got it all worked out, haven't you?" she asked, appalled. Things were moving too quickly. Trying to think, she walked into the living room.

"I hope so."

"But I can't leave. Not without some notice."

His face turned back. "You hired me for one reason— Lindsay's safety. Right? And even though you've been denying that your ex-husband is involved in organized crime, we both know you're kidding yourself! So, unless you want to take the chance that Robert will take her from you, you'd better face the facts that—yes, you'll have to hide out for a while.''

"But my job—"

"Damn your job!" he thundered. "You've got a choice, Kimberly. The bank or Lindsay. Personally I think First Cascade will stumble along without you for a few days, but what about your daughter? How will she do without a mother?"

"Stop!" she hissed. "Lindsay's more important to me than any job—"

"Is she?" he taunted. "Then prove it and do the smart thing."

She plopped down in a rocker and tucked her knees beneath her chin. "I hate to be bossed around!"

"I know, but you hired me," he pointed out. "Not the other way around."

He was right and she knew it. But she despised the thought of being manipulated by Robert. And all of Jake's talk about organized crime—she hated to face it, though deep in her heart she'd known Robert was involved in something dark and sinister. She'd hidden her head in the sand just to protect herself and Lindsay.

Squeezing her eyes shut, she tried to block out images of dark figures involved in drug deals or worse.... Though she'd finally accepted that his business dealings were shady, what Jake seemed so sure of was much more evil than she'd ever believed possible.

She felt Jake's finger under her chin. He lifted her face. "It's going to be all right," he said. "I guarantee it."

Her stomach jerked as he leaned down to kiss her with such warmth and tenderness she thought her heart would break.

"You're sure about this?"

"Positive," he said with conviction. "Now, tomorrow morning we'll pretend everything is normal, okay?"

"Okay," she whispered, but as he lifted her from her feet and carried her back into the bedroom, she had the sinking sensation that her life would never be normal again.

Chapter Twelve

Click.

Jake stirred, one eye opening. Had he heard something? Quietly, so as not to disturb Kimberly, he rolled out of bed and yanked on his jeans.

From the living room Lupus growled low in his throat.

The warning hairs on the back of Jake's neck stood on end as he moved barefoot through the darkness to the hallway. The floor was cold, the house silent. His ears strained, and his eyes, growing accustomed to the half light, searched the shadowy house.

Lupus padded up to him, his ears cocked toward the kitchen. He growled again, then started barking wildly.

"Jake?" Kimberly's voice caught his attention, and he turned. From the corner of his eye he saw a movement, darker than the house—the black figure of an intruder.

Jake scrambled for the light switch, but his hand was yanked hard behind him and something crashed down on his head. Lights exploded behind his eyes. Pain ripped through his skull. His legs gave way, and he fell to his knees. Think, McGowan, think!

"Jake?"

"Get out of here!" he yelled, but it was too late.

Kimberly found the switch, and the kitchen was flooded in intense blinding light. Her eyes moved from Jake to the intruder, a big burly blond man with a ponytail. "Jake... Oh, God!"

Lupus leaped into the air, lunging for the intruder's throat.

"Run!" Jake yelled, and was rewarded with a swift kick that knocked the air from his lungs. "Kimberly, run!" His face crashed against the cold floor. He blinked, trying to keep unconsciousness at bay. The overhead light in the kitchen was blinding, and he couldn't focus. But Lupus had the intruder down, his jaws clamped around the burly, blond man's arm.

"You damn bastard," the man yelled, trying to beat Lupus off. But the shepherd wouldn't let go.

Kimberly ran from the room. He heard her footsteps on the stairs leading to Lindsay's room.

Staggering, Jake jumped on the blond man, and his fist crashed into a stubbled jaw, sending pain jarring up his arm. Bones cracked, and the big man groaned. Jake wouldn't let up. They struggled, each pounding the other.

Breathing hard, Jake found his feet just as Burly did the same.

The man took a swing at Jake and missed, and Lupus attacked again, lunging for the intruder's rubbery legs while Jake connected with a left hook.

"Who the hell are you?" Jake growled, feeling hot, sticky liquid running down his face as the man stumbled backward. Jake curled his fingers around the bigger man's jean jacket and lifted him back to his feet. "Don't tell me, you're one of Fisher's goons!"

"He's Robert's bodyguard," Kimberly said, returning to the kitchen with a wide-eyed, frightened Lindsay huddled against her.

Jake's nostrils flared, and he pulled the man closer, meeting him face-to-face. "Call 911," he yelled to Kimberly, though his eyes didn't leave the beefy man. "Talk to Detective Brecken. Tell him to send a squad car on the double."

"Don't bother," a cool voice said from behind his head.

Jake realized with sickening certainty that Robert Fisher was there. For Lindsay!

"Let him go," Robert commanded.

Jake's fingers tightened about the denim clenched between his fingers. He wasn't about to release the man, not yet. He turned and eyed the man who was his sworn enemy. Robert, standing in the doorway, seemed calm, but his eyes were slitted, and the raincoat he'd tossed over his shoulders didn't hide the barrel of a small pistol he was pointing directly at Jake's chest.

"I said, let him go." Fisher repeated.

"Daddy?" Lindsay's small voice asked.

Robert flicked a glance her way and he actually smiled, not the cold, calculating grin that Jake associated with Fisher, but a warm smile. "I'm sorry, honey," he said, adjusting the coat to hide his pistol. "This'll be over in a little while, and we'll go for a ride."

Lindsay clung tightly to her mother. "I don't want a ride."

"Sure you do. It'll be fun." His gaze moved to Kimberly. "Pack her clothes."

"No!" Kimberly cried. "Get out of here, Robert, before I call the police! You have no right—"

"Do it, Kim!" he commanded again, momentarily distracted.

Lupus, who had been coiled at Kimberly's feet, sprang.

"No!" Jake cried.

Fisher reacted, shooting blindly. The shot blasted through the house, and Lupus's body flinched. The dog yipped pitifully and fell to the floor. Blood stained the shepherd's white coat near his hip.

"You bastard!" Jake dropped the bodyguard and took a step forward, but Robert waved the gun in his face.

"Back off, McGowan."

"No! No!" Lindsay cried, her face twisted as she tried to climb from her mother's arm and reach Lupus.

"Shh, honey, shh!" Kimberly whispered.

"Lupus!" Lindsay wailed.

"Let him be!" Fisher ordered, forcing Jake away from the dog. His gaze shifted back to Kimberly. "I mean it, Kim! Move it!"

"Daddy, oh, Daddy, you shot Lupus . . . you shot him dead. I hate you!" Lindsay cried, big, fat tears rolling down her cheeks. "I hate you forever!"

Robert's composure cracked a little. Regret darkened his eyes. "I didn't mean to—"

"You're not taking her anywhere!" Kimberly cried.

His expression turned ugly. "You've got no choice in the matter," he said, his teeth clenching together.

Lindsay buried her face in her mother's neck, and Jake moved slowly, positioning himself between Fisher and Kimberly. He glanced pointedly at the blond man huddled in the corner. Old Ponytail was holding his jaw and breathing hard. Blood oozed from his mouth.

"You'd better find yourself another bodyguard, Fisher," Jake baited. "This one's about dead on his feet."

Lupus whimpered pitifully.

"Hang in there," Jake whispered, his heart twisting, fury firing his blood.

"All those stories are true, aren't they?" Kimberly asked, eyeing the man who had been her husband. Her throat worked, and tears stood in her gorgeous eyes.

Robert didn't bother to answer. He tried to shoulder past Jake to get to Lindsay, but Jake blocked his path. "It's all over, Fisher," he said, his pulse throbbing in his brain.

Fisher barked out a cruel laugh. "It's not over until I get my daughter. Get out of the way, McGowan."

But Jake didn't budge. He noticed Kimberly inching backward toward the hall. "If I were you, I'd leave now, before the police get here. Someone's bound to have heard the shot, and there just may be people outside waiting for you. People who may have already contacted the cops."

Robert's eyes narrowed. "What do you mean? Who?"

But Jake didn't answer.

Robert motioned to his bodyguard. The burly man stepped forward and reached for Lindsay. Jake attacked, hitting the man squarely in the midsection as the front door burst open.

"Hold it! Police!" a harsh male voice boomed through the house.

Robert whirled, heading for the back door, but another policeman was on the back porch. His gun was aimed at Robert's chest. "Don't even think about it," he warned.

Robert dropped his gun, and Kimberly, still clutching Lindsay, fell into Jake's arms. A few minutes later Detective Brecken appeared. With a grin at Jake he snapped handcuffs on Robert and instructed the younger policeman to read Fisher his rights. But Fisher wasn't finished. He glared at Jake, and his gaze oozed pure hatred. "I'm not talking until I speak with my lawyer," he clipped, then his eyes turned to Kimberly. "You know, Kim, you don't have a very good track record at picking lovers. Your boy here—" he motioned to Jake "—isn't interested in you as much as he wanted to get at me."

"Shut up, Fisher," Brecken warned.

But Robert was picking up speed. "He's only involved with you because he's on some wild-goose chase, a vendetta for his brother. He's got the crazy notion I was involved in his death. Well, I wasn't. The man did himself in. And as for caring for you, get real. McGowan's a loner. Only cares about number one and, of course, vengeance. Daniel Stevens killed himself, McGowan. Face it."

"Can it, Fisher," the younger policeman said.

Kimberly sagged against the wall and held her daughter close. Her heart was thudding in her brain. Robert's wild accusations didn't make any sense.

But it was over. Thank God, it was over.

Her arms tightened around Lindsay, and she fought back the urge to break into tears of relief.

"You okay?" Jake asked, touching her on the arm. His warmth filled her with an inner strength, and she nodded weakly, still using the wall for support.

Jake snatched a clean dish towel and bent over Lupus as Ron Koski sauntered in. "I'm glad you called," Koski said. "Even if it did mean freezing my tail off."

"Thanks," Jake replied, "I owe you one."

"Make it a draft."

Jake nodded, his face white beneath his tan as he tended to Lupus's wound.

Kimberly glanced from Ron to Jake, who was trying to stem the flow of blood from Lupus's midsection.

"This is my friend, the private investigator," Jake muttered, wincing when the dog whimpered. "Ron Koski— Kimberly Bennett and Lindsay. Ron staked out the place and had told the police what he was doing. With the help of a beeper he alerted Detective Brecken the minute Fisher pulled up.''

Kimberly was stunned. So that's how the police had arrived so quickly. Jake had known Robert would show up?

"Will Lupus be all right?" Lindsay whispered.

Kimberly's heart stuck in her throat. "I hope so, honey."

Ron leaned over the dog. "I'll take this old boy to the vet," he offered. "You take care of the ladies."

"We'll be okay," Kimberly said, seeing the pain in Jake's eyes, the emotions he was trying to keep at bay. Her own eyes filled with tears, and rage burned deep inside.

She looked at the man who had been her husband and felt sick. "Don't you ever, *ever* come into my house again," she said through clenched teeth. "And stay away from my daughter!"

"She's my daughter, too," Robert reminded her.

Lindsay shook her head and cried. Kimberly carried her into the living room, away from the bleeding dog and the sight of her father being led, swearing and cuffed, to the squad car outside.

Still holding her daughter, Kimberly dropped into a rocker, barely listening to the sounds of voices and feet shuffling in the kitchen. She switched on the Christmas tree and stared at the lights, singing softly to her child, hoping the nightmare would go away. But Lindsay continued to sob, crying for Lupus.

Kimberly didn't even hear Jake approach. "We both have to go down to the station," he said softly.

She glanced up, seeing his bloodied face and loving him. "I know."

Detective Brecken entered the room. "It's just a formality."

"And my daughter?" Kimberly finally asked.

"She's been through enough tonight," Brecken replied. "If you have some place she'd be comfortable..."

Kimberly nodded. "I'll only be a minute."

"No!" Lindsay wailed. "Please, Mommy, don't leave me."

"Oh, I won't, precious." Kimberly said, her throat tight. She looked at Jake and swallowed hard. "She'll come with us," she said firmly. "I'll call Arlene and ask her to go with us."

"Good idea."

Kimberly reached for the phone.

It wasn't until they were in the police station, giving their accounts of Robert's kidnap attempt on Lindsay, that Kimberly started piecing all the facts together. And she didn't like the conclusions she was drawing.

She and Jake had finished giving their statements and were drinking bitter coffee from white cups. Detective Brecken had told them to go home for the night.

"Who was Daniel Stevens?" she asked as she crumpled her cup and threw it in the trash.

Jake's jaw hardened. His gray eyes grew cold. "When we get home," he said, "and Lindsay's asleep—then we'll talk. I have a lot to explain."

Kimberly's stomach twisted painfully, and she barely heard anything Arlene or Lindsay said all the way back to Sellwood. They dropped Arlene off, then returned to the house. Shuddering, Kimberly carried Lindsay inside.

Jake dialed the emergency veterinary clinic for a report on Lupus, and Kimberly carried Lindsay upstairs to her bed. "No!" Lindsay whispered, refusing to let go of her mother's neck as Kimberly tried to lay her down. "Mommy, please, can I sleep with you?"

Kimberly smiled sadly. "Of course you can, sweetheart." She wished she'd thought of it herself. Lindsay had just got over her nightmares, and now she'd witnessed her father shooting a favorite pet, threatening her mother and then being handcuffed and taken away in a police car. Lindsay would need time and patience to understand everything that had happened tonight. And so, Kimberly thought, would she.

"Come on, we'll take your blanket and Sebastian." She scooped up a pink elephant and wrapped the faded blanket around Lindsay's shoulders.

Downstairs Jake had cleaned up the kitchen, but his face was grim and set. He watched as she carried Lindsay into the bedroom.

"You sleep now, too," Lindsay whispered as Kimberly settled her into the bed.

"Of course I will," Kimberly said. "It's late and I'm tired." That was a lie. She was so keyed up, she couldn't imagine falling asleep. A thousand unanswered questions raced through her mind. How had Robert got in? Why had he come this night? How had Jake known? What did Robert's crazy comment about Jake's brother mean? Jake didn't have a brother—or did he?

Confused, she snapped off the light and climbed into bed beside her daughter. Lindsay instinctively cuddled closer. Kimberly knew she'd never sleep; she heard Jake in the kitchen, talking on the phone in a low voice, cleaning up, trying to be quiet and failing.

She stared out the window, watching snowflakes fall against the panes. Lindsay's breathing evened out, and Kimberly forced her eyes closed. In the morning, she thought, finally drifting off. In the morning Jake will explain everything, and it will be all right. She'd never have to worry about losing Lindsay again.

* * *

Jake replaced the receiver and shoved his hair from his eyes. He felt the matted blood on his scalp and wondered if he should've had the wound looked at. Hell, what did it matter? He was alive, wasn't he? Fisher was behind bars. Lindsay was safely with her mother for the rest of her life.

Lupus, unfortunately, wasn't doing too well. The bullet had ripped through his flank and done some internal damage. The vet had performed surgery, but it would be touch and go for a little while.

He poured himself a cup of coffee and stared broodingly through Kimberly's kitchen window to the black night beyond. Robert Fisher was finally where he should be. So, why didn't Jake feel an intense satisfaction, a lifting of the weight that had been on his shoulders for years?

He glanced to the short hallway and the bedroom beyond. Now he'd have to tell her everything and admit that he'd lied, and, yes, in the beginning, used her.

And there was Lindsay to think about, as well. A child, for Pete's sake. A child he cared about. A child he was willing to claim as his own.

And the dog—whether he wanted to face it or not—Lupus might not make it.

Damn Robert Fisher and damn this whole mess!

He finished his coffee, threw the dregs down the sink and snapped out the lights. Snatching an old quilt from the back of the couch, he headed toward Kimberly's bedroom and cracked the door quietly open.

The scene before his eyes tore at his soul. Kimberly and Lindsay, close together, their faces washed by pale light filtering through the window, were both asleep. Their expressions were calm and peaceful. Outside, the snow was falling again, promising a white Christmas, and the house was silent except for the soft ticking of a clock in the living room.

He sat in the rocker near the corner and stared at the two people he'd come to think of as his family. At least they were his for a little longer. Until Kimberly discovered the truth. He wrapped the blanket around him and waited.

Kimberly's head pounded. She had to force her eyes open against the gray light of dawn. A warm lump cuddled close to her, and she instinctively touched Lindsay's tangled crown.

Yawning, she noticed Jake seated in the rocker near the foot of the bed. His eyes, a little bloodshot, were open and staring at her. His hair had been freshly washed; beads of water still shone in his dark strands. He hadn't bothered shaving, and the dark shadow of his beard added to his innate male sexuality. She smiled because she loved him so much.

At the sight of her, his lips tightened and despite his injuries, he was handsome, and roguish looking. God, how she'd love to wake up to his cocky, irreverent smile every morning.

"Been up long?" she asked, pulling on her robe.

"About an hour."

"Short night," she observed, cinching the belt.

"Long enough."

Lindsay stirred, and they walked from the bedroom to the kitchen. Fresh coffee had already brewed, and the kitchen was clean, all evidence of the night before washed away. "How's Lupus?" she asked as she poured them each a cup.

"Still hanging in there."

She noticed the signs of strain, the lines around his mouth and eyes. "I'm sorry."

His jaw clenched, and he swallowed hard. "So am I." He kicked out a chair from the kitchen table and cocked his head toward it. "Sit down," he said. "There's something I've got to tell you."

His voice was low, his eyes sharp. It wasn't over yet, Kimberly realized with a sickening sense of dread. She wrapped her fingers around her cup for warmth and dropped into the chair.

"First of all, you were right about Bill Zealander. I called Brecken at the police department, and he had already picked him up. Zealander was new to Fisher's organization, but he was in it up to his button-down collar. He was unhappy at the bank, felt he'd been looked over time and time again in favor of you. When Fisher approached him, he was ready."

Her hands were shaking, and she swallowed hard. "No," she whispered.

"That last account Compton gave you—"

"The Juniper trust."

"Right. That was the last straw."

Setting her cup on the table, Kimberly licked her lips. She sensed this was just the start, that there was more, much more to come. She wasn't sure she wanted to hear it.

"It looks like Zealander lifted your keys and had a duplicate set made."

"When?"

"I don't know. But probably while you were working at the bank. Do you keep your purse locked?"

"No, it's usually in my desk drawer...." There were many times Bill could have rifled through her purse, many times she'd spent a couple of hours in the security cage or the safe-deposit vault. She shivered and rubbed her arms.

"Bill Zealander seemed to think that you were the single reason he wasn't advancing in the trust department. Fisher not only provided him with more money than he'd ever be able to earn at the bank, but he'd also given him an opportunity to get back at you."

Kimberly tried to sort it all out. "But why didn't Robert wait until the custody hearing? He might have persuaded Monaghan to give him custody of Lindsay. Why risk a kidnap attempt?"

"There wasn't enough time. The police were on to him. He found out that he was being set up and he panicked." Jake smiled coldly. "And he even had his escape route planned—with Kesler's plane."

"In Mulino?"

"Right. No one would think of him flying out of there, especially using Ben's name."

She blew her hair from her eyes. This was all too much to absorb. And yet she wanted to know everything. Raising her eyes to meet his, she asked, "And what about you, Jake? How do you fit into this?"

"You came to me, remember?" His eyes slid away from hers.

"But there's more."

"Yes." He muttered an oath aimed at himself. "Daniel Stevens was my half brother."

She braced herself, but her insides began to churn. Hadn't Robert said as much? Her chest constricted, and she had trouble breathing as she realized that Jake had lied to her...used her. And she loved him, Lord, how she loved him. With the drowning realization that he had never cared for her, had only agreed to be her attorney to get back at Robert, she dropped her cup. Hot tea sloshed across the table. She didn't bother wiping it up. It didn't matter—nothing did. Jake, her precious Jake, was, in his own way, as bad as Robert. She closed her eyes, squeezing them shut against the truth.

"When I saw the opportunity to go after Fisher. I couldn't resist."

"So, that's what all the questions were about—why you wanted to know about his business," she asked, dread giving way to anger. How could she have been so stupid—so fooled by his easy seduction?

"Partially," he admitted, reaching for her hand. She pulled it back. "But I wanted to help you, too."

"Help me, or hurt Robert?" she snapped, her eyes flying open. She was unable to stop the tide of rage that was roiling through her. "And is that why you slept with me?" she asked, her cheeks flaming, her throat so tight she could barely speak.

"No—"

"Did you want to know what it was like to bed Robert Fisher's ex-wife?"

"Don't be ridiculous."

"Am I?" She scraped her chair back and walked to the far side of the tiny kitchen. Ugly thoughts crept into her mind. "Was it Bill Zealander who was following me?"

"Yes."

"And what about Ron Koski? Isn't he a friend of yours—a private investigator? He was lurking about the house last night, wasn't he? That's why he showed up here so quickly!"

"I thought we needed a backup."

"And what about before?" she demanded, then felt the blood drain from her face. "You had *me* spied upon, didn't you? You were investigating *me*, weren't you—trying to find out if I was involved in any of Robert's business deals!"

"No—"

"Oh, God, Jake, don't tell me you had Ron watching me, checking into my personal life!" Her insides churned, her entire life turned inside out. She'd trusted him, loved him, and he'd repaid her by using her!

Jake's jaw grew rock hard. "I was trying to help you."

She shook her head. "That wasn't it! It was your need for vengeance, wasn't it? You know, I thought that I should know your name, but I never connected it with Daniel Stevens until now. I saw your name in the newspaper accounts of his death—as the surviving relative!" She felt as if she might throw up.

"And that's why you seduced me," she concluded, tears burning the backs of her eyes. "To get back at Robert by getting close to me and digging up anything you could on him. Well, I hope you had a good time, Jake, because it's over! And I hope to high heaven that your investigator 'friend' didn't take any pictures of you and me in a compromising position!"

"Enough," he bellowed, crossing the kitchen and placing strong, possessive fingers around her shoulders.

"What's wrong?" she went on, her emotions raw. "Have I offended your delicate sensibilities?"

He actually shook her. His fingers dug into her shoulders, and he gave her two hard shakes. "I love you," he vowed, his face twisted and pained.

"Love?" she repeated, nearly laughing hysterically. "You don't know the meaning of the word!"

"I know that I was willing to try with you, Kimberly. To take you and your daughter as part of my family. To try all over again."

She wrestled free of his painful grip. "Why? To salve your guilty conscience? Well, don't bother!"

"We're good together."

"'We' never existed. It was all a lie, McGowan. Your lie!"

"That's not the way it was!" he thundered, his eyes flashing. He placed warm hands on her cheeks and tilted her face upward. "Look at me, Kimberly," he commanded, his eyes drilling into hers. "Look at me, dammit!"

She forced her eyes to his and saw the agony deep in his soul. "You should be proud of yourself," she whispered sarcastically. "All you had to do was dance with me, buy me dinner, take me to bed—and I told you everything you wanted to know, help you set up my ex-husband."

"And are you sorry?"

"About Robert? No." She shook her head and swallowed against the hot dryness in her throat. "But I'm sorry for you and me and all the lies . . . all the damn lies."

"Are you finished?"

"Just about." She braced herself, ripping away from his grip, ignoring the pain shadowing his eyes and finally forcing the words past her tongue. "I think you should leave, Jake," she said softly, bleakly. "Send me a bill for your services, and get the hell out of my life."

"I can't do that."

"Sure you can—it's easy. Just walk out the door."

"And what about Lindsay?"

"She'll survive," Kimberly predicted sadly. "Besides, I would never want her to know that all the affection you showed for her was a lie."

"I never lied to Lindsay."

Kimberly forced a brittle smile. "You lied to her every time you walked through that door and pretended she was special. The guinea pig, hoisting her on your shoulders, making snowmen with her—those were all lies, because they led her to believe that you thought of her as a daughter, or at the very least a special niece—when you and I both know that you'll never be tied down to a child again, that you don't have room or time in your life for the pain and vulnerability a child can bring. Now, before you hurt me or my child any more, you'd better leave!"

Jake growled an oath and started for the door as the phone rang. Kimberly reached for the receiver automatically, and someone asked for Jake. She handed him the phone without really caring who it was. She felt dead inside—beaten down by a love so vital and now gone.

He took the call quietly, not saying much. When he replaced the receiver, he sighed. "Lupus didn't make it," he muttered, then walked out the back door.

Kimberly's knees gave out, and she slid to the floor. Tears welled in her eyes. Tears for a failed marriage, for a love affair based on lies and for a brave white dog who gave up his life for her and her child. She dropped her head onto her knees and felt the soft threads of her terry robe brush her cheek and absorb her tears.

She knew she should be pulling herself together, but she couldn't stop sobbing uncontrollably. Lindsay would be up soon and Arlene would be here, and then back to the bank—as if nothing had happened? Pick up the pieces of her life and go on? Without Jake?

She had to forget him.

But would it ever be possible? She sat huddled on the kitchen floor for several minutes until she forced the sobs back.

The front door opened, and Arlene's voice sounded through the house. "Kimberly?"

"In here," she sniffed, struggling to her feet and brushing away any lingering traces of her tears.

Arlene, newspaper tucked under her arm, entered the kitchen. She took one look at Kimberly and wrapped her thin arms around her. "I know, I know," she whispered, patting Kimberly's shoulder. "Now, you sit down and tell me all about it while I make us some tea."

As Arlene fussed around the kitchen, Kimberly haltingly admitted that she'd thrown Jake out.

"But why?" Arlene asked as if Kimberly were out of her mind.

Battling tears, Kimberly told Arlene the entire story.

"And you think he betrayed you?" Arlene asked, dunking tea bags into two cups of steaming water.

"Betrayed, lied, deceived. You name it, he did it."

"But I've seen the way he looks at you, how he acts around Lindsay. I tell you, Kimberly, that man's in love with you."

Kimberly let out a bitter laugh. "Sure he is." She sipped from her cup and burned the tip of her tongue. "That's why he was spying on me, using me."

"You're twisting this all around."

"No, Arlene," she said sadly, "for once I'm seeing things all too clearly."

"Well, if I were you, I'd hightail it out of here and run after him. Find him, admit you were wrong and that you love him and never intend to let him go."

"Oh, Arlene, that's crazy."

"It's the soundest advice you'll ever get!"

Lindsay, her battered blanket in tow, stumbled into the room. "Mommy?" she whispered, climbing into Kimberly's lap. "You been crying?"

"I'm just tired, sweetheart."

"Where's Jake?" She glanced around the room.

"He had to leave, honey."

"Did he go get Lupus?" Lindsay asked, yawning. From the corner of her eye Kimberly saw Arlene's lips tighten.

Kimberly's chest constricted. She couldn't tell Lindsay about the dog, not yet. But Arlene's eyes pinned her, and she said, "Lupus is in heaven, honey."

Lindsay started to cry, but Kimberly assured her that the white shepherd was happy now. "Come on, let's get you some breakfast, okay?"

"'Kay," Lindsay mumbled, her face red.

"I'll do this," Arlene said, reaching for the instant oat-meal and a bowl.

"Good, I should get ready."

"For work?" The older woman looked stricken. "To-day?"

"It's a workday, isn't it?"

"Yes, but you should take some time off."

"I can't."

"Well, think about it. Work won't be easy—you made the front page." Arlene spread the newspaper on the counter, and Kimberly cringed. A huge, grainy picture of Robert dominated the top half of the front page. She skimmed the story, seeing her name and Lindsay's interspersed in the article.

It was a wonder other reporters hadn't started calling. "I'll call in today," she said, deciding that her place was here, with Lindsay. "But let's leave the answering machine on."

"Good idea," Arlene agreed as she stirred oatmeal into hot water. "And we can all go down to my place. That way we won't be bothered."

Kimberly offered the older woman a grateful smile. "I'd appreciate it. Thanks, Arlene. You're a godsend."

"I wish," Arlene said. "Now, go on, get dressed. I'll take care of Lindsay."

Kimberly didn't argue. She walked to the bathroom, stripped out of her robe and nightgown, then twisted on the faucets.

As she stepped under the hot jets of water, she tried to pull herself together. She couldn't let Robert nor Jake nor the newspaper nor the police determine the course of her life. And she couldn't sit around the house moping for Jake and a love that had never existed. No, today she'd take the day off, take Lindsay Christmas shopping and have her daughter's picture taken with Santa. Once things had settled down, she'd get back to business as usual. And somehow she'd forget Jake McGowan had ever existed.

If she could.

Chapter Thirteen

Two days later the bank was still a madhouse, the cafeteria buzzing with gossip. Kimberly answered most questions put to her in a very matter-of-fact and straightforward manner. And she tried to ignore the speculative glances cast her way by interested bank employees.

"You were right about Robert," Marcie said, dropping a stack of mail onto the corner of Kimberly's desk. "Heather said he was moving money out of the bank so fast she could barely keep up with the transactions."

"I thought so," Kimberly replied, managing a wan smile though she found the entire subject depressing.

"And Bill! Can you believe he was involved!" Marcie threw her hands into the air and shook her head. "I thought he was a real nose-to-the-grindstone type."

"I guess we all make judgment errors," she said, thinking of Jake as she had for the past four hours. Why couldn't she stop dwelling on him? It was barely eleven, and she couldn't wait to make tracks home. She'd already been grilled by Eric Compton and Aaron Thorburn, who in turn had been interrogated by the police, FBI, and an auditor from the FDIC, who had called for a special audit of the bank's books to check for money laundering and all sorts of other crimes involving one of the bank's wealthiest customers.

"Henry Juniper is coming in today," Marcie said.

"Wonderful," Kimberly muttered cynically. The day was getting better and better.

"Oh, and Mrs. Pendergraft called to thank you for the flowers the bank sent her a few weeks ago. She said they were 'gorgeous.'"

The first good news of the day. "Anything else?"

Marcie nodded. "Jake McGowan called again."

"I don't want to talk to him."

"I know. But I thought I should tell you."

Jake. Why couldn't he just take no for an answer?

Two hours later Henry Juniper was seated on the other side of her desk, worrying the brim of his hat in his hands, blowing off steam and, in general, not listening to any kind of reason.

Marcie buzzed in. "Ms. Juniper is here," she called.

Henry's face went white. "Carole's here?"

"I asked her to stop by."

"With that snake of an attorney of hers—that Kesler fellow?" Henry demanded, his voice rising an octave.

"I don't think so." The paper had reported that Ben was having a few problems of his own—all because of his association with Robert Fisher.

Marcie led Carole into the room, and the middle-aged woman took the only available chair next to her brother. They glanced at each other once, then stared stonily ahead at Kimberly.

"I'm glad you're here, Carole," Kimberly said, picking up the document file on the Juniper estate. "I wanted to go over the terms of your father's will again, so that each of you see exactly what is in the estate and what share you're entitled to."

Henry's head was bobbing up and down.

Carole's lips pursed.

Kimberly started reading and silently hoped she could find a way to settle the mess between brother and sister without the problem of a lawsuit.

By the time she finished reading, Henry and Carole were exchanging glances. A few minutes later they argued a few points, but eventually agreed to let the bank handle all the bills of the estate, including reasonable bills presented by Carole for her father's care during his convalescence.

"I guess she's entitled to something for all her time," Henry grumbled, stuffing a hat on his head and saying, "I'll see you after the New Year."

"Thanks, Kim," Carole said, "and Merry Christmas."

"Same to you," Kimberly replied. She glanced at the calendar and felt a pang of regret. Soon it would be Christmas day. And she and Lindsay would spend it alone.

She didn't see Jake again until Christmas eve. She and Lindsay were stringing popcorn and listening to Christmas carols while the guinea pig exercised on his wheel, the metal cage clicking in time to the song.

"Can't we open just one present now?" Lindsay begged, her gaze on the little tree.

"Santa doesn't come until later."

"I know, but there're some presents under the tree already."

That there were. Half a dozen brightly wrapped packages skirted the Douglas fir.

"Besides," Lindsay prodded, climbing into Kimberly's lap, "I want you to open my package."

"And I want to wait until tomorrow morning."

"Please..."

"Okay," Kimberly replied, not having the heart to disappoint her.

Lindsay retrieved the huge package, and Kimberly pulled off the paper. Inside was a large birdhouse made from scraps of lumber nailed together. The house would hold six nests. "Lyle and I made it," Lindsay said proudly.

"And it's beautiful," Kimberly whispered, admiring it. "You're quite a carpenter."

"I know," Lindsay replied solemnly.

"Thank you very much." She kissed Lindsay's crown.

"Now, can I open one?"

Kimberly sighed. "Just one."

Lindsay hurled herself back under the tree, found a package and tore open a holiday puzzle. "I like it! I do! I do!" She beamed at her mother. "Now, your turn again."

"Oh, no."

"Just one more."

"I can't. Really."

Lindsay nodded. "Open Jake's!"

"Jake's?" Kimberly's insides turned cold. "There isn't a present from Jake."

"Oh, yes, there is!" Lindsay said, scrambling off Kimberly's lap and reaching into the thick branches of the Christmas tree. She hunted awhile and withdrew a small box wrapped in silver foil.

"When did this get here?"

Lindsay shrugged. "A long time ago."

"How long?"

"When we heard the singers in the park," Lindsay said, forcing it into her hands.

Kimberly's chest constricted. She didn't want to think about Jake—nor about this present. "I don't think I should open it."

"It's okay. He told me that it had to be a secret until Christmas eve. And that's now!"

"So it is," Kimberly said, fingering the card while her heart pounded. She opened the envelope, and her throat constricted with tears. "To Kimberly, a woman who has brought happiness and light to my life. I'll love you forever. This was my mother's. No one has ever worn it since she gave it to me."

"Oh, no," she whispered, remembering all the ugly words she'd said. Taking in a deep breath, she untied the small red ribbon and slit open the foil. The shiny paper gave way to a tiny jewelry box, and as Kimberly lifted the lid, she felt tears building behind her eyes. There, on a faded cushion of red velvet, was an antique ring. A diamond sparkled brightly in the box.

"Oooh!" Lindsay cried. "It's *beautiful*."

"That it is," Kimberly admitted, feeling a fool. Had she judged Jake too harshly? If he'd left the ring before the ordeal with Robert, didn't that mean that he loved her? She had to find out. Stuffing ring and box into her pocket, she jumped to her feet.

"Come on, Lindsay, we've got work to do."

"But I want to open a present—"

"When we get home." Kimberly found her daughter's coat, boots, mittens and hat. Then, retrieving her cape, she shepherded Lindsay out the door.

"Where're we going?" Lindsay asked.

"You'll see." Kimberly strapped Lindsay into the passenger side of her car, then slid behind the wheel. Tonight, she decided, she'd have it out with Jake. Once and for all. She'd crawl back on her hands and knees to find out if he'd really meant it when he'd said that he loved her. If so, she'd be the happiest woman on the earth. If not . . . She shuddered.

She wheeled into the parking lot of her favorite mall and smiled when she saw that the store was still open. "Come on, Lindsay. You're going to enjoy this. I guarantee it."

Jake swirled his drink, glanced in the mirror and growled, "Merry Christmas," at his reflection. He'd spent the better part of the week trying to forget that it was Christmas, that he'd hoped to marry Kimberly Bennett and that his life was much too empty. He'd failed on every count. Losing Lupus had hurt horribly; losing Kimberly had been a deathblow.

He threw the remains of his drink in the fire, snagged his leather jacket off the back of his couch and started for the door. He was going to have it out with her once and for all. And this time, dammit, he'd force her to believe just how much he loved her.

The doorbell chimed, and he swore. He wasn't in the mood for carolers, shining faces or Christmas cheer. Scowling, he yanked open the door and there, standing in the middle of the porch, was Lindsay, her blue eyes shining, her hair in two lopsided pigtails. She was carrying a box that was nearly as big as she was.

"Merry Christmas!" she sang out.

Jake's heart lurched almost painfully. "Hello," he said, filled with wonder that this little girl could burrow so deep in his soul.

"'Lo."

"Come in, come in." He stood outside of the door, letting her pass. "Your mom with you?"

"Uh-hmm." She set the box on the floor in front of the fire, and Jake was sure it moved, but his attention was diverted when Kimberly, dressed in her familiar black cape, swept into the room.

"Merry Christmas," she said breezily, her eyes deep with mischief, her mahogany-colored hair swirling behind her in a tangled red-brown cloud.

"Merry Christmas. I was just about to come visit you."

"Well, I guess we saved you a trip." She swung her cape off, and Lindsay giggled, not for a minute leaving the huge box.

To his surprise Kimberly sauntered up, wrapped her arms around his neck and kissed him long and hard.

Jake couldn't help but respond. He wrapped his arms around her waist. "I'd like to ask you what's going on, but I'm afraid to disturb the fantasy."

Winking broadly, she plucked a sprig of mistletoe from her pocket. "This man I know convinced me that mistletoe didn't need to be hung."

"A wise man," Jake drawled.

"And I wanted to thank you for my Christmas present."

He grinned, then glanced over to Lindsay. "I thought I said Christmas morning."

"I couldn't wait," Lindsay said.

"And neither could I." Kimberly slid out of his arms and tugged on his hand. "Lindsay and I went shopping to-night...for you. And we hope you like what we got. We had trouble deciding on the color."

Jake eyed the box suspiciously. "You want me to open it now?"

"Yes."

"Maybe we should wait till morning."

Kimberly laughed merrily. "Oh, I don't think that would be such a good idea."

"All right," he agreed, untying the big green bow and lifting the lid. As he did, an excited yip escaped, and a bright-eyed black puppy leaped up and washed his face with its long pink tongue.

"Hey, slow down," Jake cried, but the pup, a mix of lab and shepherd, Jake guessed, jumped on him ecstatically.

Lindsay clapped in joy. "He's perfect, isn't he?"

"Perfect," Jake agreed, smiling as the puppy made three mad dashes around the room and finally landed on Lindsay's belly. The little girl screamed and laughed, her giggles rising to the ceiling. "In fact I think we'll name him that."

"What—Perfect?" Kimberly asked.

Lindsay shook her head. "I like Snowball better."

"But he's black," Kimberly said, laughing.

"Doesn't matter," Lindsay argued.

Jake grinned, staring up at Kimberly. Her blue-green eyes were bright, and as she stood near the fireplace, she seemed to fill his house with a warmth and happiness that had been missing for a long, long time. God, how he loved her. It was frightening, yet caused his spirits to soar.

Winking seductively at him, she cocked her head toward the backyard and turned to her daughter. "Come on, Lindsay, let's see if Perfect or Snowball or Perfect Snowball needs to go outside." She helped her daughter back into her coat, mittens and boots.

Jake opened the back door, and the puppy shot through, straining against the leash and pulling Lindsay outside. Jake and Kimberly followed.

The night was quiet. The ghost of a moon dusted the snow-covered ground with a pale light, and beyond the yard the dark waters of the lake lapped quietly. Kimberly took hold of his hand. "I guess I owe you an apology," she said, taking in a deep breath. "I said awful things to you."

"You were upset."

"And I was wrong." Tilting her chin up, she stared at him with wide, blue-green eyes. "I love you, Jake. I have for a long time. I came here because I want to marry you."

Jake felt the corners of his lips twist. His heart thudded, and love surged through his veins. "Is this a proposal?"

"Oh, yes," she said, her breath misting in the cold winter air. She took his face between her mittened hands and pressed a gentle kiss to his lips.

Jake's lips twisted cynically. "You know, I think maybe I should do the asking."

"So, ask already," she teased.

"Will you marry me?"

"Only if we can have a Christmas wedding."

"But that's—"

"Tomorrow."

"You think you can find a preacher on such short notice?"

Kimberly giggled. "It just so happens that Arlene has connections at a little church. The preacher is a personal friend of hers. I bet I could get her to twist his arm. The only problem will be Diane. She'll kill us both if we get married and she's not around."

"I guess that's just a chance we'll have to take," Jake said, wrapping his arms around her and kissing her long and hard.

Lindsay and the puppy dashed by, powdery snow flying, giggles and sharp barking filling the clear night air.

"I love you," Jake whispered against her hair, "and if you think I'm waiting until tomorrow to start the honeymoon, guess again."

Kimberly tossed back her hair. Her expression turned impish as she reached into her pocket. "No reason to wait," she said, holding up the sprig of mistletoe. "As far as I'm concerned, tonight is the first night of our life together."

"Then let's make it count."

"I'm all yours, counselor."

"And I'm yours. Forever."

"I don't think that's going to be long enough," she teased, and was rewarded with a kiss that promised her a lifetime of love. In the distance, from across the lake, she heard the sound of Christmas bells ringing, sending clear notes into the wintry air as Jake lifted her off her feet and carried her back inside their home.

*   *   *   *   *

Back by popular demand, some of Diana Palmer's earliest published books are available again!

Several years ago, Diana Palmer began her writing career. Sweet, compelling and totally unforgettable, these are the love stories that enchanted readers everywhere.

Next month, six more of these wonderful stories will be available in DIANA PALMER DUETS—Books 4, 5 and 6. Each DUET contains two powerful stories plus an introduction by Diana Palmer. Don't miss:

Book Four	AFTER THE MUSIC DREAM'S END
Book Five	BOUND BY A PROMISE PASSION FLOWER
Book Six	TO HAVE AND TO HOLD THE COWBOY AND THE LADY

**Diana Palmer's fortieth story for Silhouette . . . chosen
as an Award of Excellence title!**

CONNAL
Diana Palmer

Next month, Diana Palmer's bestselling LONG, TALL
TEXANS series continues with CONNAL. The skies
get cloudy on C. C. Tremayne's home on the range
when Penelope Mathews decides to protect him—by
marrying him!

One specially selected title receives the Award of
Excellence every month. Look for CONNAL in August
at your favorite retail outlet . . . only from Silhouette
Romance.

CON-1